DESPERATE CHOICES

Other Books
by Sharon S Darrow

Bottlekatz,
A Complete Care Guide for Orphan Kittens

Faces of Rescue:
Cats, Kittens & Great Danes

From Hindsight to Insight,
A Traditional to Metaphysical Memoir

Tom Flynn, Medium & Healer

Navigating the Publishing Maze,
Self-Publishing 101

She Survives, Laura's Dash Book 1
Strive and Protect, Laura's Dash Book 2

Coming soon:
Her Triumph, Laura's Dash Book 4

Short Stories appear in the following Anthologies:
Lizard Love, in Birds of a Feather
Introduction To Chickenese, in More Birds of a Feather
Travel Means Flying, in Destination, The World, Volume 1

Desperate Choices

Sharon S Darrow

Samati Press

Sacramento, California

First Edition, 2020
ISBN-13 — 978-1-949125-14-6 (Print Version)
ISBN-13 — 978-1-949125-15-3 (Digital versions)
ISBN-13 — 978-1-949125-29-0 (Audio version)

Library of Congress Control Number: 2020943710

Edited by Sue J. Clark

Publisher: Samati Press
Sacramento, California

Manufactured in the United States of America

Dedication

This book is dedicated to my grandchildren, Stanley Young, Nicole Tilton, Christopher Wilson, Nicholas Wilson, and great-grandson, Dallas Tilton. They are unique, precious human beings who can make a difference in the world.

Spending time with them is a pleasure. Teaching them the importance of knowledge, values, and character, has been a privilege. And sharing stories with them about their family history continues to be a joy.

I wish them success, happiness, and love throughout their lives.

Contents

Chapter One

Is Papa Crying

July 1938, Aurora, Missouri

Three more days. Three more to find out if Glen would be back to his old self.

Laura watched her husband sleep, his sandy brown hair curled against his forehead. The drugs in his system kept him from dreaming, a blessed relief from the nightmares that had haunted him since his mental breakdown. Dr. Farnsworth had suggested weaning him off his medications, skipping one of his three doses each day.

The next evening, Glen didn't seem any different after taking two pills that day. She wondered if his behavior would change after being cut to one pill the following day.

When Laura woke in the morning, she was shocked to find Glen sitting on the edge of the bed, staring at the window.

"Good morning, honey." She padded around the bed, knelt down and looked into his blue eyes. "You're awake early. Are you hungry?" She kept her tone light, hoping he'd respond. His eyes were open and appeared focused, but he wasn't looking at her, he was looking through her.

"How about some coffee before the kids wake up?" Laura thought she saw a faint flicker of something in his eyes. She grabbed her old, green chenille robe and pulled it on. "Let's stop at the bathroom first, then you can keep me company while I put the coffee on and start breakfast."

Laura noticed that Glen held his head a little more erect at the table. There was a slight tremor in his hands. He didn't speak though, so she stopped trying to engage him in conversation.

"Here, Glen," Laura said, handing him his pill. She made sure he swallowed it, grateful that he didn't fuss about taking his medication. She'd better get the chores done fast, since there was no telling how long it would last.

Laura worked as fast as possible, caring for the animals and garden, keeping Glen close by. "Good thing we bought these folding chairs when we used to have people over," she said. "You can keep me company while I'm working." Glen sat, feet and knees together, back straight and eyes focused straight ahead, at the edge of the garden while Laura watered and pulled weeds.

"It was a lot easier when you helped with chores around here, honey. The kids try, but they're too young to accomplish a lot." Laura glanced at Glen, but his face remained blank.

She made many trips to the house and outbuildings to check on the children as they first did their chores, then played. She carried the chair with her when she moved from place to place, while Glen followed, sitting down when she unfolded the chair. "Here you go," she'd say each time. "Are you comfortable? Would you like a glass of water?"

At dinner, June sat on Glen's right at the table. She stared at him while Laura started filling the children's plates. She observed him following Laura's motions with his eyes. "Papa, do you feel better?" Her voice was high and full of hope. No answer, but Glen seemed to twitch as if he'd been touched.

Laura willed him to respond to his daughter, but saw no indication he was aware of her at all. If he could eat and drink at a normal pace, why wouldn't he answer his daughter? Or at least look at her. "I'm sorry, Junebug, I guess he needs more time."

June nodded, her blue eyes bright with unshed tears. "But how much time, Mama? When will Papa get well?"

Laura shrugged and shook her head. "I don't know, honey."

All four children looked glum as they finished their meal.

"I have an idea. You guys have been working so hard to help me and keep an eye on your papa this last week, I think you need some extra play time and a treat. No more chores for you this afternoon, and I'll bake a cake for supper." Laura leaned forward. "How about chocolate icing, too?"

The smiles were a little slow in coming, but then all four cheered and ran out the back door with June carrying David on her hip.

Laura spent the rest of the afternoon in the kitchen baking, first the promised cake and then oatmeal raisin cookies. The kids ran in and out, checking on the progress, while Glen sat on a chair next to the small table where she worked. "Smells good, doesn't it?" She dropped spoonfuls of dough on the cookie sheet, as the sweet aroma of the cake in the oven filled the room.

"Can we have some dough?" June begged from the washroom doorway, her brothers peeking around her. "A little bite for each of us?"

Laura started to say no, then laughed and relented. "Okay, then out you go until I'm done." She handed each child a small spoonful of dough, and waved them out the door. "Our kids are pretty special," she said to Glen.

He stayed in the room with her while she worked, but grew more and more agitated. The muscles in his face and arms twitched, his hands clenched, and his legs bounced up and down. Now and then he cocked his head as if listening to someone, and more than once Laura thought she heard him mumble under his breath. As she pulled the last batch out of the oven, Glen stood and stalked through the dining room and out the front door.

Laura left the cookie sheet on the stove top and followed, afraid to let him out of her sight. He stopped on the porch, one hand on an upright post in front of the steps leading to the yard. Laura stood about two feet behind him. "It's pretty out here, isn't it, honey? Feels good to stretch your legs."

Not a word in response, but Glen's head moved toward the right as if to hear her better. If only she could think of something to say. Then Laura noticed Dr. Farnsworth's car coming toward the house. "Glen, Dr. Farnsworth is coming to visit. He'll be pleased to find you outside." Thank goodness. Maybe the doctor could do something to help him.

Glen didn't say anything, but Laura saw his hand clench tight on the post, his knuckles white, while he tucked his other hand into his front trouser pocket. Glen's breathing sped up as they waited until the doctor parked his car and approached the steps.

"Hello Dr. Farnsworth, you're early," Laura said. She stepped from behind Glen. "Look who came outside by himself today." Her voice sounded brittle and artificial.

Dr. Farnsworth looked as dapper as ever in his dark suit as he approached the steps, his gray hair, mustache, and goatee impeccable. "Good afternoon, Mr. and Mrs. Webber. I had a cancellation today and hoped you wouldn't mind my coming out early." Dr. Farnsworth's tone and facial expression were neutral, devoid of sentiment as he approached the porch, his gaze focused on Glen. "It's good to see you outside, Mr. Webber, beautiful day isn't it?"

Laura saw Glen's jaw clench and move side to side, but he didn't speak. She placed her hand on his back, surprised when his muscles tightened and he pulled away at her touch.

Dr. Farnsworth climbed the first two stairs, one slow, deliberate step at a time. "Mr. Webber, you appear much better today. Would you mind my giving you a quick checkup?"

Glen didn't look at him, but moved back two steps toward the middle of the porch. He stepped backwards again as the doctor climbed the last two stairs, keeping the same distance between them.

Laura opened her mouth to speak, but after a quick head shake by the doctor, remained quiet. Her hands were clasped so hard she could feel the nails biting into her palms.

Dr. Farnsworth paused at the top of the steps, then moved toward two chairs and a small table grouped together near the door. He placed his medical bag on the table and removed his stethoscope. "Mr. Webber, would you mind sitting down for a few minutes? I'd like to check your heart and lungs. Won't take long, I promise."

Glen turned his body and faced the doctor. Laura noticed his forearm muscles flexing and his hands tightened into fists.

"No, I'm not leaving him," Glen said, staring at the porch floor where there seemed to be something no one else could see. He focused on the doctor. "I know he's gone, I know that, but I'm not leaving him." Glen's body was a study in defiance and pain. He dropped to his knees, threw his head back and began to wail. His entire body shook with the force of the ungodly cries that ripped from his throat.

"Please, please do something." It was hard for Laura to breathe, much less talk. "I can't bear to see him hurt like this. Can't you do something?" She grabbed Dr. Farnsworth's arm with both of her hands.

"Mrs. Webber, all I can do is give him something to knock him out. This breakdown is far beyond my abilities. The only help available to him is the Springfield Mental Hospital. I've spoken to them about your husband, and they have room."

"How can I do that to him?" Laura clasped her hands together, kneeling near Glen.

He continued to rock on his knees, arms tucked around his torso, screaming and moaning. "What am I supposed to do?"

The screech of the screen door opening behind her startled Laura. "Mama, what's wrong? Is Papa crying?" Laura leaped to the door, pushing hard to keep a frightened June from coming outside. "Stay inside, sweetheart, you and your brothers need to stay inside."

"Dr. Farnsworth, do what you've got to do. Please, the kids can't see this."

The doctor, his own eyes glistening, nodded, pulled a syringe from his bag and filled it. Glen didn't react to the needle plunging into his arm, just continued rocking and yelling. In minutes he stopped making the awful noises and his body relaxed. The doctor pulled him to his feet and began walking him down the steps. At the foot of the stairs, he turned to Laura. "I'm taking him straight to the hospital before the shot wears off. I'm sorry there isn't more I can do for him."

Laura's entire body shook as she watched the men make their way toward the car. She realized June had stopped screaming and banging on the door, then heard footsteps pounding away from the door toward the hallway. Within minutes June and her brothers came running around the side of the house as Dr. Farnsworth was putting Glen into his car.

Laura ran down the steps and caught June in her arms, holding her tight until the doctor's car pulled away. "Honey, your papa is sick, and the doctor is taking him to get help."

"No, no, bring him back." June's fists beat into Laura's chest as soon as her arms were free. The boys clustered together next to Laura. June, crying and calling for their papa to come back, stared at the car as it disappeared from view.

Laura didn't even try to stop June's blows, absorbing them until June wore herself out. She dropped to her knees and wrapped her arms around all four children. "I want him here, too, I didn't want him to go away. But Papa's hurting and we can't help him. You don't want your papa to be in pain, do you?"

Their cries and tears hurt Laura much more than June's punches, and the worst pain was not being able to help them. "Dr. Farnsworth is taking Papa to a special kind of hospital. They have a room all ready for him, and know how to make him well again."

The tears and cries diminished, but all four children held tight to Laura. "Mama, when will Papa come back?" June's raspy voice was hard to recognize.

"I don't know, sweetheart. I wish I knew."

"But they will fix him, won't they?" Raymond's eyes were huge, and his voice was filled with longing.

"Of course they will, honey." Laura tightened her arms around her babies. "That's what doctors and hospitals do."

Laura almost added the words "I promise" but somehow held them back. Memories of sad endings when she worked in the hospital in Tulsa flashed through her mind. More memories came of doctors ready to "let nature take its course" and nurses who let patients die who'd been deemed hopeless.

"Papa will be fine, but it may take a while for the hospital to find the right medicine to make him well," Laura said, trying to soothe the children she held in a tight huddle, rocking until the sobs subsided.

At long last, Laura stood and lifted David into her arms. The other children stayed close to her sides as they walked back into the house. Please God, if you're listening, please help him.

"God always listens, honey, but sometimes his plans aren't easy to understand."

Laura's steps faltered as the words rang inside her head. Ma? Can't you help me? I can't stand this. It's too much. Laura hadn't heard her ma's voice or felt her presence in a long time.

"Yes, you can. You're a strong woman, and can do whatever you have to. Your children need you. I know you won't let them down."

Laura started to reply, but her ma was gone. She'd left right after she'd delivered her message.

CHAPTER TWO

Children Need Their Papa

Aurora, Missouri, Two Weeks Later, August 1938

A loud knocking on the front door surprised everyone. Before June or Raymond could get up, Laura motioned them to stay in their seats. "Can't imagine who that might be. Stay put and finish your breakfast while I get the door."

"Papa, I'll bet it's Papa come home," Jimmy said, dropping his fork on the table.

June and Raymond looked at each other, eyes wide, then bolted toward the front door with Laura right behind them. "Get back, both of you." Hands on her hips, she glared at the children. "I'll get it." Turning away from them, she took a deep breath and reached for the doorknob.

"It's not Papa." Jimmy peeked out the curtained window next to the door. "There's a big guy on the porch wearing a hat, but not Papa." Jimmy dropped the curtain closed, and trudged back to the table. He sat sideways in his chair, so he could still see Laura and hear what she said.

Three more hard knocks shook the screen door. "You two go finish your breakfast and keep an eye on Jimmy and David." Laura waved June and Raymond back, waiting until they had resumed their seats across from Jimmy before opening the door.

A strange man stood on the porch. "Can I help you?" Before he spoke a word, her heart raced at his somber expression.

"Mrs. Webber?" The man, tall with a weathered face, dark pomaded locks smoothed back, and well-groomed facial hair flecked with gray, wore shiny shoes and a blue suit. He removed his black felt fedora and held it in his left hand. When Laura nodded, he continued. "My name is Mr. Bannon. I was your husband's supervisor at Connor Construction."

Laura's breath caught at the past tense. She glanced at the children seated at the breakfast table, wide-eyed and focused on her conversation. She opened the door and closed it behind her, joining Mr. Bannon on the porch. "What do you mean you *were* his supervisor? Has something happened to him at the hospital?"

"No, ma'am. I mean, I haven't heard anything about something happening to him." He looked down and cleared his throat while he played with the brim of his hat with both hands. Then he brought his gaze back to meet Laura's eyes. "It's just that since he's been in the hospital for over two weeks, the company can't continue to keep him on the payroll."

"What does that mean, you can't keep him on the payroll?"

"Well," he said, turning the hat in his hands faster. "He's not working now. He hasn't worked since the accident."

Laura crossed her arms, feeling warmth creep up in her face. "That's right, since the accident. The accident on the job site where that young man, Ralph, I think his name was, got buried at a cave-in and Glen helped the other guys on the crew dig him out. My husband was a hero that day and always worked harder than anybody. He's not working because of that accident, and it wasn't his fault." There was a huge lump in Laura's throat, so big it was hard for her to get the words out.

"I understand, Mrs. Webber." Mr. Bannon's voice sounded thick. "But the accident didn't hurt your husband. The truth is that he's been out of work for almost a month. We heard that he went to the mental hospital in Springfield two weeks ago. Connor can't keep someone on the payroll who isn't working."

"You fired him?" Laura's fingers flew to her lips as if to hold back a cry. "He did nothing wrong, and he worked hard to save that young man. In fact, the men who brought him home said the man who died caused the cave-in. They told me no one could have done more than Glen did. And they're the ones who called Glen a hero." Laura's voice broke. She wiped her eyes hard. She would not cry in front of this man, no matter what.

"Yes, he tried as hard as he could. Nobody could have done more," Mr. Bannon said. He paused, staring at his shoes, then stroked his beard before looking up at Laura. "But the fact remains that your husband wasn't injured at work. The cave-in didn't hurt him, and his breakdown wasn't a result of the accident. Dr. Bailey, the doctor who pronounced the death at the cave-in, said your husband suffered a complete mental collapse. He said your husband didn't know what was happening, was crying and shouting gibberish."

Laura squeezed her eyes shut trying to block out the picture Mr. Bannon painted. "But it all happened after the accident, you can't deny that. Trying to save a man and having him die under your hands would have a horrible effect on anyone." She opened her eyes, but her stomach muscles remained cramped tight.

Again, Mr. Bannon cleared his throat, then took a deep breath. "I understand how you feel, Mrs. Webber, and wish things were different. However, our work crews have tight deadlines to meet and we can't keep his position open any longer. Your husband was an excellent worker. He can reapply for a job at Connor Construction as soon as he's able to come back to work."

〜〜

"We're done, Mama." June's voice was soft as she slipped out the front door, holding David in her arms, to join Laura. Raymond and Jimmy crowded onto the porch behind her.

Startled by their presence, Laura turned and looked into four upturned faces. She forced a smile on her face for the children, then turned back to Mr. Bannon. "Please excuse me for a few moments. I'll be right back." She pushed the children through the door, not waiting for a response.

"Did he make you cry?"

"Who is that man?"

"Did he work with Papa?"

"What's happening?"

The questions from the children came quick and fast, words tumbling out on top of each other. "SSSHHH, I'll explain later. Please clear the table and stay inside. I need to finish talking to Mr. Bannon." Laura raised her hands, palms facing the children. "I won't be long, I promise. There's nothing to worry about."

The kids looked at one another, then nodded and stayed put. Laura looked at the worried expressions on each little face, then turned away and went back out on the porch.

"I'm sorry for the interruption."

Mr. Bannon waved his hand and shrugged. "No problem. You have a lovely family."

"Thank you. But our children need their papa."

"Yes, ma'am." Mr. Bannon paused, resumed twisting the brim of his hat between his fingers, and cleared his throat again. He reached into his jacket and pulled an envelope from the inside pocket. "I brought his last check for you, well, I brought the cash since it might be easier for you to deposit at the bank. Management added an additional two weeks pay since he was such a good employee."

Tears stung her eyes, but she blinked them away as fast as she could. "Thank you." Her voice broke, but she held her composure.

Mr. Bannon nodded, "I almost forgot. The men took up a collection for your family."

He reached back inside his jacket, pulled out another envelope and handed it to her. "Your husband was a good man, and everybody wanted to help as much as they could."

"My husband still is a good man." Laura took a deep, shuddering breath as she reached for the envelopes. "Please thank them for me."

"Yes ma'am, I'll do that." Mr. Bannon put his hat on and stepped back. "I'm real sorry for what happened and hope Mr. Webber will be well soon." Then he turned and rushed off the porch toward his vehicle.

Laura stood rooted in place until the car was out of sight. She clutched the envelopes so tight her fingers ached.

"Mama, who was that man?" June said. "Did he tell you when Papa's coming home?"

Laura turned to see June and Raymond's faces pressed against the screen door, Jimmy and David behind them. It hurt to see the worried looks on their faces. Her first impulse was to say nothing, but she'd always been honest with her children. "No, he doesn't know. Come sit with me."

She opened the screen so the children could join her on the porch. Jimmy continued down the four wide steps, David backing down on his knees beside him, to play with a wagon they'd left in the grass. Laura sat on the edge of the porch, her feet on the step below. June and Raymond joined her, one on each side.

"Was that one of the men who brought Papa home?" Raymond's voice quivered. "Looked like them."

"No, honey. But they worked together. In fact, he was the boss."

"Why did he give you envelopes?" June asked. "I kind of peeked through the curtain and saw him."

Laura sighed and swallowed the impulse to scold her.

"You looked real scared, Mama. What did he say?" Raymond's eyebrows drew together while he chewed on his lower lip.

"Nothing for you to worry about, sweetie." Laura hugged him close, pressed her face into his hair, and started again. "Yes, I was scared. Mr. Bannon said they can't keep paying him while he's not working. The envelopes had Papa's last paycheck and some extra money from the men he worked with"

The children digested her words, then June said, "But you told us he was a hero. You said the accident made him remember when his brother died, and he was so sad he couldn't stop thinking about it."

"Yeah," Raymond chimed in. "You told us Papa was sick in his mind. The doctors at the special hospital are supposed to fix him. Doesn't his boss care? It's not Papa's fault."

Jimmy, with David close behind, climbed up to the second step and leaned against Laura's legs. "I want Papa." A single tear ran down his cheek, and his hands fisted on Laura's lap. "Please, Mama."

Laura pulled Jimmy into her lap and hugged him close, then opened her arms and wrapped them around June and Raymond, too. "I want him home too, but he needs help first."

Before the children could protest, she continued. "It's time to get some answers, and I'll need your help. We need to be strong for Papa." She looked into each child's face, including David's, who'd squirmed into the huddle with the others. "I have to walk to town and see Dr. Farnsworth. That means I'll need to leave you guys alone. Can I trust you to be good for me while I'm gone? It's important that you follow the rules and stay safe, or I can't go."

Each child nodded and promised. After one last family hug, then Laura said, "Okay. Your Papa will be so proud of you when I tell him how good you are. I've got to clean up the breakfast dishes, then get changed for town. And you kids need to take care of the chickens."

Laura had cleaned the kitchen and changed into one of her day dresses by the time the children brought the eggs inside. "You look real pretty," Raymond said, handing her a basket of eggs.

Laura put the basket on the long counter next to the kitchen sink. "Good job collecting the eggs." She looked at the other children clustered around Raymond. "Did you remember to feed and water the chickens and spread fresh straw on the floor of the coop?"

June snorted and rolled her eyes. "Yes, ma'am, and we latched the coop door open so the chickens can go in and out from the yard. We know what we're supposed to do. We're not babies."

Laura suppressed a smirk at the pained look on June's face. "Great job." She smoothed the nubby fabric of the navy blue skirt that reached halfway down her calves, then adjusted the wide belt at her waist, centering the cloth-covered buckle in front. Laura wished she didn't have to dress up just to go to town. "I don't know how long I'll be gone, but until I get back, June's the oldest, so she's in charge."

The boys sputtered and protested while June drew herself up and folded her arms across her chest. "I'm depending on each of you to be on your very best behavior. As long as you boys follow the regular house rules, June won't need to bother you at all." Laura looked from one face to another. "Is that understood? When I get back, we'll do something nice, but only if you all behave."

After reluctant nods and mutinous glances from Raymond and June, Laura slipped into her bedroom to retrieve her pocketbook. She slid the envelopes from Mr. Bannon inside, along with the bank book she'd found in the top drawer of Glen's nightstand, glancing in the mirror as she snapped the purse flap closed. She grabbed a wide-brimmed straw hat from the top of the armoire and put it on, then yanked it back off. Forget it. I've got business to handle, I'm not going to a tea-party. She smoothed her Peter Pan collar and the puffed sleeves that reached her elbows, then pulled the narrow handbag strap over her shoulder and left the room.

The children followed her outside on the porch. Laura felt their eyes on her as she started marching at a steady pace down the driveway. She'd never left them alone like this before, but they'd be fine. Please, God, watch over them and keep them safe for me.

CHAPTER THREE

Feels So Wrong

Laura's thoughts were in turmoil as she walked. How was she supposed to cope with no additional money coming in? What were the doctors doing to hasten Glen's recovery? How long would it take before he returned home? The questions alternated with memories of the awful days since the accident.

Worst of all was reliving what happened when they brought Glen home that day. She kept seeing the three vehicles in their driveway, and the man, embarrassed and sad, who brought her the keys to Glen's truck. Then a doctor met her on the porch and explained that Glen had had some kind of mental collapse.

"Your husband kept crying and screaming the name Bobbie, over and over, after the young man he'd tried to save had been pronounced dead," the doctor said. Laura explained that Glen's brother, Bobbie, had been killed in the war. "That explains it," the doctor said. "His breakdown was probably shell shock. The sudden, accidental death reminded him of when his brother died. The accident could have triggered that awful memory, and caused him to feel guilty about failing to save his brother or the man at the worksite." Then the doctor and another man half-led, half-dragged a sedated Glen to bed.

Laura's steps slowed as she remembered, and tears filled her eyes. Enough. Thinking about what happened doesn't change anything. She wiped her eyes, straightened her back, and hurried along.

Laura went to the bank first, but kept waffling back and forth about depositing the contents of both envelopes. Pushing through the bank's double doors, she decided to deposit the salary money into the bank account, and put the rest into the mason jar where she and Glen had been saving emergency money since the day they'd gotten married.

Laura approached a large mahogany desk in the lobby. "May I help you?" said a short, wiry man with a lush, black handlebar mustache and shiny black hair that gave off a faint aroma of Brylcreme. He introduced himself with a slight nod, hands clasped behind his back. "My name is Mr. Tibbits, and I'm the Assistant Manager. How can I be of service to you today."

Laura bobbed her chin, both hands holding her pocketbook tucked against her side. "Thank you, Mr. Tibbits. I wanted to check the balance in our account and make a deposit."

"I can help you with that." Mr. Tibbits pointed toward an armless ladder-back chair at the side of his desk, then sat down in the leather executive chair behind it.

"Thank you," Laura said. "Here's the bank book." She reached inside her handbag and pulled out the small, green, leather-bound book with the bank's name and logo in gold lettering on the cover. "Mr. Webber, my husband is ill in the hospital, so I must take care of our finances until he recovers. Checking the balance before depositing his wages seemed like the smart thing to do."

"A wise decision." Mr. Tibbits opened the book and copied the name and account number on a piece of paper. "Please be patient for a few moments, and I'll get that information for you, Mrs. Webber." He stood, glanced at the paper in his right hand, and strode toward a curtained glass door at the back of the bank.

Laura watched people move in and out of the lobby, twisting her fingers in her lap. Most of them made their way to one of three teller windows, framed in the same polished wood as the counters and Mr. Tibbits' desk. She noticed all the customers waiting in line were men. Goodness, it's been a long time since I've taken care of my banking and bills. Glen handled our finances since we got married.

While she waited, she checked the balance printed in the bank book again, even though she had the total memorized, $142.38, and hoped it was accurate. The knowledge that there wouldn't be any more of Glen's paychecks terrified her. Her mind careened from one idea to another about how to survive until he was back home and working again.

Mr. Tibbits opened the door, turned for some last words with the person inside, then focused on Laura as he returned to his desk. "Sorry to take so long." He settled back into his chair and placed a few sheets of paper in the middle of his desk blotter. "We seem to have a slight problem."

"What do you mean? My husband is always meticulous about entering everything in the bank book." Laura's pulse throbbed in her ears, and the warmth drained from her face.

"No, no, the balance in the book is accurate. The problem is that the account is only in your husband's name." Mr. Tibbits placed one piece of paper, which had the bank's logo embossed at the top of the page, in front of Laura and pointed half-way. "You're listed as the beneficiary, which means you'd receive all the money if your husband died, but his is the only name on the account." Mr. Tibbits paused, smoothing non-existent creases out of the paper with his fingers. "That means you can deposit money but can't make a withdrawal. Since you said your husband is in the hospital, all the funds in the account have to remain there until he's well enough to withdraw them himself."

"But while my husband is in the hospital, I have to feed four small children and pay the bills. How can I do that if I can't use our money?" She fought hard to keep her voice even, to not let her panic and anger bleed through. Her palms hurt where the edge of the desk pressed into her skin. "You have to know that this is not what my husband wanted. I can't believe anyone told him I wouldn't have access to our money."

Mr. Tibbits reached across the desk and patted Laura's hand. "I understand, Mrs. Webber, and I wish there was something I could do, but I'm bound by the bank regulations. I asked the manager," he said, pointing at the office he'd visited earlier. "But he told me we couldn't make an exception"

Laura leaned forward and clasped both her hands together. "Please, there must be some way around this."

"Well, I do have an idea. If you obtained a doctor's letter certifying that your husband can no longer take care of his own affairs, we'd release the money."

"What?" In spite of her best intentions, Laura's voice crept up. "You want me to have a doctor write that he's crazy? That he can't manage his own affairs? I can't do that to him. And besides, we expect him to get better and come home soon."

"I hope he does, Mrs. Webber, but until that happens we can't let you remove the money from the account. And remember, the doctor's letter could be reversed after he's released, so there wouldn't be any lasting problem for him," Mr. Tibbits said. "Until you can get the doctor's letter, you can open a new account in your name with the money you want to deposit. We'll order you some checks to use until he comes home, then you can merge the two accounts and put both names on it."

Laura stared at Mr. Tibbits, aghast at his suggestion. It felt so wrong, like she was giving up on Glen, but it seemed to be her only choice. And a letter like Mr. Tibbits wants? How embarrassing for Glen when he recovers and sees it. Even if she could get a letter like that from the doctor, how hard will it be to get a new letter restoring Glen's rights? It seemed so final, so public to put his problems in writing. She wondered whether it would hurt him when he returned to work? Who wants to hire someone with a letter saying he's mentally ill? She hated this.

᭟

Laura walked out of the bank with a new bank book in her purse, and a dozen checks tucked inside. Seventy-Five dollars. Two week's wages. Almost twice that amount in the other account, but no way to touch it.

Dr. Farnsworth's office was her next stop, and he better have some answers.

The doctor's office was only two blocks from the bank. The nurse sitting at the corner desk waved Laura toward the only empty chair in the room. She sat, tapping her foot and playing with the clasp on her handbag while she waited for an hour, getting more worried about the kids with every passing minute. She almost gave up before her name was called, then she followed the nurse through a short hallway into a tiny inner office.

"I'm sorry for barging in like this, but it's urgent that I talk to you." She sat down in a small chair next to the desk.

Dr. Farnsworth's small, wiry frame, topped by short gray hair and sporting a matching goatee, was parked in his chair behind the metal desk. "Are you sick, Mrs. Webber?" he said. "You've been under a terrific strain since your husband became ill."

"No, I'm fine. Well, physically." Laura stopped and watched the doctor tap his pencil on the desk blotter, three taps, then a pause, then three more. She shook her shoulders, straightened her back, and tried to find the right words. "Doctor, my children and I have been doing our best, but they don't understand why their papa is still gone. They've started fighting all the time and have trouble sleeping. Every single day they beg for Glen to come home, and I don't know what to say. More than anything, they need something to hold on to." Laura' took a deep breath to calm herself. "When do you think my husband will be released? He's been gone for over two weeks now and the accident was almost a month ago. I haven't heard a word from the Springfield Mental Hospital about how he's doing or how they're treating him."

Dr. Farnsworth leaned back in his chair, putting a little more distance between himself and Laura. He stopped tapping the pencil and started sliding it end to end, over and over, between his fingers. "Mrs. Webber, treating a mental illness isn't like treating a sprained ankle. We know very little about how the mind works or what to do when someone seems to lose touch with reality."

"What are you saying?"

"Look, I don't mean to be vague, but I don't treat mental illnesses. I have no idea when your husband will be able to leave the hospital because the doctors who are treating him now are in charge. If you want to know what's happening, you need to talk to them."

Laura's head jerked back, and she took a sharp intake of breath. "How can you not have any idea? What are they doing with him? Haven't the hospital doctors stayed in touch with you? You've been our family doctor since we moved to Aurora and I trusted you to do what was best for him."

"I mean exactly what I said." Dr. Farnsworth rested his elbows on the desk, palms together. "Even though I've been caring for your family for several years, Mr. Webber is now under the care of the staff at Springfield Mental Hospital. They don't give me updates. You need to talk to them. I can give you the name of the person who admitted him. You should go there and talk to the doctor in charge of your husband's case."

"I, um, I assumed you'd be in charge." Laura blinked her eyes, then shook her head to clear it. "I guess I'll have to find a way to go there then. But can you give me any idea of how they might treat him?"

Dr. Farnsworth dropped his chin onto his clasped hands. "Remember the first week after the accident when Glen was at home? You gave him three pills a day because we hoped it would help him escape the scene he kept seeing in his mind, the death of his brother? The only drugs I had to give were barbiturates, but they can only calm him down, not cure the condition. He stayed in a kind of fog, able to follow simple directions but not quite aware."

"I remember every minute. The kids didn't understand why their Papa wouldn't talk to them or do anything by himself."

"Then we tried reducing the daily drug use and hoped he'd come out okay." Dr. Farnsworth reached across the desk and touched Laura's hand. "But when the drugs wore off, he was right back where he started, on his knees crying and screaming. Had I not been there, you'd have had to go get the sheriff to take him away."

Laura's face felt like stone. "How could I ever forget?" She closed her eyes as if trying to escape the memory. "Then you injected something that almost knocked him out. I remember how you walked him to your car." Laura took some deep breaths, then refocused her gaze on Dr. Farnsworth's face.

"Only the doctor treating him can give you a full update, but I can give you a general idea of things they might try."

Laura nodded, unable to speak.

"I know that when drug therapy doesn't seem to work, even after experimenting with different medications, singly and in combination, his doctors might put him into a drug coma for five to ten days to see if that will bring him back when he awakens. Two weeks is not even enough time to test a drug's effectiveness on him. They may test several individual drugs or combinations to find something that works."

"And if none of those things work?"

"If medications don't help, they may need to resort to electric shock therapy."

Laura gasped and wrapped her arms around her stomach, which felt like she'd been kicked. "Oh dear God. I've heard that's a horrible, barbaric treatment." She couldn't stop tears from welling up. "But you can't be sure if that will be necessary, can you?"

"No, and they won't try shock therapy until after they attempt putting him in a drug coma."

"But doctor, my children need their father. Can't you give me any idea at all?"

"My dear Mrs. Webber, I wish that were possible, but I'd be misleading you. Please just let your children know their papa is in good hands."

🦇

When she found herself outside on the sidewalk, Laura was shaking as she headed home. Dr. Farnsworth had given her a piece of paper with information about the hospital, who to ask for, and some questions she should ask. He'd even drawn a crude map of the route she should take. She felt numb, overwhelmed by what she'd learned, as yet unable to process all that she needed to do.

Laura stopped at the post office since it was on the way home. She was glad customers were behind her in line because her focus was on planning the trip to the hospital, and she wasn't in the mood to chat. The postmaster, Mr. Niedermann, had become a dear friend, but she wasn't able to say a word. He had a quizzical expression when he handed her the mail, so she tried to smile before turning away from the counter. Laura shoved the envelopes in her purse, but lacked the energy to even look at them.

After stepping around the people behind her in line, she made her way outside, moving without paying attention to her surroundings. Normal sounds like cars, pedestrians, and the barking of two dogs almost disappeared, unable to penetrate the wall of fear surrounding her.

What am I going to do? The same phrase repeated itself in Laura's mind for the hundredth time.

"You'll do what you have to do, whatever is best for your children." The voice was firm but kind. Laura felt each word in every atom of her body rather than hearing them.

"Ma? I've missed you," she said. "It's been so long since you've come to me." She stopped in place on the sidewalk, then looked around, hoping nobody had noticed her talking to herself. Ma, I need your help. This time Laura spoke only in her mind.

She waited, but knew her ma was gone. Okay, Ma, I get the message. It's time to stop whining and figure out what to do. She couldn't help a stubborn, petty little part of her that wished her dead ma would be more helpful with her messages, maybe give some actual suggestions instead of cryptic guidance.

CHAPTER FOUR

I Told Them to Pick Bugs

When the house came into view, Laura stopped a moment, remembering the day they'd moved in—the same day she and the children had seen it for the first time. She loved the single-story, brown house. A deep porch spanned the length of the front, with posts holding up the roof. A neat picket fence, with a wide rail on top, edged all three sides of the porch. Four wide steps in the center led up to the porch and straight to the front door with a large window on either side. When she resumed walking up the long curved driveway, the kids spotted her, and Raymond and Jimmy ran to meet her. June stayed seated in a rocker on the porch, plunging back and forth at full speed. David sat in the grass next to the wagon.

Uh oh, never a dull minute. She pasted a smile on her face, ready for the boys.

"Mama, June told us we had to pick bugs. You told her she's not our boss, but she wouldn't leave us alone," Raymond's said, his face flushed. Jimmy was right behind him, nodding at every word.

"Don't worry, we'll talk when we get to the porch." Laura smiled at the looks on both boys' faces as they marched next to her.

When the trio neared the porch, June bounded out of her chair and ran to meet them. "They didn't follow the rules, Mama, so I told them to pick bugs. They said no and ran off. You told me I was the boss, so you need to make them do what I say."

Laura raised her hand. "Quiet! I don't want to hear another word from anyone." She stared at all four children. "Except for you, David. Did you have fun today?"

David grinned, nodded his head, then resumed playing with the wagon.

"Okay, sounds like you three had problems while I was gone." June and Raymond both started talking at once, pointing at each other. "Before you say another word, I have some questions for you. Did anyone get hurt?...Did anything get broken?...Did anything get spilled or wasted?...Did anything happen to the animals?" Both kids shook their heads no after each question.

"Are any of you bleeding?...Is anything on fire?...Did you kill anything?" This time they grinned while shaking their heads.

Laura chuckled and crossed her arms. "It looks like you survived your first time alone, and I'm proud of you. Let's have the rest of those oatmeal cookies with some milk."

Hours later, Laura rocked on the front porch, her eyes closed, listening to the sounds of nightbirds. The children were asleep, exhausted from all the things that had taken place during the day. Poor kids, they listened to what she'd told them about Glen, but all they cared about was having him home. How were little children supposed to understand matters adults couldn't even figure out?

Laura sipped from a glass of iced tea, turning the events of the day over and over in her mind. The most important thing was figuring how to travel the thirty miles to the hospital. She'd have to drive the truck, something she hadn't done since before June was born. She hoped she'd remember how. Would it even start after not being driven since the accident?

Thirty miles each way, and no telling how long she'd be there. Better plan for the trip to take a whole day. Laura realized she'd have to take the children with her, since they couldn't be left alone that long, and she had no place to leave them.

Laura thought of all the friends that used to come every Saturday night before David was born. All the children would spread pallets in the kids' bedroom while their parents played music and danced in the living room. She'd play the piano while Glen accompanied her on his guitar or the harmonica, taking dance breaks when their guests took turns with the music. Laura missed those days so much. After David was born, Glen became obsessed with working and building their savings, and stopped their Saturday dance nights. They'd lost touch with those friends, so she didn't feel like she could ask them for help.

She worried about money, too, but refused to let that become the children's problem. Laura hoped their money would last until Glen came home, so they didn't have to resort to their mason jar emergency savings. He had created that emergency fund through the years to protect Laura and their children if something happened to him. Glen's memories of how his family had been left destitute when his father died haunted him, and he was determined not to let that happen to his family.

Even the farm was a huge potential problem if Glen stayed away for an extended time. Caring for the landlord's animals and garden, plus giving him half of the produce and milk, was a good deal for not paying rent, but how long could she handle everything alone? She and Glen had shared the responsibilities, with him handling the toughest ones. Was it even possible for her to do everything by herself?

The stars held no answers, so Laura gave up and went inside. She checked the children, curled together like a litter of puppies in their bed, then returned to her room. The bed felt so empty without Glen next to her. Funny, she hadn't loved him when they got married, just wanted a family of her own like her sisters all had. She knew he was a good man, so when he proposed she said yes. But now, she missed him so much it hurt.

🦇

Sleep drained away bit by bit, like sand sliding off warm skin. Laura reached for her husband, then opened her eyes in a room lit only by moon glow through the window. Her fingers found Raymond, slumbering next to her. She smoothed tendrils of damp hair away from his face. In my bed again? Your pa's been away over two weeks now and I don't think you've stayed in your own bed even half the nights. Poor baby, seven is too young to go through all this.

Laura planted a soft kiss on Raymond's forehead, turned away and sat up. She pressed

the alarm button on the clock twelve minutes
before it was due to go off, grabbed her robe
from the hook by the door and pulled it on as
she left the room. Her bare feet were silent on
the cool wooden floor, as she made her way
down the hallway to her children's bedroom.
She stepped inside and crept forward until she
stood beside their bed.

Moonlight illuminated three small
figures. Look at June. Just turned ten years old a
couple of months ago and already such a
comfort to David. Laura pulled the sheet up
over her daughter's shoulder, smiling at the way
June's body cradled her baby brother. David
stirred in his sleep, but June's arm pulled him
closer without either of them waking. Would
David remember Glen if he stayed away much
longer? Poor little guy was only one. Laura
shoved the thought away, determined not to
consider that possibility.

Jimmy, uncovered and stretched out flat
on his back with arms and legs spread out like a
starfish, occupied half of the double bed. His
breath whistled in and out of his open mouth.
Good thing Raymond joined me in bed.
Jimmy's taking all the room for both of them.
She started to cover the sprawled out six-year-
old, but changed her mind when she touched
his little warm, damp foot. Hot body when he
sleeps, just like his papa.

That thought pierced her heart with longing for Glen. Lord, I hope those doctors fix him up and send him home soon. Shaking her head to clear it, she retraced her steps through the hallway toward the living room, through the dining room and into the kitchen. She stopped at the sink on her left and stared out the window. Five years in this house and she still couldn't believe they lived here. Better get moving though, gawking and daydreaming wouldn't get the animals taken care of.

She moved through the kitchen into the washroom where she donned a long-sleeved shirt, trousers, canvas coveralls, work gloves, and rubber boots. She rolled up the coverall cuffs since they were Glen's, and tucked them inside the top of the boots. A rooster crowed as Laura passed the chicken coop on her way to the barn. "Sorry Rufus, you and your girls will have to wait for the kids to wake up and feed you after they finish breakfast."

When Laura opened the barn doors and let herself in, the sound of cows lowing greeted her. "Hold on ladies, I'll get to you in a minute." She grabbed a three-legged stool and a large bucket and headed for the nearest stall. After she milked all the cows and transferred the warm, frothy liquid into large, metal, milk cans, Laura let the animals out into the pasture. She filled all the feed bins and made sure the water troughs were full before heading back to the house. Sure was easier when Glen did the animal chores each morning.

Laura pulled off her mucky boots and left them on the back porch, then hung the work gloves and coveralls in the washroom. She heard laughter coming from the kitchen and grinned. "You guys are up early," she sang out.

Laura scrubbed her hands and arms in the washroom sink, then entered the kitchen and found June pouring glasses of milk for Raymond and Jimmy. "What would you like for breakfast?"

"Fried eggs and bacon," Raymond yelled, always ready for his favorite.

"I want pancakes." Jimmy waved his hand, trying to catch her attention.

"Scrambled eggs and potatoes would be great," June said, stepping out of David's way as he ran circles around the table.

Determined to avoid the tension of the previous day, Laura kept a smile on her face. "That'll teach me to ask a dumb question." She walked to the refrigerator to look inside.

"Would you like to try again? I'm only cooking one type of breakfast, so you four can figure out what you want. My vote is for pancakes with sausages."

Sausages won the vote. Laura mixed batter, June washed David's hands and face while supervising Raymond and Jimmy, both of whom insisted they didn't need her bossing them. The children attacked the steaming pancakes and sizzling sausages when they grabbed their forks, laughing and making silly faces as they ate.

After she filled all the plates, Laura sat joined the children at the table. She loved watching them laugh and tease one another as they ate. What a difference from meals when she was growing up. She'd take giggles and jokes over frozen-faced scared silence any day. She reached over and ruffled Jimmy's hair, then poked his nose to make him laugh. There had never been laughter at the table when she was a child, only the fear that ruled her family's table, and the sound of her pa's belt striking tender skin whenever his rules were disobeyed.

Whatever it takes, whatever I have to do, my children will not grow up in fear.

CHAPTER FIVE

The Best Summer Ever

Laura propped the garage doors open, then walked around their truck. She stroked the left front fender, leaving a streak in the thin coating of dust. "You've missed Glen, too, haven't you. He always kept you in tiptop shape."

She remembered the day Glen arrived home with the truck after he'd traded their car for it. It was a complete surprise to her, but later she'd learned it was part of his grand plan to leave their apartment and jobs in Tulsa and move to Seminole at the start of the oil rush there.

She opened the driver's door and climbed into the seat, then rubbed her right hand over the threadbare upholstery. Memories of their trip echoed within the quiet, empty truck. The two of them, excited about their future and confident of their ability to create it together.

"There you are, Mama. No wonder we couldn't find you." June and Raymond, excited grins on their dirty faces, peeked through the open door. "Look what we caught." Raymond held up a Mason jar full of pollywogs swimming in brown water.

June clasped her hands in supplication. "Can we keep them? It'll be fun to watch them grow and turn into frogs."

"Fun for you, but the poor little pollywogs need room to swim." Laura held the jar, peering at the teeming throng of wiggly creatures. She handed the jar back to Raymond.

"Go put them back, honey. If you go to the creek and check every few days, you'll be able to watch them change without hurting them."

Raymond raced off, but June climbed on the running board. "Do you know how to drive?"

"I used to drive," Laura said. "But that was before you were born. Since then your papa has always driven so I could take care of you kids."

June leaned inside. "Sure was crowded with all of us inside, even without David." With that pronouncement, June jumped down and headed for the garage door. "I'd better make sure the boys put the pollywogs back where we found them."

Laura nodded, lost in memories. June was just over a year old when they left Seminole for South Dakota, urged on by messages from Laura's ma. Glen had been angry and suspicious when he learned about Laura's "second sight," but was convinced when she told him things about his past that she had no normal way of knowing. Her predictions proved accurate, saving them from losing all they'd accumulated when the oil boom crashed as fast as it had risen.

Stop daydreaming. You need to figure out how to start this thing.

Laura checked to be sure the emergency brake/neutral lever was all the way back. Her heart started beating a little faster, and her fingers shook when she put the key into the ignition. Next, she had to move the spark advance lever all the way up to retard position, but where the heck was it? She released the emergency brake and grabbed the lever behind the steering wheel on the left side of the steering column and shoved it up. Then, with her right hand, she reached for the throttle lever on the right side. She remembered her original lessons from Glen, and how he'd put his hand over hers and cautioned her about not moving the throttle more than a quarter of the way down. Okay, now to make sure the Magneto-Battery switch is in the battery position.

Laura took a deep breath, pressed the starter button on the left side of the dash. A few sputters, and the engine roared to life. She'd done it. Sweaty hands tight on the steering wheel, she guided the truck outside into the sunshine.

She let the engine run for awhile, remembering Glen's words about the importance of not letting a vehicle sit idle for too long. Relief flooded over her when she turned it off, confident that she could start it again whenever she had to.

She climbed out of the truck, then walked around to check the box in back. Once the double doors were open, she saw the space was clean and empty, with just a light coat of dust. Glen was right, the truck had been a lifesaver for them. Three of them rode in the front during the move to South Dakota, with all their belongings packed on top of the roof and in the back. At night they slept on mattresses stacked in front of the doors. They never could have done it without the windows Glen cut in the sides for light and air.

Laura closed the back doors, thinking about how different the trip from Seminole to Dennis and Gladys' place in South Dakota had been with June, compared to what it was like when they left with three children to care for and no set destination in mind.

Dennis, Glen's uncle, had welcomed them when they needed a place to go, offering a tiny house once used by his farmhand. They might still be in Geddes now if Gladys, Dennis's wife, hadn't been cruel to the children. Laura still felt guilty about hurting Dennis by insisting they leave, but she couldn't stay after Gladys whipped June and Raymond with a tree branch.

"Mama, David just woke up," June said, leading her brother by the hand. "He's hungry."

Laura laughed, "When isn't he hungry? I'll fix us some dinner. Go get Raymond and Jimmy for me."

June nodded, started back to the doors, then turned and walked to the truck. She lifted David up on the running board and asked. "When we go see Papa, can we stop at the bridge on the way back?"

"The bridge?"

"Maybe we could even go play underneath it where we lived." June looked pensive. "That was the best summer ever."

"Living under a bridge was the best summer ever?"

Laura was surprised when June nodded.

"Yes, it was so much fun. Don't you remember, Mama?" June said. "I mean, we got to play in the creek every single day. We had fun digging worms so you and Papa could fish, and everything tasted better cooked outside over the firepit. Even when it rained and we had to stay all squished in the back of the truck, we could still sing songs and play games."

Wow, not how Laura would describe seven weeks living under a bridge. Glen bicycled to work each day, but she'd never been able to leave or speak to another living soul for fear of being discovered. "Maybe on the way back from the hospital we can stop. We'll see how it goes."

Before going to bed, the children filled a wooden crate with toys for the trip and placed it next to the front door. Laura filled another box with food—apples, crackers, a loaf of bread, jar of peanut butter, some boiled eggs, a bag of cookies—and placed it on the counter. Then she placed three mason jars full of water in the refrigerator. "That should be plenty for the trip," she said. "No telling how long we'll be at the hospital, but we'll all be thirsty and want to snack before we get home."

In spite of good intentions, it was almost ten when Laura pulled out of the driveway. The children's enthusiasm, fired by the prospect of seeing their papa, made short order of their chores, but Jimmy forgot Laura's instruction to leave the chickens in the coop for the day. By the time the unhappy birds were rounded up and locked inside, she had to change David's clothes and wash his face, arms, and legs.

The excitement of speeding down the highway lasted about fifteen minutes.

"Ow, you stepped on my foot," June hollered, elbowing Jimmy off her side.

"You and David are hogging the window. I want to see out, too." Jimmy leaned across June, trying to shove his face even with David's.

"What are you complaining about?" Raymond retorted. I can't see through either side window from here in the middle." He glanced at Laura since he had begged to sit next to her. "Just looking through the windshield is boring."

"Are we almost there yet?" June said.

"Not even close. It's only been a few minutes." Laura glanced at the four sweaty, flushed children squashed on the seat beside her. "Why don't you guys play word games or sing some songs?"

"Will you play with us? You can even pick the first song." Raymond said. The others nodded, eager to see what she'd choose.

"Not this time. I need to concentrate on my driving." That was a lie, well, sort of. Laura was having a hard time focusing on the road because she couldn't stop worrying and wondering about what she'd find at the hospital. She was determined to get some answers, and she needed to see Glen for herself.

It took just over an hour to arrive. The words, Springfield Mental Hospital, were carved into the stone lintel above the double glass doors. Laura found a shady parking spot at the side of the lot, turned the engine off and set the emergency brake. The clicking sounds of the cooling engine broke the silence as everyone's attention was riveted by the biggest building they'd ever seen.

CHAPTER SIX

Someone Please Help Me

Three stories tall, the dull red brick building's front was broken only by the glass double-wide doors and three lines of identical barred windows. The doors were centered in the first floor, with twelve windows on each side. Laura counted twenty-five windows on each of the top two floors, all identical. She saw two wide chimneys at each end of the steep shingled roof, and five gables with small windows spaced at even intervals from what must have been an attic. A low hedge grew along the building front and the walkway that led from the parking area to the doors, but no flowers or trees had been planted to add color or soften the grim lines.

Raymond's eyes looked enormous when he turned to Laura. "That place is so big. How will we find Papa?"

Thinking the same thing but not wanting it to show, Laura said, "Don't you worry about that. We'll find him if we have to check every single room." She opened her door, stuffed some toys and snacks into a canvas bag, and slung it and her pocketbook over her shoulder. She beckoned the children out of the truck and said, "Remember what I told you. I'll do all the talking. You need to stay with me, no running or fussing. And don't interrupt me when I'm talking to the hospital people." She stared into each child's eyes. "Okay, here we go."

Laura pushed her way through the heavy doors, then led the wide-eyed children up to a long, u-shaped counter in the middle of the room. Laura tried to catch someone's attention. "Excuse me." She said as she stood at the counter waiting, while several white-coated women went about their work on the other side.

"Can someone please help me?"

A short blonde nurse looked up from her desk. "Hold on. I'll be with you in a minute." She finished writing, then tucked the paper into a folder before joining Laura at the counter. "What can I do for you, ma'am?"

"My husband has been here for a couple of weeks. His name is Glen Webber, and I'd like to speak to his doctor."

"What's his doctor's name?"

"I don't know. Our family doctor, Dr. Farnsworth, arranged for his admission," Laura said.

The nurse sighed and tapped her pencil. "I can't track your husband that way. If you don't know his doctor's name, how about his room number?"

"I don't know that either."

"Your husband has been here for over two weeks and you don't know who his doctor is or his room number?" The nurse raised one eyebrow as her voice rose.

Warmth crept up Laura's face. She must think I'm an idiot or someone who doesn't care. "I thought Dr. Farnsworth was directing things. Until I saw him yesterday, I didn't know he'd transferred Glen's care to the staff here." Laura twisted her fingers together just below the edge of the counter. "I'm here today to find answers, so please, can't you check the records? I need to talk to his doctor and see my husband."

The nurse shook her head and rolled her eyes. "It's going to take some time. You said his name is Glen Webber? Is that spelled W E B B E R?"

Laura watched the nurse go back to a line of metal file cabinets. "Mrs. Webber, you might as well take a seat." She waved at a row of chairs behind Laura next to the front door. "This will take awhile."

Laura nodded and led the children to the chairs.

"Where's Papa?" June whispered.

"Is he coming to see us out here?" Jimmy's voice rang out.

"Sshh, keep your voice down," Laura whispered. She sat and pulled the children close. "The nurse is looking for your papa's information."

"Did they lose him?" Raymond said.

"No, honey, but they take care of lots of people here."

The conversation stayed low as Laura tried to keep the children calm. Raymond and Jimmy were playing with two cars on the floor next to Laura's chair, while June sat next to her reading The Story of Ferdinand to David.

A grey-haired nurse approached them holding a manila folder in front of her. "Mrs. Webber, we found your husband's records. He's being treated by Doctor Vaughn. If you'll please come with me, I'll take you to the doctor's office."

The children jumped to their feet, then dropped their toys and books into their mom's bag. "Thank you," Laura said.

The nurse led them around the right side of the counter, pulled a full keyring from her pocket, and unlocked a door to her right. "This way, please." She waved the family through, then locked the door behind them. "His office is at the end of the hallway. Don't mind the patients. They won't bother you."

The children stayed close to Laura as they made their way behind the nurse. They passed three men in the hall. One of them stood against a wall, staring at another who sat on the floor at his feet. Neither spoke, but the man on the floor made soft moaning sounds as he rocked back and forth, ignoring the one who loomed above. The third man shuffled toward the family as they walked, his gaze skittering around, never looking anyone in the eyes.

As he passed them, June whispered, "Mama, why are his sleeves wrapped around behind his back?"

"It's all right, Junebug, I'll explain later." The boys pressed against Laura's sides, their eyes wide.

"Here's Doctor Vaughn's office." The nurse opened a door, waved them through, then closed it behind them. Laura was relieved when she left without locking it.

"Mrs. Webber, I'm Doctor Vaughn. please take a seat."

Everything about Dr. Vaughn's appearance was average—average height, average weight, brown eyes, brown straight hair combed back from his high forehead, and an unremarkable face. Only his voice was memorable, nasal with a heavy southern accent.

There were only two chairs facing Dr. Vaughn's desk. Laura sat in one, placed her purse in the other. She handed the canvas bag to June. "Thank you," she said. "Kids, the doctor and I need to talk, so take the bag and sit on the floor by the door. You may play or read, but you must remain very quiet."

"I'm surprised to meet you, Mrs. Webber." Dr. Vaughn leaned back in his chair after tossing the folder into the center of his desk. "I saw from Glen's file that he was married, but since I never heard from anyone, I assumed ..."

"You assumed what? That his family didn't care?" Laura's voice rose. "Dr. Farnsworth has been our family doctor for five years. When he brought Glen here, I thought he'd be involved in his care and keep me advised. I just learned yesterday that he turned everything over to your staff."

Dr. Vaughn's smile had no warmth in it. "And yet you made no attempt to contact us for two weeks? I find that difficult to understand." He shook his head, then opened the folder. "Be that as it may, what questions do you have about your husband?"

Laura jerked back at his words, but her shock turned to anger. "I beg your pardon. You find that difficult to understand? I have four children, Doctor Vaughn, children who miss their father and can't be left alone for me to travel. We don't have a phone, and live thirty miles away. I just found out yesterday that Dr. Farnsworth is not handling Glen's care, and we are here today. Do you even have children, Doctor Vaughn?"

Dr. Vaughn opened his mouth to reply, then stopped. "I apologize, Mrs. Webber. We have so many patients who are ignored by their families. I shouldn't have made an assumption."

"That's terrible."

"Yes, it is. But having a loved one you can't handle at home, one you can't control or understand, isn't easy. Many of the families find it easier and less painful to turn their backs and leave their relatives to the system."

"I have no intention of doing that." Laura took a deep breath, and folded her hands in her lap. "I need to know how Glen is, and what your treatment plans are. We love him and want him home as soon as possible. The children and I need to see him, too. Not knowing and not seeing him makes this situation harder."

Dr. Vaughn shook his head. "I'm happy to tell you what I know about your husband, and what the treatment options are, but it's not a good idea for you and the children to see him right now."

"I don't expect it to be easy, Doctor, but we must see him. He can't be worse today than when he was screaming and crying on the floor, seeing things that weren't there. I don't lie to my children. They can face what's going on better than imagining a reality that is even worse."

"I have to disagree," Dr. Vaughn said. "Besides, your husband is in a ward with many other patients. Taking you and your children in that room would be upsetting for not only the children, but to the other patients. Be reasonable."

"Doctor, we are not leaving without seeing Glen. I don't care if you have to curtain off his bed or move him to a different space where we can be with him. One way or another, you need to make this happen." Laura paused to calm herself. "Now, can you tell me how he's doing?"

Dr. Vaughn agreed with Dr. Farnsworth's tentative diagnosis of shell shock, and also concurred with his statement that very little was known about treating it. Glen had been kept under heavy medication since he'd arrived. The plan was to start reducing the dose gradually. Unlike what Laura had tried, the reduction would be over a period of weeks instead of days.

"Weeks?" Laura whispered the word, not wanting to believe what she was hearing. "And if he doesn't come out of it after you've reduced the dosage?"

"Well, there are a couple of other drugs we can try. But the course for those drugs would be the same. Full strength at first, then a gradual tapering off."

Laura buried her face in her hands, heartsick, then straightened up. "Are drugs your only options?"

"No. We've found that patients such as your husband can be helped, at least made much calmer, through the use of hydrotherapy."

At Laura's puzzled look, he explained. "The patient is greased to protect the skin, then they are kept in warm, moving water in a deep tub for long periods of time. Only their heads are above the canvas tub cover, and the warm water circulates around them."

Dr. Vaughn waited, but Laura didn't respond. "If medications and hydrotherapy both fail to bring good results, the next step would be electroshock therapy."

Laura shook her head. "No. I've read up on that, and it sounds barbaric. I don't want you to do that. I won't give permission for that."

Dr. Vaughn started to explain the benefits and techniques for electroshock, then gave up. He assured Laura that he'd do his best with medication first, and keep her informed.

She gave him the telephone number for the post office, sure that Mr. Niedermann wouldn't mind taking a message for her. After he'd answered all her questions, the doctor stood to escort Laura out.

"Wait, Doctor Vaughn. We need to see Glen before we go."

"But I thought you understood he's not in shape for visitors," he said.

"Doctor, I appreciate all you've told me, but we need to see him. We can't go home without seeing him first." Laura's voice radiated determination.

"I'm only trying to make it easy on you. If you insist, fine. I'll have the nurse take you to him." Dr. Vaughn stalked past them, down the hallway.

꙾

The ward smelled sour, a combination of vomit, bleach, and ammonia. Ten beds lined one wall, each with a chair at the foot. About half of the patients were in bed, with the rest sitting in the chairs.

"Wait here." the nurse said, leaving Laura and the children just inside the ward door. "I'll draw the curtain around Mr. Webber's bed for some privacy."

The nurse walked down to the third bed from the end, where a man rocked back and forth on his chair. The metal rings screeched on the bar as the curtain was pulled around his area, shutting him off from the rest of the room. "Come on, now," the nurse called, motioning the family forward.

Almost running, the children tugged Laura forward. The nurse pulled the curtain aside for them to get inside, then left after telling them to stop at the front desk when they were through visiting.

Laura stared hard at Glen's face. His eyes were open, but not focused on anything. His dry, cracked lips were parted just enough for a string of drool to crawl down his face from one corner. He was in a straitjacket, arms invisible in sleeves that wrapped around his torso and tied in the back. The pajama bottoms he wore were wrinkled and stained, pooling on top of scuffed slippers that looked much too big.

"Glen, honey, we're here." The words sounded ridiculous as Laura said them.

The children stayed close to Laura, keeping their distance from Glen. He kept rocking, rocking as if they weren't there. When he made no moves toward them, June and Raymond moved closer on either side. Jimmy leaned against his legs and patted his knees. "Papa. Papa, come home with us."

CHAPTER SEVEN

Beans Stuck To The Ceiling

As the family started home, the silence in the truck was thick and oppressive. The children sat still in their places, but Laura felt their glances on her face.

"I'm so sorry you had to see your papa like that," she said.

"He looked awful." June's voice was soft, but full of pain and accusation. "You said they took him away to make him better."

"That's right." Raymond's face was flushed. "He was better at home. And why did they have him tied up in that shirt?"

"I didn't like that doctor." Jimmy stared at Laura. "We shouldn't have left Papa with him."

"I know how you feel, but we have to trust the doctor and the hospital to do what's best for him." Laura felt waves of hostility and hurt from the children. And she didn't blame them. It was an awful shock to see Glen in that condition. She didn't trust the doctor, either, but had no other place to turn for help.

Silence filled the truck cab for a long time, broken only by David making engine sounds as he played with a small wooden truck, running it up and down his legs.

"Ma, is that our bridge?" June said, pointing ahead through the windshield.

"Sure is." Laura slowed down and pulled to the side of the road before they reached the bridge. "I'll check it out. The way down under it is steep, and I'm not comfortable trying to drive there." She climbed down, pushing the door closed behind her. "Stay in the truck until I get back."

Laura picked her way on the gravel turnout toward the slope that tilted down toward the water, remembering all the times she'd watched Glen maneuver the hill on his bicycle to and from work. She was about half-way down when she heard male voices interspersed with rough laughter and what sounded like glass breaking. So much for letting the kids play for awhile. Laura turned and climbed back up, careful not to make a sound.

"Sorry kids," she said when she reached the truck. "Sounded like some fellows were down there having a party. We can try again after our next trip to the hospital."

"Can we go see Miss Cecilia and Miss Inez?" June said. "They're close by, and they were awful nice to us when we lived here."

"Miss Cecilia and Miss Inez?"

"You remember them. They're the twin sisters in the yellow house. Remember when they saw me pulling the wagon from the store?" June said. "They gave me lemonade on their porch, then filled the wagon to the top with all kinds of food for us."

"Oh, of course, I didn't remember their names." Laura kept her tone light, but her insides twisted. They hadn't been able to shop when they lived under the bridge, even though Glen was working. In desperation when their supplies ran out, they sent June to the nearest store with a small list and a dollar bill, but when she was on the way back, she met the sisters, who filled the wagon with food for the family. Neither Glen nor Laura wanted to accept the charity, but couldn't deny their children. On the day they'd moved, they'd left an envelope with money and a letter thanking the sisters for their generosity.

"Well? Can we stop at their house or not?"

Laura could see that June was becoming impatient after all the sitting they'd done that day, and she didn't blame her a bit.

Laura wasn't at all sure that stopping to see the ladies was a good idea, but perhaps the twin sisters would like to see June again. "We can drive by their house. It wouldn't be polite to just drop in, but if they're home we can stop."

June examined each house as they drove down the road. "I'm sure that's the house, but look at it." The once bright yellow paint was dull and peeling. What had been a lush green lawn was now overgrown and brown. The flowerbeds surrounding the trees, as well as the bright-colored ceramic pots on the porch, were filled with dead plants. Even without the boarded-up windows, the house would have looked forlorn and lifeless.

Laura stopped in front of the house. "I'm so sorry, sweetheart, but it looks like they've moved on."

June sank back into the seat without a word, and remained silent the rest of the way home.

🦇

Laura shuffled to the couch, then dropped on the cushions with a groan. "Oh, my feet hurt. Heck, everything aches." She turned sideways, stretched her legs out and closed her eyes. She'd kill for one of Glen's foot rubs right now. She kicked her shoes off and wiggled her toes. "If I had to spend another day standing in the kitchen putting up produce, I think I'd shoot myself. Thank goodness it's all done and put away on the basement shelves."

Laura loved gardening, but hated canning. Standing in a sweltering kitchen for hours was miserable, but there was no putting it off after harvesting the vegetables. She'd spent the last two weeks pickling and canning. Since the children were too young to be much help, they'd spent most of the time outside under the threat of dire punishment if they interrupted the canning process.

"When that pot of beans is done cooking, I don't even want to look at the pressure cooker for at least a month." Laura, eyes closed as she rested on the couch, heard the back screen door slam and the sounds of squabbling and running steps coming down the hall.

All of a sudden, June's piercing scream propelled Laura straight up off the couch and into the kitchen. June and her brothers were standing in the middle of the room with their mouths hanging open, staring at the ceiling. Brown beans and juice were shooting out of the top of the pressure cooker like bullets from a machine gun. Lots of the beans stuck to the ceiling, while the rest rained down along with the dripping juice. Laura saw the kids weren't hurt, just in shock and covered in brown streaks.

All four turned to her, eyes wide. Before
Laura said a word, she burst into laughter,
surprising everyone. Not a sedate little giggle
either, but a loud belly laugh that doubled her
over.

"Mama, it's not funny." June stamped
her foot, then looked at Raymond for help.

"You're funny looking," Raymond said,
licking juice off his fingers. "Tastes good."

Jimmy pointed at David, who was
holding his hands out to catch beans and juice
that dripped from the ceiling. "Look at David.
He's got a bean stuck on his nose."

That did it. The children pointed at each
other and started laughing along with Laura.
The pressure cooker stopped spitting beans and
hissed a last puff of steam, which struck
everyone as hilarious. They laughed until it
hurt, then looked around at juice-streaked faces
and started laughing again.

When it was quiet at last, Jimmy said,
"I'm hungry."

"Well, honey," Laura waved around the
room. "We were having beans for supper."

That started all of them laughing again,
which tapered off as they looked around at the
incredible mess. Laura wiped their hands and
faces with a wet dishtowel, fed the children
peanut butter sandwiches, then sent the three
oldest to the bathroom to wash their hair and
bathe. She scooped David up and plopped him

into the washroom sink. Once the children were clean, she put them to bed and headed back to the kitchen to tackle the monumental cleaning job.

॰॰॰

Hours later, beyond exhaustion, Laura stretched out on her bed, wishing Glen was next to her. She closed her eyes, and pictured Glen in the kitchen during the bean scene as if he had been there. "How you would have laughed, Glen. I can just see you lifting the children one by one to let them pick beans off the ceiling. They always had more fun with you, and you loved playing and being silly with them."

Laura kept her eyes shut, enjoying the thought of Glen with the children. She whispered to him. "You would have helped them clean up, then put them to bed while I started on the bean mess. I can see you returning to the kitchen after tucking them in, then wrapping your arms around me, murmuring in my ear that we should hurry and finish so we could go to bed." She almost felt his arms around her, and his breath against her cheek.

She held that image in her mind, including the faint smell of his scent. "I'd turn to you for a kiss, enjoying the warm, familiar sweet taste of your mouth. We'd head for our room and..."

Laura opened her eyes and sat up straight. "Stop it, just stop it." She clenched her fists. Daydreaming about having him home didn't help, in fact, it made her miss him even more. She could dream about him coming home after driving to the hospital tomorrow, that is, if there was any improvement. He had to be better. Having him gone was just too hard.

CHAPTER EIGHT

A Matter of Survival

They hit the road early, even though Laura was still glassy-eyed with fatigue. The children started played and giggled, full of bean jokes, but grew quiet when the hospital came into view.

Laura steered into a parking spot near the entrance. "You guys were great last time, and I need you on your best behavior today, too." She looked into each child's face, now solemn, then turned and opened the truck door.

The kids clustered around her as they started toward the hospital doors. Laura's heart raced and sweat dampened her armpits as they entered and approached the long counter. "Excuse me, miss," she said to a nurse writing on some cards. "I need to see Doctor Vaughn."

"Do you have an appointment?"

"No, ma'am, but he's my husband's doctor. If we can't see him, then I want to visit my husband." Laura's voice was firm even though her hands were shaking.

The nurse frowned, then said, "I'll check with the doctor. Take a seat. It may be awhile."

She was right. Over an hour passed before she ushered Laura and the children into Dr. Vaughn's office.

"How can I help you, Mrs. Webber? It's only been two weeks since your last visit."

Irritated and tired of dealing with fussy kids, Laura resented his condescending tone. "Two weeks is a long time. How is my husband doing? Have you seen any improvement?"

"We've lowered his medication dosage just a little, but as I explained last time, the goal is for him to adjust over time, and that means a lot longer than two weeks." The doctor leaned back and crossed his arms. "There's nothing more to tell. We have him on a schedule of exercise, walking with an orderly twice a day. He also spends several hours in the men's common room with other patients, so we can watch how he interacts, if he does interact at all."

"Is my papa still tied up?" June put her hands on her hips. "How can he get better if he's tied up?"

Shocked, Laura started to speak, then changed her mind. After all, it was a good question. She turned her attention to Dr. Vaughn and waited for his answer. He didn't say a word, just stared at her and tilted his head toward the children as if to encourage her to speak to them. Laura could see he wanted her to handle June, but she decided to let him answer the question.

"Yeah," Raymond said, "Tying him up was a mean thing to do."

Dr. Vaughn cleared his throat and cast a disapproving look at Laura. "Your papa isn't tied up. When you saw him, he was wearing a special shirt to keep him calm and to prevent him from hurting himself or anyone else."

"We want to see for ourselves." June and Raymond leaned against Laura. "Please, Mama, can't we see Papa, now?"

"Mrs. Webber, I'm sorry, but we don't allow children in the common rooms and it's important for your husband to stick to his routine. If you'll take them back to the lobby, I'll have an orderly accompany you to visit Mr. Webber."

Dr. Vaughn's voice was firm, brooking no argument. "There are numerous other patients with him, some of whom might be uncomfortable with children moving in their midst. For the sake of everyone's safety and peace of mind, only adults are allowed and only one visitor in the room at a time."

After major protests, the children left the room with a nurse, sending Laura venomous looks over their shoulders on the way out. June held both Jimmy and David's hands, while Raymond carried the canvas bag that held toys and cookies.

"Doctor Vaughn, before I see my husband, I need your help on a financial matter." Laura spoke fast, not wanting an orderly to overhear. "Our bank says I need a letter from you stating that Glen can't manage our money due to his condition. His name is the only one on the account and I need to access our funds to care for the children while he's in the hospital." She paused, took a deep breath, then raised her eyes from the desktop to the doctor's face. "I hate to ask, but this is a matter of survival."

Dr. Vaughn nodded and patted Laura's hand. "I understand. Can you give me the name of the bank and the person who requested the letter?"

Before Laura could respond, a big, burly man in a white uniform entered the room. "You called for an orderly, doc?"

"Yes, Gary, please take Mrs. Webber to see her husband in the men's common room.

Hang on just a minute." Dr. Vaughn looked at Laura. "The names?" As soon as Laura furnished the information, he said, "Your letter will be at the front desk waiting for you."

Laura's heart was racing by the time Gary unlocked the common room door and ushered her inside, locking the door behind them. "If you have a problem or need help, ma'am, just let me know." Gary crossed his arms and stood with his legs apart, a immovable against the door. "When you're ready to leave, I'll take you back to the doctor's office."

Laura nodded and stepped away from the stone-faced orderly. The room was large, and held what looked like about thirty men. A line of identical rocking chairs faced a bank of windows opposite the door. Silent men staring forward occupied eight of the chairs. Five small tables were scattered around the room, each with four chairs. The tables were sized for board games or cards, but no cards or games were in sight. Some of the men seated at the tables gestured with their arms and appeared to be talking, but none seemed to be listening or reacting to activity or conversation around them.

Laura studied each face. After what seemed like a long time, she recognized Glen among a small group who paced around the room, weaving between the tables.

"Glen," she blurted out. When he didn't respond, she picked her way to his side. "Honey, it's so good to see you." She touched his shoulder and looked into his face. His eyes flickered from side to side, but never focused on her. His lips moved, but no sound emerged. She shook his arm, but he just pulled away from her and continued pacing.

Tears began to flow, but Laura rubbed them away. She refused to cry here. She could fall apart when she was alone, but not here in this room full of damaged men. After watching Glen walk the perimeter of the room, round and round, over and over, with no change of pace or expression, Laura gave up and asked Gary to take her back to the doctor's office.

☙

"Why'd you take so long?" Raymond said, once they were settled back in the truck cab for the drive home. "It was boring in that room."

"I'm sorry, but I had to talk to the doctor afterwards." Laura waited awhile to resume, trying to compose her response. She didn't want to discuss the letter to the bank that rested in her purse, but was also determined not to describe the miasma of hopelessness that filled the common room where she'd watched Glen pace.

"What did Papa say to you?" June had greeted Laura with mutiny in her eyes. Her expression hadn't softened now that they were headed home. "You had lots of time to talk to him. Did he even ask about us?"

"Honey, your papa didn't act like he recognized me. He seemed to say some words as we walked around the common room, but I couldn't understand him." Laura hesitated, not wanting to lie but not wanting to hurt the children more either. "I'm afraid he didn't say anything that made sense. There wasn't any real change from before, except that he was up and around instead of sitting in a chair."

"If Papa could walk around and say words, he could have talked to you." June sounded bitter and angry. David slid forward off her lap and she jerked him back hard, causing him to yelp in surprise.

"Quit being mean to him," Jimmy glared at his sister. "Is June right? Is Papa pretending or is he mad at us?"

"No, honey, neither one. He's not pretending or mad."

The kids remained subdued when they got home. They played outside, but Laura didn't hear much out of them while she tended to chores and fixed supper.

The mood in the house remained somber throughout the rest of the day and into the evening. Once the children were asleep, Laura made her way to the front porch where she and Glen had spent so many evenings holding hands and talking. The silence was broken only by the sound of frogs and nightbirds, and the swish of tree branches swaying in a light breeze. Laura's head rested against the back of the rocking chair while she stared at the countless stars in the distant sky. Had she said the right words to the children? How could this have happened? And the worst questions of all, could she have stopped Glen's mental deterioration and was it her fault?

No answers came, only more questions about their future. She fell asleep with one arm extended over the chair arm next to her, reaching for Glen.

CHAPTER NINE

Clocked By a Girl

One week later, September 1938

The children were excited about school, which began the week after Labor Day, which was one week later. Laura was less excited, since she had to buy new shoes for June, Raymond and Jimmy. She could have insisted on Jimmy wearing Raymond's old ones, but remembered how hard it was to always be stuck with hand-me-downs. Besides, Raymond's old ones had worn heels scuffed beyond repair. David had to make do with old shoes from his brothers, but he spent most of his time barefoot, anyway.

School clothes were a bigger problem. Dr. Vaughn's letter met the bank'srequirements, so Laura had access to the family funds, but every penny spent was money they couldn't replace. She bought two dresses with puffy cap sleeves and full skirts for June, along with two petticoats. She purchased two pairs of pants and shirts each for Raymond and Jimmy, plus suspenders, and three sets of underwear and socks for all four children. Because David stayed at home and was too young to know the difference, his things came from a second-hand store.

Since it was Jimmy's first day of school, Laura walked with them, pulling David in the wagon. From then on, Jimmy walked with Laura and Raymond each day, all three carrying their lunch pails and books.

"Mama, today was so much fun. I love school," Jimmy said. He was breathless with excitement, and a huge smile creased his face, when he reached the porch ahead of June and Raymond.

"That's wonderful, I can't wait to hear all about it." Laura pulled Jimmy close for a hug, then put her arm out to block all three from entering the front door. "All of you need to change clothes before you do anything."

"Okay, but I need a drink first," Raymond said, "I'm awful thirsty."

"No, change clothes first, then you can do whatever you want."

From day one, the routine was the same. Laura washed the school clothes each night and hung them to dry, so they'd be clean, dry and ironed for wearing every other day. Before going to bed, Laura cleaned and polished their school shoes. Her children might only have two sets of school clothes and one pair of shoes, but they would never go dirty or looking unkept.

※

"Couldn't live without chickens, but sure wish they weren't such dirty creatures." Laura stretched her shoulders and back to get the kinks out, then eyed the interior of the coop. She'd scraped all the wood surfaces and cleaned out all the nesting boxes except for the two occupied by brooding hens. "All I've got left is to shovel up the muck on the coop floor and spread fresh straw. Guess I shouldn't complain too much about their mess, since it makes fine fertilizer for the garden."

"I help, Mama, I help."

Laura whirled around to see David, who she'd left playing on a grassy area outside of the henhouse, sitting right inside the coop door spreading dirty straw and feathers around with the grimy scraper.

"Oh, no." Laura started to scold him, but the sweet, delighted smile on David's dust covered face made it impossible. "Great job, son, but let's move you to a different digging spot."

Keeping David clean was no longer possible, so Laura scooted him over to a wide area outside the coop that the chickens used for their dirt baths. She let him keep the scraper for digging and moved his toys from where he'd left them. "I know you want to help, so how about smoothing all the dirt out so the hens can make fresh spots for their baths."

David nodded and started moving the dirt mounds around. Watching him was more fun than shoveling the nasty stuff out of the coop.

"Mama." June's voice rang out from the back porch, followed by the sound of the door slamming. "Mama, Raymond and Jimmy got hurt in a fight."

"I'm out here by the coop," Laura shouted. She glanced down at David and motioned for him to stay put, then started running toward the house.

The three children met her halfway, with June in the lead. All were still in their school clothes, but it was far too late to worry about keeping them clean. Raymond's nose was bleeding, and he had a huge shiner blooming around his almost closed right eye. Jimmy's pants had split at the knees, with blood leaking down both legs. Bruises colored part of his face, and the heels of both his hands were scraped and bloody. June had no visible wounds, but her dress and legs were filthy.

"What in the world?" Laura dropped to her knees and examined both boys. All three children started talking at once. "Quiet, all of you, I can't understand what you're saying." She looked at June. "Did you say they got hurt in a fight?"

June nodded, but Raymond answered. "It wasn't our fault. A big boy, older than me, yelled at us at recess, saying awful things about Papa. He said Papa's crazy because only crazy people get put in the nuthouse. Jimmy yelled and hit him, but the boy shoved him down."

Laura bit back an angry retort and hugged Jimmy. "Then what happened? Did one of the teachers stop it?"

"No, the bell rang, and we went back inside. We were mad, but nobody was hurt, so when class was over we started home like always."

June couldn't stay quiet another minute. "That boy was waiting for us down the road with two of his friends. As soon as we got close, he started shoving Raymond and Jimmy, and calling Papa crazy as a loon, and a nutcase from the nuthouse."

"Mama, I hauled off and hit him in the stomach as hard as I could. I know we're not supposed to hit people, but what he said wasn't right." Raymond's chin jutted forward. He was proud of defending his papa's honor.

"I hit him, too," Jimmy said. "But then the other guy hit me and pushed me away." Jimmy looked down at his ripped pants, dirt and bloodstained below his knees. "I'm sorry, but I fell on my hands and knees. Didn't mean to rip my good pants."

"It wasn't his fault," June said. "Both boys were pretty big. After the one knocked Jimmy down, the other punched Raymond in the stomach, sat on him, and started punching him in the face with both hands."

"How did you get away?" Laura said. "Did an adult see the fight and make the boys leave you alone?"

Raymond and Jimmy stared at each other, grinning. "No grown-ups, it was June."

"June? What in the world could June do?"

Raymond grinned at his sister. "She swung her book bag at his head as hard as she could and knocked him right off me."

"I didn't want him to keep hitting Raymond, so that was the only thing I could think of." June looked pleased with herself. "You should have seen him, Mama. He fell right off of Raymond. Yelled like a little, bitty kid, too. He gave me a real mean look too, so I started swinging the book bag like I was going to hit him again, and he and his friend took off."

"Good for you, girl. But tomorrow we'll have to have a talk with the principal so those boys won't bother you again."

"They won't dare say anything now." Raymond laughed and winked at his sister. "If they do, we'll tell everybody that the big guy got clocked by a girl. He'd get laughed out of school."

With the excitement over, Laura sent the children inside to clean up and put some cloverine salve on the cuts and scrapes. Relieved she could find no real damage, she still felt heartsick at the cruelty of children.

Once the older kids headed into the house, she went back to check on David. She found him digging fresh holes and throwing dirt with abandon. Like it or not, that coop wasn't going to finish cleaning itself. Since David was occupied, she grabbed the shovel and started filling the wheelbarrow.

🦇

Supper was fast and easy, tomato and fried egg sandwiches with tall glasses of milk. Laura was worn out after hosing what looked like pounds of dirt off David in the washroom basin before she could let him loose in the house. She checked the children's homework, tended to the boys' injuries, then tucked them into bed.

Poor kids. Not fair they should get picked on because their Papa's sick. Bad enough that they miss him so much and have to work a lot harder to help me. Wish I could spank both those rotten boys, but most likely they're just repeating what they heard from their parents.

Laura examined the grubby school clothes, looking for any additional damage other than Jimmy's torn knees. Sure enough, Raymond's shirt pocket was almost torn away. June's dress had a spot on the hem that needed repair, but no telling how that happened. She carried them to the back porch, together with her sewing basket, preferring to make the repairs first instead of waiting for the wash cycle to finish.

"Glen, you'd have been proud of our kids today." She imagined Glen next to her, and the way he'd smile as he listened. "Don't hold with fighting, but they didn't hesitate to protect family." She bent down and bit the thread after sewing Raymond's pocket seam. "And June? That girl isn't afraid of anything. Hate to say it, but I kind of wish I'd seen the bully's face when he got bested by a girl."

Laura took her time, then started the washing. Not a big load, but David's things had enough dirt for a whole wash load all by themselves. She settled in a rocker on the back porch, leaving the washroom door open so she'd hear when to run the pieces through the ringer. The night sky was clear, and the air smelled sweet. Laura caught sight of a shooting star, closed her eyes, and made a wish.

Her ma's soft chuckle filled her mind and wrapped all around her body. "Sweet wish, honey, but you know it doesn't work like that. Connecting with someone's mind isn't like turning on the radio and dialing your favorite channel."

"Sure wish it did." Laura spoke out loud, knowing the children were asleep. "It's so good to hear your voice, Ma. But what I wouldn't give to be able to sense what Glen's thinking right now. Is he awake or asleep? Is he dreaming? Does he even remember us?"

"I know." The familiar voice was comforting and full of love. "The second sight isn't something you can control. It comes in its own time, with information you need to have."

"That's not very helpful." Tears welled up and were blinked away. "We miss him so much, and I hate feeling helpless. Do you think I could connect with him easier if he wasn't so far away?"

"Distance and time don't work the same in visions as they do in the regular world. Wouldn't matter if Glen was next to you or half-way 'round the world. You'd feel him if you were supposed to." The sense of being wrapped in an invisible hug intensified. "Just be patient and do your best. No one could ask more than that of you."

There was a long pause. "Thanks, Ma. I'm trying."

"I know. Just keep your focus on doing the right thing for your children."

CHAPTER TEN

The Worst Type of Nightmare

Two weeks later, September 1938

"You kids better get a move on or you'll be late," Laura said. She was at the kitchen table writing a note.

"I can't find my shoes," June yelled. "Somebody stole my shoes."

"Who'd want your stinky old shoes?" Raymond said.

"I left them on the bench in the washroom like always." Laura didn't even look up.

"There're not there. I looked on the bench, under it, and all over the room." June's voice got louder with each word.

Jimmy started laughing. "David's wearing them. Come see. He looks pretty funny."

Laura rose and joined Jimmy in the living room where he was watching a grinning David clomp around in June's Mary Janes.

"No, David, give those back to your sister." Laura lifted David out of the shoes before June reached him. "Enough complaining, June. Put your shoes on." She reached into her pocket and pulled out a piece of paper. "Here, I've got a note for you to take to the office before you go to class. It's an excuse for you all to stay home tomorrow, so we can drive to the hospital to see Papa."

"No, I don't want to go." Raymond's face looked grim.

"What?" Laura said, shocked at her son's statement. "Of course you're going. You need to be there in case Papa's better. He loves you and seeing you might make a difference."

June looked at Raymond, then back at Laura. "He's right. It's awful there, and when we go back to school the other kids will ask where we'd been. We love Papa, but we don't want to go there anymore."

Laura bit back a retort as she looked at the three children. They'd moved closer together, standing in solidarity against her. It hurt, but she understood. "Okay, I'll take David and go alone. If we're not back by the time you get home, I want you to change clothes, then do your homework and chores. Can you do that? I don't know how late it'll be."

June nodded after looking at Raymond and Jimmy. "We know what to do. You can trust us."

After giving them all a fierce hug, Laura watched as they disappeared down the driveway. "Okay little man, it's you and me today."

Laura felt like nails had pierced her head right above the eyes, pulsing deeper in sync with her heartbeat straight through to just above her neck. She wanted nothing more than to close her eyes, curl up in a ball, and go to sleep. That was impossible, though, since she had a long drive home from the hospital with a cranky toddler.

It had been a horrible day. David got bored in minutes with no one to play with, and wouldn't sit still. Laura's only option had been to stop by the side of the road and move him to the floor on the passenger side. She'd put his toys on the seat and told him he had to stand

and look out the window, or sit down and play, but the whining needed to stop.

When they pulled into the hospital parking lot, David announced his need to go potty, and almost didn't make it to the bathroom. Dr. Vaughn was adamant about not letting a child enter the men's common room, not caring that David was too young to leave alone. If the nurses at the reception station hadn't offered to watch him, Laura wouldn't have been able to see Glen at all.

Once again, there'd been no signs of recognition from Glen. Laura saw that he was a little more animated and seemed to twitch in response to sounds near him, but he hadn't responded to her voice or presence. Dr. Vaughn told her he was progressing, but couldn't, or wouldn't, provide any indication of how long the process might take.

Laura's headache had appeared during the initial conversation with Dr. Vaughn and intensified throughout the day. Now the pain was making her nauseous. "Please David, play with your toys like you did before."

"No, go home. Go home now."

"We are going home, honey, but it takes time. If you don't want to play, you can stretch out on the seat for a nap."

"No. Go home now." David's voice rose in volume, and he started pounding on Laura's arm.

"Stop that. Mama's got a headache. You need to behave until we get home, then you can run and play outside all you want."

Laura's entreaties didn't work. David started crying, then segued into a full-blown tantrum, kicking the door and dashboard and screaming at the top of his lungs. Giving up on words, she tried to ignore him and concentrate on her driving. After what seemed like hours, he wore himself out and leaned against Laura's side.

Thank goodness. She'd almost started screaming with him, except her head hurt too much.

David didn't sleep long. He sat up and stared at her. "Go home? Get out now."

"Don't start again, David. You can get out when we get home. I don't want to hear any more from you."

That worked like pouring kerosene on a fire. David stood up on the seat, took a deep breath, and started yelling. But then he slipped forward and fell, face first, into the dash. The screaming ratcheted up even higher, and when he turned to face Laura, his face was covered with blood.

"Oh my goodness. Hold on, baby." Laura pulled over to the side of the road and stopped the truck. She jumped out and ran around to the passenger side, pulled David out and sat him down on the running board. "Here, honey," she said, grabbing a small towel out of the canvas supply bag. "Hold still so I can clean you up." David's nose was bleeding, but not broken. His mouth was swollen where his front teeth had pierced the inside of his upper lip. Once the bleeding stopped, she wet the towel with water from a jar stored behind the seat and tried to clean the blood off David's face and hands.

"My mouf hurts," David said, touching his ballooning lip.

"I know. I'll give you an ice cube to suck on when we get home." Laura patted his face, and helped him into the seat.

Laura noticed wisps of white floating above the hood as she turned the key. Her headache slammed back tenfold as she realized she'd forgotten to fill the radiator that morning. "Oh please, Bessie," she patted the dash and begged the truck, "it's just a little ways to go. Don't quit on me now."

The engine started, but sounded louder and rougher than usual. Laura kept the speed down, trying to drive as slow and careful as possible. Their driveway was in sight when the truck shuddered, and loud banging noises erupted under the hood. She turned into the driveway, pleading under her breath, but the engine died with one last clang and a plume of smoke.

"No, no, no. I can't take this." Laura rested her head on the steering wheel, eyes closed tight, whispering under her breath. "No more, please God. I don't know what to do."

"Yes, you do. Get on your feet, help your child down, and start walking." Ma's voice wrapped around Laura, but instead of comfort she was propelled into action. "No time to feel sorry for yourself, just do what you need to do."

Laura resisted the urge to curl up and cry. Instead, she helped David down from the truck. "Come on, big boy. We're walking the rest of the way." She put her pocketbook strap over one shoulder, grabbed the canvas bag of toys and supplies, and trudged toward the house.

David meandered at her side until he spotted his sister and brothers on the front porch, then ran to meet them. June swooped him up in her arms, gasped, and shouted. "What happened to David's face? Who hurt him?"

Raymond and Jimmy stopped to check David out too, then continued on to meet Laura. "Why are you walking? Where's the truck?" Raymond peered down the driveway.

"Yeah, Mama, what happened?" Jimmy's eyes widened at the sight of blood on Laura's dress.

"The truck broke down, but nothing for you to worry about." Laura's pasted-on smile seemed to reassure the boys. June, now with

David on her back with his arms and legs wrapped around her, caught up.

"I'll tell you all about the trip," Laura said, "when we get inside and I kick these shoes off. How was school?'

Bloody clothes soaked in cold water. David sucked on an ice cube, and Laura's headache was almost gone. She leaned against the warm flank of one of the cows, teasing frothy milk into the bucket beneath swollen udders. The children clustered nearby, giggling about the hazards of standing behind a cow. "Sounds like you guys did just fine by yourself today. I'm proud of you."

When Laura finished milking the last cow, she and the children trooped back to the house. Laura kicked off her muck boots in the washroom, then followed the children into the living room. She put her tired feet up on a small table, wiggled her toes and sighed, pulling David up to stretch out on her lap. The others dragged chairs close so they could put their bare toes on the table with hers.

The silence almost lulled Laura to sleep, when Jimmy's soft voice brought her back. "I miss Papa. Doesn't he want to be with us?"

"I miss him too, honey. Your papa loves you kids more than anything, and loves being with you." She paused a moment, trying to find the right words. "It's kind of like Papa is half-way between being awake and lost in an awful nightmare. They're trying hard to help him wake up all the way, but the nightmare is powerful. If he were awake right now, he'd be here."

"Why is it hard to wake him up? When David was little and had bad dreams, you'd just pat his back and talk to him until he woke up or the dream went away." Raymond and Jimmy both nodded at June's question.

"I don't understand it, except he seems to be lost in a special kind of dream. He saw something so horrible, the death of his brother, that the experience keeps coming back as the worst type of nightmare. His bad dream hurts so much that he can't hear people talking around him or feel them touching him. The doctors are trying different medicines to help him wake up, but so far nothing has worked."

"Will Papa ever get better?" Raymond's whispered question sliced through Laura's heart.

No perfect words of reassurance came, and Laura had vowed to always tell her children the truth. "I want that, we all want that, more than anything." They deserved an answer, but what to say? "The doctors say there is hope for him to recover, but they don't know whether he will or not. That's not a good answer, but we can't stop thinking about him."

Laura didn't want the children mired in the hopeless pain and worry she felt, so she tried to divert their attention. "Do you remember when your papa taught you guys to swim in the creek under the bridge? You learned fast, then you'd gang up and throw water on him until he could hardly see. I laughed so hard watching you my stomach hurt."

"I remember," June said. "And sometimes he'd throw us up high in the air one at a time to see who made the biggest splash when they landed in the water."

"Yeah, and he taught us how to ride his bicycle when we got big enough," Raymond said. "That was fun."

Jimmy smiled and said, "Remember when Papa would play his guitar and sing silly songs? He'd make up funny words instead of the regular ones."

"Remember how Papa would chase us, then catch us and tickle until we laughed so hard we almost wet our pants."

The stories kept coming, each bringing new memories.

"Uh oh, David's asleep. I guess it's time for us to call it a day." Laura stood, cradling David's body in her arms. It wasn't long before all four children were asleep on their bed, curled together like peaceful puppies.

Laura stared at her children as they slept. "What beautiful babies we have, Glen, and they're growing into amazing little people." She couldn't feel Glen's spirit around her, but said the words out loud, anyway. "We love you so much. You need to be here watching our children with me, helping them and playing with them, teaching them..."

CHAPTER ELEVEN

What Are You Afraid Of

October 1938

Laura's worst fears about the truck came true. Mr. Giddings, manager of the Texaco station and the best mechanic in Aurora, checked it out and confirmed that overheating when the radiator ran dry had caused the engine to seize up. Even though he offered her a good deal to replace the engine, there was no way she could afford it. "Here's the key," she said, declining the offer. "I'll remove all our personal things before you come for the truck." Laura squeezed his hand and accepted a check for $50.

"I'm sorry, Mrs. Webber. I wish I could give you more for it, but I'll just be parting it out since it would cost too much to repair and sell it." Mr. Giddings walked her to the door. "I'll tow it away some time tomorrow."

"I understand. Thank you."

"Mrs. Webber? Next time you see your husband, would you give him my best? He's a darn good mechanic, and a good man, too."

A lump formed in Laura's throat. She nodded once and left the shop. Guilt ate at her all the way home. If only she'd filled the radiator before driving to the hospital. If only she'd noticed the first wispy threads of overheated steam and pulled over. If only she hadn't tried to push on for that last mile or so. "Quit wasting time. Can't go back, so just do what you have to and stop feeling sorry for yourself." Squaring her shoulders, she marched home, making plans on how to adjust to not having a vehicle.

Laura planned all her errands with care, and tried to complete her trips to town while the children were in school. David walked as much as he could, then climbed into the trusty wagon as they went from place to place. Sometimes she would walk along with the older children on their way to school, other times she would meet them on their way home.

The biggest change was the inability to drive to the hospital to see Glen and talk to the doctor. She'd long since turned off their phone service as an unaffordable luxury, and long distance calls cost too much to make on pay phones. She couldn't ask anyone to let her use their phone for such expensive calls, so she had to depend on letters.

Laura's first letter to Dr. Vaughn, mailed just two days after the truck died, was a struggle. She agonized over every word, wanting him to understand that she had no way to reach the hospital, rather than believing she no longer cared. She begged him to send her updates on Glen's progress at least once a week, and to keep her informed on what was happening with his medications and other treatments. It seemed like forever before she received his first response, but their correspondence from then on was on a regular basis. Of course, his letters were always too short and curt, but there was little she could do about that.

By mid-October the weather had turned wet and cold, and a nasty rainstorm put a major damper on Halloween. The kids celebrated in their costumes at school and during their traditional walk through downtown visiting the businesses, but arrived home soaked, shivering, and ready to stay in for the night. Laura gave them oatmeal raisin cookies fresh out of the oven and cups of hot cider to warm their hands and insides while they sorted through their bags of goodies.

Laura celebrated with the children, but her thoughts stayed on a letter she'd received from Dr. Vaughn that day. She hadn't wanted to open it in front of them at the post office, so left it stuffed in her purse. She was anxious to see what it said since Dr. Vaughn's correspondence had been less frequent, but waited until the children wore down and fell asleep before pulling it out of her purse.

Curled up on the sofa, feet resting on the table, she pulled the envelope flap open and read it twice, pulse racing, before putting it down on her lap. "I can't believe this. Doctor Vaughn wants my permission to use electroshock therapy on Glen." She picked the paper back up and read it a third time. "After all this time on medication, after he seemed to improve as they lowered the dose a small amount at a time, Glen's regressed back to where he started." She leaned back, closed her eyes, and rubbed her forehead. All this time for nothing. But electroshock therapy would be messing with Glen's brain, and was supposed to be painful. And nobody knew why or how it worked, just that the violent convulsions caused by the therapy were supposed to have a calming effect. There was a huge chance for side effects, too, and no guarantees.

Laura read the letter again several more times, then tucked it back into her pocketbook. "I'll sleep on it and decide in the morning."

Falling asleep proved impossible. After adjusting positions countless times, Laura gave up, grabbed her robe and a blanket, and slipped outside. The air was cold, but still. She stared at the sky, watching invisible clouds move across the heavens, blanking out swaths of flickering stars as they went.

Laura kept asking herself if she should go along with Doctor Vaughn's request, or beg him to keep trying different medications. It had already been so long. With no guarantees of any better outcome, was it worth putting Glen through the horrors of the new treatment?

"What are you afraid of?" Not soothing this time, Ma's voice was quite matter-of-fact.

Startled, Laura answered out loud. "Afraid? I'm not afraid. I just want to do what's best for Glen."

"Are you sure? Go deeper and think this through. What are you afraid of?"

Before Laura could answer, Ma's presence was gone. "Am I afraid?" Laura didn't think so, but tried to organize her thoughts. Perhaps it would work if she thought of what might happen with each potential choice.

"Ma, if you can hear me, I don't get it. All I can figure is that I'm scared of failure either way. If the drugs don't work, he won't get any better. If the electroshock therapy doesn't work, he won't get better either." No answer, and Laura still couldn't decide. "Help me here. I've only got two choices, and no idea if either of them will do any good. So how can I..."

Then she got it. Laura realized that she was not just afraid of the electroshock not working, but that if it didn't work, there were no new options waiting in the wings. If the shock therapy didn't help Glen, she would lose hope, and hope was what sustained her. "Thanks, Ma. I understand now. For his sake we have to try."

Laura padded back inside to the kitchen table and wrote her letter giving permission to Dr. Vaughn, but asking him to let her know what the process would entail and how often it would be administered.

CHAPTER TWELVE

Electroshock Therapy

November 1938

L aura was at peace with the decision she'd made, but anxious to learn how Glen was doing. The days and weeks of November flew by with no word. Rain and wind made every trip outside miserable, with the children coming up with ever-more creative excuses for staying home each day instead of walking to school. Laura made them go, but met them with hot cider each afternoon when they got home. David sprawled on the living room rug in front of the hearth with the others while they worked on their schoolwork.

The day before Thanksgiving was cold and dry, a welcome change since Laura needed to go to town. The older children didn't want to go, preferring to revel in their freedom to stay home. David, though, was ecstatic to be with Laura. He rode in the wagon most of the time, but climbed out and walked next to her at the grocery store, the shoe repair shop, and the post office.

"My goodness, that boy's growing like a weed, Mrs. Webber." Mr. Niedermann leaned down and patted the top of David's head.

"Yes, he is," Laura said. "Smart, too. Never misses a thing."

Mr. Niedermann took three letters from Laura. "Writing to your sister, Ruth, and Mrs. York, I see," he said, handing her one in return. "I sure hope this one has good news about your husband."

Laura saw the hospital logo on the envelope and glanced down to see if David was paying attention. "Me too, Mr. Niedermann, and thanks for your concern." She stuffed it in her coat pocket and led David on their way.

The envelope kept calling all evening, but Laura resisted until the children were asleep and she was alone in the kitchen. Dr. Vaughn, in his usual clipped style, wrote that Glen would receive two electroshock therapy treatments per week. He cautioned her about expecting too much, since it might take several weeks of repeated applications to bring about a change. She double-checked the dates in the letter. "It's happening. According to this, the first treatment was today, and he'll have another on Friday." She smoothed the paper out on the table, then picked it up and put it back into the envelope. "Now we wait...wait and pray."

Raymond and Jimmy chased one another through the house, stopping only to sneak cookies from the side table in the kitchen. June stood at the counter on a low stool drying dishes and keeping an eye on David playing in his highchair. Laura jabbed a fork into potatoes simmering on the stove.

"Mama, why aren't we having a turkey today?" June said. "We always had turkey on Thanksgiving. Just because you put the chicken in the oven doesn't mean it'll taste like turkey."

"I know, but we couldn't afford a turkey this year." Laura cracked the oven door open and spooned melted butter over the skin that was just beginning to crisp. The bird lay in a bed of stuffing, fragrant steam surrounding the baking dish.

June made a face. "Still just chicken, and we have that a lot."

Laura bit back a retort, not wanting to scold on Thanksgiving. Her children might not be grateful for the jars of food she'd put up during the summer, but she refused to make it worse for them by complaining about their financial straits.

It was the second week in December, and the post office was full of people. Laura waited, tapping her foot, until the lobby cleared out, then asked Mr. Niedermann if she could use the pay phone. She'd brought a full coin purse, determined to get Dr. Vaughn on the phone. There'd been no word since the letter at Thanksgiving, and she had a bad feeling about the silence.

Laura had David climb in the wagon and opened her canvas bag. "David, look at the books while I use the phone. I need you to stay very quiet until I'm done, and don't get out of the wagon. Can you be a big boy and do that for me?"

As soon as he nodded, she placed a piece of paper with the hospital's phone number and her coin purse on the shelf under the phone. When the hospital receptionist answered her call, she told Laura it would take a little time to find Dr. Vaughn, and to please hold on. Laura dropped more coins in the slot before she was told that Dr. Vaughn wasn't available.

"Not available? Is he at the hospital today? He takes care of my husband, Glen Webber, and I need to talk to him."

"I understand, Mrs. Webber, but he can't come to the phone right now. I'll let him know you called and have him call you back."

"He can't call me back. I'm at a pay phone at the post office here in Aurora. I need to hear from him as soon as possible. Can you ask him to write me a letter right away? It's been a long time since his last letter, and I'm really worried."

"Yes, ma'am, I'll pass your message on. Bye now."

Laura stared at the phone. Something was wrong, she could feel it. She wanted to reach inside the phone and shake somebody. Instead she put the phone back in its cradle, closed her eyes a minute and took some deep breaths.

"Thanks for being such a good boy, David." She waved at Mr. Niedermann, who was once again facing a line of people, and headed for the door.

With all the extra holiday mail, would she receive anything before Christmas? It was only ten days away. How on earth could she stay cheerful for the children when she was twisted up with worry?

"Merry Christmas, Mrs. Webber," said Mrs. Hunter from the middle of the line.

"Thank you, Mrs. Hunter. Merry Christmas to you and your family, too." Laura's smile had no warmth. She hadn't thought about the holiday, but somehow she'd make sure her children had warm holiday memories in spite of what was happening to Glen.

CHAPTER THIRTEEN

Wake Up, It's Christmas

Christmas, 1938

Laura stood inside the barn door, inhaling the sweet smell of fresh straw and warm animals, and listening to the soft night sounds. It was Christmas Eve, and every creature on the farm was bedded down for the night except her. The lantern at Laura's side provided the only light, since invisible clouds hid the moon and stars, and a steady downpour filled the air.

She leaned against the door, not ready to venture out in the rain to the dark house. Laura missed Glen so much, it was hard to breathe just thinking about getting through the holiday without him. All of a sudden, the memory of their first Christmas Eve together popped into her mind. They lived in Tulsa in the apartment Glen had rented for them before they got married.

"Let's go for a walk," Glen said. "We'll have the streets all to ourselves."

"Because everyone else will be inside where it's warm?" Laura remembered her surprise at his suggestion.

"Warm is overrated. Besides, we can bundle up and cuddle while we walk." He led her toward the door, pulling their coats, hats, scarves, and gloves off the rack.

The sidewalks were almost deserted, so it seemed like the shop decorations were shining just for their pleasure. Twin frosty breath plumes led them on the way. The air was cold but dry, and the sky formed a brilliant dome of sparkling lights framing a moon that looked ripe for plucking.

"Admit it, this was a great idea." Glen squeezed Laura's waist, holding her close.

Laura nodded and wrapped her arm around Glen's back, tucking her head against his shoulder. They walked all the way around the city block holding each other. No need for words.

The memory faded, but Laura realized she had fallen in love with her husband that evening so many years ago. She'd married him because she wanted a family. There'd been another man she'd loved before Glen, but he had betrayed her and soured her on the concept of romantic love. Laura had always known Glen was a decent, honorable man, and she was determined to be a good wife. But that sweet walk on Christmas Eve was when she knew, for the first time and without any doubt, that she loved him.

Laura blinked her eyes. Back in the present. She pulled the barn door closed, then picked her way through the muddy yard to the house.

"Mama, Mama, wake up, it's Christmas." All four children bounced on the bed.

"Not yet, please, give me a little more time." Laura pulled the pillow over her head, even though she knew it was hopeless.

"You can stay in bed and we'll fix breakfast for you," June said.

Visions of the kitchen after her children prepared breakfast filled Laura's head and propelled her out of the bed. "That's sweet, honey, but I'll get up. Let me get my robe and slippers on. Did you check your stockings yet?"

The children whooped and ran to the living room, David's short legs churning as fast as they could.

"Look, the stockings have our names sewn on them." June pointed to the bright green letters embroidered on each sock.

"There's mine." Raymond yelled, then handed both Jimmy and David the stockings with their names.

Laura sat on a chair near the hearth. She was pleased that they liked the lettering. Sewing the names after the children fell asleep each night had been a chore, but the bright smiles were worth it. Each stocking had a big bulge near the heel, with odd-shaped bumps in the toe.

"Look, an orange," Jimmy crowed, holding the bright-colored globe up in the air.

The other oranges appeared seconds later. Much excitement, then laughter when David tried to bite into his.

"No, honey, I need to take the skin off first," Laura said. "Did you check to see if there's anything else?"

A handful of walnuts and two hard candies followed the oranges out of the stockings.

"Can we eat them now?" Raymond said.

"Just one bite of walnut now. Save the rest for after breakfast." Laura crossed the room and opened the curtains. Outside, the rain had turned to drizzle, but dark clouds covered the sky. "Guess we'll skip church this morning. Don't want to risk get soaked on the way"

Raymond and June looked at each other, then June said, "Don't want to go, anyway."

Laura started to ask why, but held her tongue. "Okay, we can have more fun by celebrating Christmas here."

Breakfast was salt pork, with fried eggs cooked in the meat drippings and bread smeared with honey. When they finished, everyone got dressed and trooped outside to take care of the animals together, teasing and laughing the entire time.

"Mama, what do you think Papa's doing for Christmas?" Jimmy sat cross-legged, his stocking on the floor nearby, all the goodies tucked back inside.

"I have no idea, sweetie." Laura and the children were sitting on the floor around the fireplace enjoying the warmth. "I know he'd be here with us if he could."

"But I want Papa here now." Jimmy's lower lip trembled and his eyes glistened.

"Me, too," both June and Raymond said together.

"I know you do." Laura thought a minute. "I have an idea, let's do the things Papa would do if he was here. He always made things fun, and I'll bet if he were here, he'd start ... a tickle fight."

Laura lunged between David and Jimmy and started tickling their ribs, one hand on each wiggling boy. They shrieked and giggled, then

June and Raymond tackled Laura, trying to tickle her. No chance for tears or sadness while the family rolled around, hugging, laughing, and tickling one another.

"That was fun," June said, after they all quieted down. "But Papa was always the winner of our tickle fights.

"Yes, he was," Laura said. "What would you like to do now? We can tell stories, play games, make music and sing silly songs, or whatever you want to do."

"Anything?" June said. When Laura nodded yes, she scooted over and whispered in Raymond's ear.

"How about outside games like hide and seek or Red Rover?" Raymond said. "You said anything."

"Smarty pants." Laura glanced at June, knowing where the suggestion came from. "I said anything, so we can do them inside. But no running."

Laura watched them play one game after another, reveling at the freedom to play outside games inside. When they slowed down, she pulled out the piano bench, sat down and flexed her fingers, then started playing and singing Jingle Bells. In minutes, David and Jimmy joined her on the bench, while June and Raymond leaned against them.

Silent Night, Oh Christmas Tree, and The First Noel were followed by every

Christmas song Laura remembered. They all sang with great enthusiasm in every imaginable key. "What shall we sing next?"

"The Ants song." David shouted the only title he knew, pumping his arms in the air.

The older kids groaned, but Laura launched into the chorus. "The ants go marching one by one, hurrah, hurrah..." They took turns picking songs after that, including every silly song the kids could think of. When the selection slowed down, Laura played popular tunes, making up funny words that kept them laughing.

Hours later, after stories, more music, and a meal of chicken soup with a few of their orange sections for desert, the kids curled up on the living room couch to listen to holiday music on the radio. Laura headed outside to care for the animals. When she came back inside, they scooted to the sides of the couch and made room for her in the middle.

"This was a great Christmas," June said.

"Yeah." Raymond sighed, then reached over Jimmy to take Laura's hand. "If only Papa was here, it would be perfect."

CHAPTER FOURTEEN

Just a Bad Sprain

The day after Christmas, 1938

"Can we stay in our pajamas and play inside today, like we did yesterday?" June yawned and stretched, arching her back against the kitchen chair.

"No, that was just for Christmas. You may be on school vacation, but the holiday is over and you've got chores to do."

"Aawww, I don't want to work today. It was fun playing all day yesterday." Jimmy crossed his arms, glancing at June and Raymond for support. "Can't we have one more day?"

"Sorry, son. In fact, I have to go into town for flour, sugar, and cornmeal, so you can help June and Raymond take care of David while I'm gone."

Laura ignored the grumbling and was soon on her way, wagon behind her with a folded canvas tarp in the bed to protect the sacks of food in case it rained again. She stopped at the post office first, disappointed to see Miss Potter behind the crowded counter. Miss Potter substituted when Mr. Niedermann took a day off. Laura often wondered if she ever smiled.

"Good morning, Mrs. Webber, how was your Christmas?" Mrs. Brighton, wife of the Aurora Baptist Church pastor, peered back from the front of the line, leaning around two ladies in line behind her.

Laura smiled, "It was very nice. Thank you for asking." Of all the people to see in here today, why had she run into the biggest gossip and most mean-spirited woman in town?

"We would have loved seeing you in church yesterday, dear. After all, Christmas is the holiest day of the year. I think you would have enjoyed my husband's sermon about the importance of repentance and living a godly life."

"Yes ma'am, I'm sure it was lovely, but it was too far for the children to walk in the rain."

"Walk?" Mrs. Brighton paused, her head cocked to one side, then she smiled and said, "Oh, that's right. I heard your truck broke down and you couldn't get it fixed because of your husband's breakdown. He's in the Springfield Mental Hospital, isn't he?"

Laura felt her face turn red. All the other people turned to look at her, curiosity and pity in their eyes.

"Next, please," Miss Potter called Mrs. Brighton up to the counter.

Good thing that old biddy was next or I might have said something I'd regret. Laura took a deep breath, focusing on the feather pinned to the side of Miss Potter's hat, bobbing with every movement of her head. She refused to look at anyone else until everybody stopped staring at her. When it was her turn, she grabbed her mail, shoved it in her pocketbook without a glance, and marched out as fast as possible.

Still irritated, Laura turned into her driveway, the wagon heavy and awkward with the weight of three twenty-pound bags. That irritation was forgotten when Jimmy ran around the side of the house just before she reached the front steps.

"Mama, come quick. Raymond's in the barn. He hurt his leg and can't get up."

Laura dropped the wagon tongue and sprinted past Jimmy. She found Raymond on his back next to a bale that had fallen from the hayloft. His face was white and sweaty, and his left ankle and foot swollen and dark blue.

"He fell, Mama, and the bale came down on top of him. It was an accident." June, sitting next to Raymond, looked scared and relieved to see her at the same time. David sat on June's lap, leaning forward and patting his brother's arm. "He can't walk on it, so we were staying with him until you got home."

"You did fine." Laura squeezed June's shoulder, then knelt down next to Raymond. "I've got to check it out, but it's going to hurt."

Raymond nodded, fisted his hands and held his breath.

Laura ran her hands over the swollen foot, the ankle, and up the calf. The skin was tight and hot. "Tell me where it hurts." After Raymond nodded, she slid her fingers all around and over his foot. Nothing. She pressed on the side of his ankle.

"Ow." Raymond yelled and tried to pull away.

Laura kept moving her hands, but only the ankle seemed painful. "Can you move it?"

Raymond rotated his foot around, grimacing, but not making a sound.

"I don't think anything's broken, just a nasty sprain." Laura looked at June, still with

David in her lap, then turned to Jimmy. "Honey, can you get me a roll bandage from the tack room? The thick white ones we use to wrap the mules' legs."

It didn't take long for Laura to wrap Raymond's foot and ankle, which stabilized it enough for him to stand and walk to the house with her help. Once she was sure he was out of danger, Laura delivered a stern lecture about disobeying the rule about not climbing into the hayloft to play. She didn't punish him, though, since he'd done an excellent job of that all by himself.

"Thank you, lord, for watching over that boy." Laura whispered the heartfelt prayer from the front porch rocker after the children had fallen asleep. She thought about Glen's Aunt Gladys, who had changed from a warm, vibrant woman into a bitter shadow of her former self after her twin sons had both drowned. "I'm trying my best, but please don't let anything happen to my babies."

She relaxed, soothed by the rhythmic motion, then stopped. "I never looked at the mail. Maybe there was news from the hospital." Laura stood and started looking for her pocketbook. "Where in the heck did I put it?" She rechecked her bedroom and the kitchen. "Now I remember, I had it with me when I ran to the barn."

She grabbed a lantern from the washroom and headed for the barn. Once inside, she saw the handbag on its side behind the fallen hay bale, the corner of an envelope sticking out. She put the lantern down, grabbed the pocketbook, and settled herself on the bale to read. She pulled the letter out, staring at the hospital logo. "Please, please let there be good news." She whispered. Taking a deep breath, she slipped the folded paper out of the envelope.

The barn disappeared when her fingers touched the paper. She was aware of the letter in her hand, as well as the soft sounds of the animals in the barn around her, but those sensations were faint. They disappeared within seconds, replaced by a swirling blackness that swept her away into one of her visions.

CHAPTER FIFTEEN

Don't Fight Us

Different colored streaks of soft light leaked into the dark, disorienting and strange. The remote sound of a car engine intruded, then got louder. Laura found herself inside the back seat of a car, staring at the side of Glen's head. "Just relax, Mr. Webber, you'll feel better when we get you to the hospital."

Laura recognized the voice of Dr. Farnsworth, and the clothes Glen was wearing on the day he was taken away. Glen's facial muscles were slack, his eyes unfocused. She couldn't feel any coherent thoughts from him, just disjointed sounds and flashes of color that disappeared before she could tell what they were. The doctor's voice droned on, the tone soothing, but the words meaningless, unable to penetrate the confusion of her husband's mind. The scene faded away, like a color poster left out in the sun, until Laura was once again surrounded by darkness.

Two voices now, both male but commanding instead of soothing. "Quit fighting. You need to stay in here until you calm down."

She could see Glen flailing, his arms held by two heavy-muscled men dressed in white. They were walking, half dragging him into a small, bare room that held only a single metal-framed cot with a thin mattress and pillow. Laura couldn't tell how much time had passed from the car scene, but Glen's face was covered in stubble. His eyes were wide open, his body rigid as he resisted being pulled to the bed. His efforts were in vain. The men laughed as they left him locked in, his limbs buckled into leather restraints fastened to the bed frame which was bolted to the floor.

Glen bucked and screamed, his eyes and mouth open wide. Laura could see the muscles in his forearms, hands, and neck corded and rigid as he fought. Even his screams couldn't escape the room, which was lined with thick padding to absorb the sound of anguish, panic, and pain. It was agony to watch him. When the scene dissolved away, Laura was sobbing, overwhelmed and helpless.

"No more, please," she begged, grateful for the darkness that followed. Laura rested in the void until her heart rate slowed and her composure returned. A series of scenes followed. Some only took seconds while others seemed much longer. There was no sense of time passing, but Laura noticed that Glen's hair was different lengths, and he changed from clean-shaven to stubble and back again. She watched him sleep, walk around, and eat. She saw him vary from almost comatose to raging anger.

Anger and aggression were the hardest emotions to watch because of the way they were handled. She watched Glen forced into what looked like a normal cast-iron bathtub, a canvas cover over the top that sealed his entire body in the water, except for his head. At first glance, the tub looked normal. A closer look revealed the differences. No faucet, just tubes that fed and drained the body-temperature water to keep it circulating. Judging from the way he always calmed down, the treatment was effective, but he remained in the tub for hours.

Then Glen was confined in a straight jacket. He fought like mad to avoid it, but was always either overpowered by several powerful men or injected by a nurse with something that knocked him out. Sometimes he struggled for hours, screaming and cursing. Other times she watched him withdraw, eyes blank, mouth slack, motionless until someone came to free him, often hours later after he'd soiled himself.

Then a vision appeared of a treatment Laura hadn't seen before—electroshock therapy. Glen was led into a small white room and told to sit in a row of chairs along one wall. He appeared quiet from his medications and ignored the moaning and crying of the men who waited with him. The end of the room contained four curtained cubicles, each containing a bed and medical equipment.

When Glen's turn came, he was led into one of the narrow spaces and helped onto the bed. A doctor checked his vitals, then signaled for three large men to space themselves around the cot. A headset was placed on Glen, with round metal paddles positioned against his temples. The doctor's nurse tightened a thick leather strap around Glen's neck so the wide flat section rested between his teeth. By this time, he'd started to struggle, his eyes flickering around the room, but he was unable to move. The men around the bed held him down with their massive bodies. Then the doctor twisted the dial and turned the machine on. Glen's body tried to arch upward, and his teeth clenched the leather, almost biting through it. The muscles and veins in his neck corded against his skin. Laura watched it happen three times, with just a short minute of rest between each episode, nearly retching at the sight. When it was over, a bone-white Glen, shaking and covered with sweat, his gown stained with urine, was helped into a wheelchair and taken from the room.

The same scene was repeated three times, and Laura knew they were separate events because different people took part. The second and third times Glen showed fear of what was going to happen. He fought and cried, terrified, struggling until the switch was thrown.

Laura cried in the darkness that wrapped around her after the last time Glen was wheeled from the room. She saw the incredible amount of pain he was in and was filled with guilt for setting it in motion.

Then she was in Glen's room, watching him sleep. His eyes opened, he blinked a few times, then looked around. She didn't believe it, but he was awake—conscious and aware for the first time in months. He sat up, stared around the room, then stood and strode to the door. He looked surprised to find it locked and started shaking the doorknob and calling for someone to let him out.

The door opened, almost knocking Glen to the ground. "Stop all that noise. Do you want some time in the padded room to calm down?" The orderly filled the doorway, one meaty hand pointed at Glen.

"Padded room? What are you talking about? Why am I locked in?"

"Well, well, Mr Webber, good to see you back. Hold on and I'll go get your doctor."

"Doctor? What's going on?"

The door closed before Glen got his last question out. He grabbed the knob, but heard the lock click in place. Laura watched him pace around the room, trying the door now and then, until the orderly returned. He had another man with him, and they led him out of the room.

"Doc, it's hard to believe what you've told me." Glen sat in a chair in front of Dr. Vaughn's desk. The orderlies who had escorted him stood on either side. "And I'm grateful for your help, but I've got to get out of here. I've got a family depending on me."

"Yes, I know," Dr. Vaughn said. "Your wife and children have been here to see you. But we need to make sure this isn't temporary. We have to run some tests and watch you to make sure you don't relapse."

"I feel fine." Glen started to stand, but an orderly's hand on each of his shoulders kept him in the chair. "Please, I'm begging you, let me go home."

"I can't do that, yet. You need to stay calm and go back to your room while I write up new orders for your care."

Glen tried to say more, but found himself on his feet and moving toward the door.

Laura wanted to touch him, to let him know she was there. He tried to fight against the orderlies and return to the doctor's office, but they were too strong.

"Calm down, Mr. Webber. If you don't cooperate, we'll have to write you up and that won't help you get out of here."

"Please, fellas, my family needs me. I've got a wife and four little kids to support."

"We know that," the second orderly said. "And we're trying to help you. Doc's a paper pusher and this place is funded by the government. He won't release you until every "i" is dotted and every "t" is crossed. Play the game and do what you're told."

"He's right," the other one said. "Don't fight us and don't make trouble. That's the only way out of here."

The men left Glen locked in his room again. Laura watched him pace faster and faster, pounding one fist into the other.

Once again, the vision faded out, then was replaced by scenes that flickered for mere seconds. Like before, she saw Glen in his room sleeping, in the common room pacing in a circle, eating in the kitchen, and more than once arguing with Dr. Vaughn. She could feel the energy changing, building with Glen's frustration.

Next Glen was in his room with an orderly, both smiling and talking. Laura recognized the orderly, Gary, since he'd escorted her to the men's common room twice. She was surprised to see that Glen's smile looked forced, and his forearm muscles bunched under his skin. When the orderly turned to lead the way out of the room, Glen attacked. He slammed the man's head against the door jam then rode the body down to the ground where he pounded Gary's face against the floor, once, twice, then a third time. Blood pooled around his head. He tried to lift his head once, then didn't move again. There was no resistance when Glen reached under him to remove a key ring from his belt.

"Oh my god, Glen, what have you done?" She watched him stand and back away from the body, his face a mask of conflicting emotions. Expressions of horror, determination, regret, then resolve flashed one after another. After one last look at the orderly at his feet, Glen crept out into the hallway.

Laura clenched her eyelids closed, afraid of what she'd see next. It didn't help. The vision continued behind her closed lids. Glen running, hiding, crossing fields and a shallow river. She saw him burrow deep under a fallen tree in a forest. Next she saw him against the backdrop of a sunrise, covered in dirt, emerging from dry stalks in an abandoned cornfield. He lifted his head, a look of panic on his face, when he heard the faint sound of dogs.

Terror filled Glen's eyes, and he took off running as the sound of baying got closer. Laura watched him run as fast as he could, breathing loud and his arms pumping, toward a creek she could see in the distance. He hit the water without slowing, then ran hunched over, his body hidden by the trees and shrubs on the shore.

Laura didn't know whether to pray for his escape or for his pursuers to not hurt him. Neither helped. Three snarling dogs caught up with Glen, followed by three men on horseback bearing shotguns and chains.

"Well, well, boys, look what we've got here," the lead man said. "The dogs done found our runner."

The other two laughed, staring at Glen. He stood dripping in water up to his thighs, his eyes glued to the three dogs on the shore, snarling and growling.

"Come on out now, we don't have all day."

Glen's shoulders drooped. "Yes sir, but call the dogs off first."

One sharp whistle from the leader, and all three dogs trotted back to the horses.

Glen trudged forward as the men watched. He reached the bank and pulled himself out of the water.

"What are you waiting for? Come on over here. Don't make me chase you anymore."

Glen eyed the dogs, then walked toward the man who appeared to be in charge, stopping just a few paces short of the dogs.

"Tell me, was it worth it? I mean, was running away worth almost killing Gary?" The man paused, leaning forward over his horse's neck and stared at Glen. Then he sat back and looked at the men by his side. "I don't think so, seeing as how Gary's my brother. You put him in the hospital with a broken nose, busted lip, and a broken bone around his eye. The doc might just say you're crazy, but I think you deserve being hurt just as bad as Gary was." He whistled again, and the dogs jumped forward.

Glen turned and ran, but the dogs caught him. Laura bit her lip and tasted blood when Glen screamed and fell to the ground, the dogs biting at his back and legs.

"Hey, Nate, what are you doing?"

"Yeah, we can't take him back all chewed up, since he surrendered."

The leader, Nate, loosened a chain he had around his waist and dismounted.

"Surrender? Hell no, he didn't surrender. He tried to ambush us and we fought to subdue him."

Nate kicked the dogs away from Glen's bloody legs and swung the chain across the back of Glen's head. The links bit into bone, blood spewing. Laura covered her mouth as her stomach twisted and heaved.

Glen, who had been trying to push himself up, dropped face down on the ground, blood coating the back of his head and streaming through his hair. The chain came down twice more before the other men were able to pull Nate away.

"Holy cow, Nate, I hope you didn't kill him."

"Don't matter if I did. You just remember the story. We caught up with him, and he suckered us close by raising his hands. When we got close he started swinging and kicking. We had no choice but to use force to bring him down. Nobody will question us as long as we all say the same thing." Nate stared at the other men, the bloody chain still swinging from his fist. "Got it?"

No more scenes appeared. Instead, she found herself back in the barn, sitting on the hay bale with the lantern next to her. The letter was still in her hand, a hand that shook so hard she couldn't read the words. Laura rubbed her shaky, sweaty hands on her legs, took several deep breaths, then pressed the paper against her leg s to hold it still.

Dr. Vaughn had written the letter, informing her he was no longer her husband's treating physician. The letter said Glen had shown some slight improvement, when with no provocation or warning, he attacked one of the guards. The assault was so vicious that it took several men to pull Glen off and subdue him. The orderly's facial injuries were severe enough to require several surgeries. Because the behavior was so savage and unexpected, law enforcement had been involved, and a judge decided it was no longer safe to keep Mr. Webber at the Springfield Mental Hospital. He'd been transferred to the Marshall Rubenston's Asylum for the Criminally Insane, located in Galeston, Illinois. The judge committed him to their care until such time as he was considered safe for release.

The letter dropped from Laura's numb fingers. She doubled over in agony, holding herself tight to keep from falling apart. If she let the screams out, she didn't think she'd ever be able to stop.

CHAPTER SIXTEEN

Cry It Out, Baby

Laura remained silent, but her nails pierced her palms, and her clenched jaws hurt. She rocked, eyes closed but unable to stem the hot tears that poured from under the lids and burned her cheeks. Her nose ran and the mucous dripped into her lap, joining the tears that fell from her chin. Laura's entire body shook with the wails she held inside, building pressure in her head until it felt ready to explode.

"Oh God, how could you let this happen? Poor Glen. All he wanted was to come home, and now he might as well be on the moon. That letter is full of lies. Nobody cares, they're covering everything up to protect themselves."

The words burst from her raw throat, spat out with pain and venom. "I don't know what to do. I can't take this, I can't take anymore. Please, please, no more."

"Cry it out, baby, go ahead and cry." Ma's voice was strong, echoing inside Laura's mind. Her warm energy filled the room, wrapping Laura like snug, protecting arms. "Then when you're finished, stop whining, clean yourself up, and straighten that spine."

"I can't, Ma, I really don't think I can."

"Don't use that word to me. As long as you're breathing, you'll do whatever you need to." Ma's tone was tough, but her comforting warmth remained.

"I don't know what I can do. This is as bad as it can get." Laura sniffed back the last of her tears. "Glen's hurt and hundreds of miles away. No telling if I'll ever see him again since we only have a kid's wagon for transportation. He's not coming back and that means no money coming in. The bank account is almost empty. All we have is the mason jar money, but if I dig that up we'll have no emergency fund at all." She paused and wiped her face on her skirt. "How can I tell the children? It will break their hearts to hear what's happened to their papa." Laura's eyes started stinging again, so she blinked back fresh tears. "I feel like pulling the covers over my head and giving up."

"Stop it." The command was firm. "You've lived through just as bad before. Remember how you felt after your pa attacked you?"

Laura's mind flashed back to the river where she'd sat in water up to her chest so long ago. She remembered the cold current pulling at the fabric of her dress while she scrubbed at her legs, determined to rid herself of the sweat, dirt, and blood. She'd continued until her skin was raw, long after all visible signs disappeared, wanting nothing more than to die and float out to sea. She thought of pressing her face under the water, but hadn't been able to do it.

"That's right," Ma said. "You suffered through the worst a daughter can endure, but you picked yourself up, finished filling the water barrels and drove the wagon back to the house."

Laura trembled, remembering the awful, sick feeling of being in the same room as her pa, pretending nothing had happened until after everyone had fallen asleep.

"Remember? You waited, then sneaked outside and ran miles into town in the dead of night. Barefoot, wearing only a nightgown, you escaped."

"I was so scared," Laura whispered. "I knew the road like the back of my hand, but I was terrified, convinced every single sound was Pa or Ben, or both of them, coming to take me back."

"You were only twelve years old. You still have that same determination and courage."

"But Ma, I knew Ruth would take me in," Laura said. "I wasn't alone then."

"So what." Ma sounded annoyed at the excuses. "Remember when you saw the vision of Bonnie's death while you were living at Emma's place. Ruth had told you she'd died, but hadn't given you any details. You saw Ben in the barn, his body pressing her into the hay, his hand covering her nose and mouth while he violated her, not aware that she'd suffocated until he finished. Do you remember what Ruth said?"

Laura bit her lip, trying to keep from crying out. "Oh God, Ma, seeing that almost drove me out of my mind. I knew I was seeing what had happened, but it hurt so bad." She paused a moment, picturing the shocked look on Ruth's face when Laura told her what she'd seen. "Ruth didn't want to believe me, but somehow knew I was telling the truth. She made me promise to never tell anyone about my visions or having the second sight. She told me people would think I was either an agent of the devil or possessed."

"You believed her and thought you were alone with your secrets, but built a beautiful family anyway."

"True, but our family depends on Glen, and he's gone. My children need to be fed and clothed. And they need a parent to depend on...I don't know how I can do it. I've got nothing left."

Laura closed her eyes and dropped her face into her hands. She couldn't escape Ma's energy surrounding her, but did her best to hide.

"You don't need all the answers. Just keep your focus on those babies and do what's right. Minute by minute, or day by day. Don't matter, just do what you can."

"Mama...Mama..." June's voice drifted through the barn door from the back porch. "Where are you?"

In that instant Laura felt her ma's energy disappear, but the words stayed. "In the barn, Junebug." Laura's voice sounded raspy when she called out. "I'll be back in a few minutes."

"Are you okay?"

"I'm fine, honey."

Laura knew she wasn't fine, but didn't want to worry her daughter. She stuffed the letter back inside her purse, stood, then smoothed her dress. Taking a deep breath, she made her way out of the barn on shaky legs, purse in one hand and lantern in the other.

How could the night look so peaceful when she was consumed with despair? The moon peeked between tattered cloud banks that slid across the sky. A light breeze lifted her hair and caressed her body, cooling her skin and the fire in her swollen eyes. With the lantern lighting the path, Laura saw June in her nightgown, hugging herself against the cool air, leaning against the post at the top of the porch stairs.

"It's cold out here, Junebug. Go back inside. I'll be right behind you."

June nodded and dashed through the open screen door, leaving it open behind her. "Are you okay? I was worried when I woke up and couldn't find you." June tilted her head and tightened her eyebrows as Laura neared the porch. "You're still wearing your day dress. What's going on? You always change into coveralls to take care of the animals at night."

Laura hugged June tight, put the lantern down and shut it off. "I just realized I'd left my handbag in the barn when we wrapped Raymond's ankle, and went to get it. All the animals are fine." Laura could see that June wasn't satisfied with her answer. "What are you doing up? You should be sound asleep with your brothers."

"I had to go to the bathroom, then I saw light in the barn," June said. "Your face looks funny and your eyes are all puffy." June followed Laura into the kitchen.

Laura realized, too late, that the hospital envelope was sticking partway out of the handbag. She started to push it deeper but wasn't fast enough.

"Is that letter from Papa's doctor?" June's voice rose, fear giving it wings. "What happened? That's why you were out there alone, isn't it? You were crying, weren't you? What's happened to Papa?"

"Nothing you need to worry about, honey. Papa's just not improving. They don't know when he'll be any better, which means it may be a long time before he comes home." Laura told herself she wasn't telling a lie, just not giving more information than June could handle. She wrapped her arms around her daughter and pulled her close. "Don't worry, the doctor's will keep doing all they can, and we'll just have to manage until he can come back to us." She kept one arm around June's waist and led her through the dining room and toward the bedrooms. "We both need to get some sleep before the animals wake up and need breakfast."

It took some work pushing three little boys and rearranging their limbs for June to have room in bed. None of them woke up, so Laura tucked them in under the thick quilt, then brushed June's hair out of her eyes. "Sleep tight, sweetheart. We'll talk in the morning."

Laura took off her shoes and carried them to her room, enjoying the feel of the cool wood on the bottoms of her feet. Once in bed, she curled toward Glen's side and cradled his pillow in her arms.

CHAPTER SEVENTEEN

My Boots Have Lips

January 1939

"Wake up, sleepyheads, it's back to school today." Laura pulled at the quilt covering the children, jolting them out of a sound sleep.

"No, it's too early." June pulled the pillow over her head.

Raymond and Jimmy tried to hide from the light, too, but David didn't even stir.

"Come on. You've had your time off. Vacation's over, so get moving." Laura pulled the blanket all the way off and started tickling feet. The complaints turned into giggles, then a full-blown tickle fight. In minutes, the three oldest jumped out of bed and chased Laura down the hall, laughing all the way, followed by a sleepy-eyed David.

Halfway through breakfast, rain started pouring down the windows. Raymond and June stared at each other. June said, "Mama, we can't go to school if it's raining hard."

"Oh, yes, you can," Laura said, smiling. "You have to wear your raincoats, hats, and boots, but you're not made of sugar so you won't melt."

"Ah, come on. It's a long way." Jimmy sat back and crossed his arms. "We'll get all wet."

"I wish we still had the truck so you could take us to school," June said. Raymond nodded along with her.

"So do I, honey, so do I. We don't have it anymore and there's no other choice." The kids protested, but she cut them off. "Nothing's more important than your schooling. Unless there's a blizzard outside, you're walking to school and that's final."

When all the fuss was over, Laura walked out on the porch and watched her children until they disappeared around the curve of the driveway. Covered in their bright yellow rain-gear, they marched close together with their heads down, boots splashing through puddles. "David, stay back here where it's dry," she said when he headed for the steps. She remembered how much she'd hated walking to school in the rain. They didn't have fancy rainwear when she was young, and always were damp and uncomfortable for the first hour or so of class on wet days.

Laura stood in the open door of the empty garage. She'd finished her morning chores, and David was down for his nap. "Might as well get this over with," she said, hearing the tremor in her voice. She pulled a trowel from among the tools arranged on the wall above Glen's workbench on the left side of the garage, knelt down on the dirt floor in the corner just past the end of the bench, and started digging.

About four inches down the trowel tip hit a hard surface. She scraped the dirt away from the top of a flat rock and pulled it out of the hole, revealing the top of a quart jar. Laura worked the jar out of the ground with her fingers. She brushed at the dirt clinging to the light blue-green glass. Most of the damp earth fell away, but some remained stuck to the lettering that spelled out Ball Perfect Mason on one side. The jar, almost full with bills and coins, was heavy.

Laura filled the hole and put the trowel back in its place, then carried the jar back to the house. She rinsed the dirt off and left it in the washroom basin to dry while she checked on David. Once satisfied that he was still sleeping, she retrieved the jar and moved it to the kitchen table. Instead of opening the lid, Laura traced the lettering over and over, remembering all the years she and Glen had carried it with them.

Glen gave Laura the jar when they got married, suggesting they make it their emergency fund and put away whatever they could each payday. Later they'd agreed on making it their down-payment fund for purchasing a house of their own someday. Even through the hardest times, they'd never pulled money from the jar, in spite of the fact that the dream of owning a home looked impossible.

Laura teared up when she thought about the real reason for the jar, which Glen had revealed after the family had been living under a bridge for seven long weeks. He'd told her about his father's death and how desperate his poor mom had been, trying to provide for three children all alone, and his determination to never let that happen to his own family. He'd loved his father, but hated him for leaving the family with nothing. The charity his family received had sometimes been all that kept them alive, but he'd been ashamed of their accepting it. The memory of the pain on his mother's face when she'd been unable to support them on her own had haunted him.

"That's enough. Stop feeling sorry for yourself and get on with it." Laura wiped her eyes, twisted the lid off, and dumped the money into a pile. She counted it with care, sorting the money and coins into neat stacks, then counted it again. The total was the same each time, $183.92. She knew the bank account was down to $67.38. The combined amount, $251.30, was all they had to live on.

They paid no rent and had half the garden produce and dairy products that the farm produced, but that was in exchange for taking care of the animals and the garden. Laura had managed on her own since Glen had been taken away, but knew she couldn't keep it up much longer. Like it or not, it would be impossible to stay where they were. Somehow she had to find them a new place to live, figure out a way to move with nothing but a child's wagon, then find a job. It sounded impossible with a baby not even two years old.

Right on cue, Laura heard noises from the bedroom, and figured David was looking for her. She raked the money back into the jar and put it out of sight in the highest cabinet in the kitchen, minutes before he appeared in the doorway.

Laura might be in almost the same situation as Glen's mother, but she vowed never to let her children go through what he had. It would be difficult to move from the home they loved, but she promised herself they'd never feel the desperate pain he'd endured. Her resolve to not put their financial problems on the kids was tested as soon as they got home from school.

"Mama, look, my boots have lips." Jimmy shouted from the washroom where the children removed their rainwear and boots. With one boot in each hand, he ran into the living room waving them, soles flapping up and down. His socks trailed wet tracks behind him.

Raymond dumped Jimmy's books on the dining room table along with his own. "I told Jimmy his boots can't be fixed. Can I get new boots, too? His are ruined, but mine are getting too small and hurt my feet."

"If they get new boots, I should too." June chimed in. "It's not fair if they get new boots and I have to keep using old ones."

Oh, lord, what next? Laura kept the desperation out of her voice, but it was a struggle. "We'll talk about boots later. You've got chores to do, then homework."

"But what about tomorrow?" Jimmy said. "Can I stay home if it's still raining?"

June and Raymond spoke at the same time. "If he stays home tomorrow, we want to stay home too."

The next morning was still drizzly, with heavy clouds threatening much more rain. Nobody stayed home, but none of the children were happy. Jimmy wore Raymond's boots, with the toes stuffed with newspaper. Raymond wore June's boots, mortified to be wearing something

from a girl even if they looked identical to his.
June wore Laura's boots with two pairs of socks
and stuffing, same as Jimmy. They all stalked off
the porch with sullen expressions.

"Sorry kids," Laura said under her breath
after they marched down the steps. "But we
can't have you missing school and we don't have
money for new boots. Besides, your feet are all
growing fast, so this solution will work for
awhile." She went back inside with David, glad
that she could still carry him outside and avoid
buying him rain boots, yet. "Good thing I've got
a pile of old newspapers. I've got to stuff Glen's
for me since June has mine."

CHAPTER EIGHTEEN

A Jew and a Dirty Kraut

After caring for the animals, Laura took an inventory of their food supplies. The root cellar was full of shelves with canned tomatoes, beans, peas, corn, beets and carrots. They had bins of onions and potatoes, and a wire basket of eggs. Their portion of the beef and pork provided by their landlord was almost gone, and they wouldn't have chickens available for food after they moved. They also had the sacks of beans, flour, and cornmeal she'd bought days ago. It looked like a good list, but viewed as all they had for the foreseeable future? No matter how careful they were, it wouldn't last that long. "Looks like we'll be living on soup and beans," Laura said to David as she closed the cellar doors next to the house and carried him inside through the back door.

"Better start making a list of what we have and what we'll need. Chances are when I find us a place there won't be time to dawdle around."

David, sitting at her feet in the kitchen, grinned and clapped his hands.

"Love talking to you, little man, you're happy no matter what I say."

The washroom door slammed against the wall as June burst into the room. "We're home, Mama." Raymond and Jimmy crowded through right behind her, all three dripping on the floor.

Laura folded her list, then shoved it out of sight into her pocket. "Put your wet things away and come tell me about your day." She kept all her fears locked away in the back of her mind, and a smile pasted on her face.

The fire crackled in the fireplace, hissing like an angry cat when stray raindrops dropped through the flue. Laura sat on the couch, feet in front of her on the table. David was already in bed, so Laura had Jimmy on one side, sandwiched between her and June, with Raymond on the other. Everyone was silent throughout The Lone Ranger show on KWTO, hanging on each word.

"Let me up. I need to stoke the fire."
Laura wiggled her way free right after the Lone
Ranger's theme song ended, stretching and
rolling her shoulders on the way to the hearth.
She knelt down, moved the fire screen aside and
poked at the logs, watching the sparks fly.

When The Hour of Charm program
came on, featuring Phil Spitalny's All Girl
Orchestra, the kids groaned, raced for the
bathroom and then to the kitchen for drinks of
water. They returned to find Laura dancing
around the room, singing along with the music.

"Hey, Mama, I forgot to tell you we had a
new girl in school today." June plopped on the
piano bench, swinging her legs.

"Really? We don't get new people in
town all that often." Laura settled into a chair
near the fireplace. "What's she like?"

"She's pretty. Her name's Helga Cohen,
and she has brown, curly hair and blue eyes.
She's older than me, but they put her in my
class, anyway."

"That's because she doesn't talk right and
can't read very well," Raymond said, as he and
Jimmy settled on the couch, feet touching on
the middle cushion.

"She can't read? What do you mean she
doesn't talk right?"

June gave Raymond a dirty look. "She
talks fine, and she reads better than you do."
June turned to Laura after sticking her tongue

out at Raymond. "She comes from Germany. Helga said they lived in a place called Pankow, outside of Berlin. She's in my class, and told us she was born in Germany, but her papa is from America, so they moved here."

"Yeah," Raymond said. "Delbert, from June's class, told me she's a Jew and a dirty Kraut, and that she should go back where she came from."

"What did you say?" Laura's voice was low, but her fury was clear.

Raymond looked surprised and confused. "Delbert told all the boys she's a Jew and a dirty Kraut."

"Don't you dare ever repeat that again." Laura took a deep breath to calm down, since she knew Raymond had no idea what the words meant. "All of you, listen to me and pay close attention. First of all, Helga grew up speaking German. How would you like to move someplace where no one spoke English? Wouldn't you feel scared and lonely? And if you tried to speak or read another language, I'll bet everybody would make fun of how you sounded, and say you were stupid because you couldn't read."

Raymond shrugged his shoulders and hung his head. "I'm sorry. Guess it wasn't very nice to laugh at how she talked, even if it did sound funny."

Laura patted his shoulder, then continued. "Do you even know what a Jew is or what it means to call someone a Kraut?" Three heads shook side-to-side. "A Jew is someone who believes in the Jewish religion. You've all seen the church next to the school, right? Well, that's a Baptist Church, so people who go there are called Baptists. Folks who go to the big church near the lumberyard are Catholics."

"So Helga goes to a Jew church?" June said.

"Well, sort of. Jewish people call their churches synagogues, but it's kind of the same thing. Lots of people are afraid of things they don't understand, and make fun of people who are different than they are. So when you hear someone use the word Jew as an ugly name, that shows their ignorance. Promise me, all of you, that you won't use it like Delbert did ever again."

The children promised, then Raymond asked, "Why was it wrong to call her a dirty Kraut? What does Kraut mean, anyway?"

Laura sighed, wishing Glen were here to help with all the questions. He was always so good at explaining things. "Honey, don't call people names when you don't know what the names mean. Kraut is an ugly nickname for people from Germany. Calling Helga a dirty Kraut was a mean way of making fun of her. I'll bet she comes from a nice family and is as clean as you are, probably cleaner since she's a girl. If her papa is American, she's both American and German, and has just as much right to be here as you do."

"Delbert better not call Helga names tomorrow, or Raymond will sock him in the nose," Jimmy said, punching his fist in the air.

"No punching tomorrow, please," Laura said.

"Not tomorrow? Well, when can Raymond punch him in the nose?"

Laura smirked under her breath. "No punching at all, honey. No punching, period"

"Helga sat all by herself at lunch and recess," June said. "I'll see if she wants to play with me and Lizzie tomorrow. She looked kind of sad all by herself."

"Great idea, Junebug. She could probably use a friend."

Once the children were asleep, Laura's thoughts turned to Helga's family. She hadn't wanted to try to explain the ugliness of the Nazi regime to the children, even though she feared she'd have to in the future. Laura was heartsick for Helga's parents and what they must have endured as Jews under the hideous Nuremberg Laws put in place by Hitler. She and Glen had watched the newpaper stories since 1935, when Nazis deprived Jews of German citizenship and the right to marry non-Jews, then later when additional laws took away so many other basic human rights. Every single time they'd listened to radio programs about what was happening in Europe, Glen became more and more terrified of the potential for another war.

Laura climbed into bed and wrapped her body around Glen's pillow. How she missed the warmth and comfort of his body next to hers. "Oh, Glen, you'd hate seeing this poison reaching our family, hearing our children spout ugly, hateful words." Laura closed her eyes, shutting out the faint light that filtered through the clouds and the window. She opened her mind, reaching out through the darkness, searching for Glen. If she could just see him in her thoughts, or touch his mind, it wouldn't feel so lonely. She focused her breathing and extended her consciousness as far as she could, but heard only a low, scratchy hum like the sound you'd hear on the radio between stations. No vision came, either, only intermittent flashes of light that reminded her of lightning in far-away clouds.

CHAPTER NINETEEN

Only Have Children To Talk To

Laura startled awake. The house was silent and dark, lit only by the faint glow of moonlight through the window. She glanced at the alarm clock and saw it was just past midnight. She tossed the quilt off her body, stood and padded to the bathroom. Next she peeked into the children's room. They slept, piled in the middle of the bed, limbs tangled together in a warm, lumpy mass that emitted soft snores and snuffles. Laura chuckled under her breath and patted a stray foot sticking out from under the quilt. Thirsty, she walked past her bedroom door and headed to the kitchen for a glass of water.

They look so innocent when they're sleeping.

Laura's fingers trailed along the wall, the only guidance she needed in the dark, passing through the living room and around the corner into the kitchen.

"Ouch!" Laura hopped on one foot, holding the other in her hand as she rubbed her tender instep. She limped closer to the wall and turned on the light to find out what she'd stepped on. "Doggone jack. I've warned June over and over to make sure to pick them all up." She leaned down to pick up the spiked metal toy turned treacherous torture device and put it on the table, then filled a glass from the sink faucet and sat down. A long swallow cooled and soothed her itchy throat. While she rubbed at the sore spot on her foot, her gaze caught the corner of the hospital envelope peeking out of her handbag.

Anger bloomed, hot and sudden, then was replaced with doubt. Had she read it right? Maybe she'd missed something.

She pulled the letter out and reread it, eliminating the doubt and stoking the anger back up. The doctors were wrong. Glen wasn't insane, and not a criminal. He just wanted to come home to his family. Her breathing increased and she could feel her face flush. She read the dry, curt words again. "Without any warning or provocation" it said. Lies, nothing but ugly lies. Laura remembered what she'd seen in her vision when Glen attacked Gary, the orderly, and realized that the doctor was, in fact, correct about the assault. But they'd left out so much of what happened. Not a word about his desperate pleas on behalf of his family. Not a word about the way he'd been attacked by the dogs and beaten with chains. Poor Glen had been in a panic. He hadn't wanted to hurt anyone. If they'd only let him come home, nobody would have gotten hurt.

She bent forward, and kneaded her forehead. She couldn't erase the picture of Gary on the floor in her vision, his body still, blood spreading in a pool from beneath his face. How bad were his injuries? The letter said he'd needed several surgeries. Would he be disfigured for the rest of his life? Did anyone understand how desperate Glen had been to get home? Laura knew he was sick at heart at what he'd done, but must have thought there was no other choice but to escape.

Laura stood and carried the glass back to the sink. She looked at the window, but saw only her reflection. Now what should she do? What could she do? Horrible as it was, Glen had attacked a man. She realized that the letter hadn't said a word about Glen being beaten with chains by his captors. How bad had he been hurt by the chain blows to his head? Had he suffered any permanent injuries?

She read the last sentence again, which said the judge had committed him to their care until such time as he was considered safe for release. What did that mean? Were they afraid that he'd snap and turn violent and hurt somebody else? How on earth could he, or she, convince them otherwise. "Guess I'd better quit whining and get some answers."

Energized by the prospect of doing something, Laura found a piece of paper, an envelope, a pen, and a stamp from a drawer and started writing to the new hospital.

Dear Sir,

I have just learned that my husband was transferred to your hospital from the Springfield Mental Hospital. His name is Glen Webber. I don't have a car, so I cannot come to speak with his doctor. I don't have a telephone at home, so I will need to correspond by letter or by using a pay phone. I'm very worried about him, and would like to know the name of his doctor, and how to contact him.

I was also told that my husband cannot be released until it's safe, but don't understand exactly what that means. I will appreciate any information you can provide.

My husband is a good man who suffered a breakdown, the doctor called it shell shock, because of an awful experience during the war when he saw his brother shot dead next to him on the battlefield. Now that he's in the hospital, our four small children and I are in very bad shape. We need him well and home, so if there is anything we can do, please let me know.

Sincerely,

Mrs. Glen Webber

Laura read the letter twice, then folded it and put it in the envelope. After putting the pen away, she tucked the envelope deep inside her pocketbook, yawned, and headed back to bed.

The heavy storm clouds had disappeared by morning, replaced by a brilliant blue sky which the radio announcer said would remain for the next few days. David, bundled in his warmest clothes, climbed in the wagon, thrilled at the chance for a trip. The older children piled their books and lunchboxes around him, then took turns pulling the wagon for Laura.

"I go school," David crowed, waving his arms and kicking his legs.

"Hey, don't kick my books." June pushed David's legs away from her book bag. He waited until she let go of his legs, then grinned and gave her bookbag one final hard kick.

"Mom," June said. "Make him stop."

"Enough, David. If you've got that much energy, climb out and walk with the boys for awhile." Raymond and Jimmy took David's hands, swinging him between them. June grabbed the wagon handle and walked next to Laura behind her brothers.

Raymond and Jimmy got tired of lifting David before he was bored with the game.

"Back in the wagon, David." Laura lifted him in after they left the end of their long curved driveway and started down the road. "You aren't going to make your brothers late for school, kiddo, so don't you dare start fussing."

David pouted a bit, but was smiling and waving at everyone they passed by the time they reached the school grounds.

"There's Lizzie. Got to go." June grabbed her stuff and ran. Raymond and Jimmy followed her, leaving David and Laura alone on the sidewalk in front of the schoolyard. The school's front doors were closed, so the children milled around in groups waiting to go inside to their classrooms.

Laura noticed one girl with long brown braids standing with a small woman on the opposite side of the schoolyard. The woman wore a long brown coat that was too big for her, and a muddy-colored scarf covering her hair. They looked so alone. People circled around them, but no one acknowledged them at all. Laura couldn't hear what they were saying, but saw the child clinging to her mom. The woman loosened the girl's arms, turned her around, and gestured toward the school. Laura ached for the girl, who looked miserable as she trudged toward the doors with her shoulders slumped and her head downcast.

The school doors swung open, a signal for the children to head inside. David climbed out of the wagon and tried to follow them. "Oh, no, you don't." Laura grabbed his hand and led him toward the woman who stood and watched her daughter's reluctant progress toward the doors. "No school for you, yet. You can walk, but stay with me."

The poor woman looked lost and sad, the determined expression she'd held for her child dissolved away. She plunged her hands into the deep pockets of her over-large cloth coat, and hunched her scarf-covered head down between her shoulders. Laura couldn't stand it. "Good morning," she said. "I haven't seen you around before. I'm Laura Webber, and this little guy is David."

A tentative smile creased the pleasant, pale face ringed by unruly brown curls that sprang from the edges of the scarf. "Gut mornink, Mrs. Vebber. Ve juzt moved here. I am Magda Cohen."

"Cohen? Oh, you must be Helga's mother."

Magda tilted her head, scrunching her eyebrows together. "You know my Helga?"

"No, but I heard about her." Laura looked down at David, who was hanging off her fingers, kicking the side of the wagon. "Okay, you can play while we talk, but stay close and don't sit down in the wet grass." Eight steps later he plopped down on his bottom and started pulling at the blades of grass."

Magda giggled, then clapped her hand over her mouth. "Sohry, I should not loff at yur son."

"Why not? He's a funny little character. I laugh at him all the time. Your daughter is in the same class as mine. June told us all about her." Laura could see Magda's face close up, and took note of her flawless complexion and long feathery eyelashes.

"Magda, I know Helga had a hard time yesterday. Kids are ignorant and can be cruel, repeating stupid things they've heard from thoughtless parents."

Magda nodded, and Laura could see the glimmer of tears in her hazel eyes. "Yess, she did not vant to go back."

Laura reached out and touched Magda's shoulder. "I'm very sorry. I'm ashamed to admit that my sons called Helga names along with other boys, using words they didn't even know. We had a long talk last night. I explained a lot of things about the world to them that I'd hoped they didn't need to hear about at this age. They promised it would never happen again, and felt really bad about what they'd done. In fact, the boys are ready to sock anybody who teases her, and my daughter is planning to invite Helga to join her and her best friend at lunch and recess."

Tears welled up again, but this time above a tremulous smile. "Sank you."

"You're welcome." Laura picked up her soggy-bottomed son and put him in the wagon.

"We're headed for the post office. Are you going that way?"

"Yess, ve live abof the tailor shop down the street. Not far."

The two women parted in front of the post office. Laura felt comfortable with Magda, as if they'd known one another for ages. She reminded her of Willa, her best friend.

Laura watched Magda walk away toward the tailor shop, thinking about how Willa had come into her life. They'd met while traveling from South Dakota, looking for work. Willa, her husband Isaac, and their son Ruben, were stopped by the road with a flat tire. They had the first Hooverwagon, a car being pulled by a big blonde draft horse, Laura had ever seen. Everything the family owned was packed inside or lashed on the outside of the car, which had broken down shortly after leaving Sioux Falls. The two families spent the night camped together so Willa, very pregnant at the time, could rest. Even though they'd gone separate ways the following morning, they'd stayed in touch throughout the years.

Both women seemed frail, but had incredible inner strength that belied their appearance. "Too bad Willa lives in California," Laura said to David after they waved a final goodbye to Magda. "They'd like each other, I think."

"Come on, little man." Laura opened the post office door and pulled the wagon inside behind her.

"Good morning, Mrs. Webber." Mr. Niedermann stood at a long table behind the public counter, sorting mail. "I've missed you and young David."

"We've missed you, too, but I didn't want to bring him when it was raining." She glanced down at David, who was climbing out of the wagon, then pulled the letter to the hospital from her pocketbook and handed it to Mr. Niedermann.

"Hmmm, that's a new address," he said. "Did they move Mr. Webber? Galeston is a lot farther away." Mr. Niedermann's voice radiated sympathy and unspoken questions.

"Yes, it's a very long way, but that doesn't matter much since I don't have the truck anymore." Laura was grateful there weren't any other people standing around. "I need to know what's happening at the new hospital where Glen's been transferred. I want to call and get some answers, but first I have to find out who to talk to." She pointed to the letter in his hands. "I'm hoping they'll write back with what I need."

Mr. Niedermann shook his head. "You're right. When you get the information you need, come here and use the phone. I'll keep David occupied for you." He reached under the counter and retrieved a small stack of letters. "You hit the jackpot today, letters from Lizbeth, Willa, Becka, and someone named Barbara."

"Barbara?" Laura looked up, trying to place the name. "Oh, my goodness, that might be Glen's sister. Goodness, we haven't heard from her in almost a year."

"Well, I hope it's good news," Mr. Niedermann said. "And the others, too. It's been a while since you heard from Ruth, so I hope all is well with her family."

Laura tucked the letters in her handbag, lifted David into the wagon, and waved goodbye to Mr Niedermann. She pulled David through the door and headed down the sidewalk toward home. Her thoughts turned to the last time she'd seen Barbara. They'd still been living in Tulsa. How many years had it been? Her face burned with shame at letting so much time go by.

"Mama, go potty," David yelled, his voice cutting into Laura's thoughts. "Go potty now." His tone was urgent and his eyes were wide open.

Laura turned around, knowing Mr. Niedermann would let him use the bathroom in the post office, but saw two women going through the door with three large parcels. She didn't want to ask him now, but it sounded like David couldn't wait until they got home. "Hold on, son, just a little bit." The tailor shop under

Magda's apartment was only three buildings down. "Let's see if Magda would let us in."

They parked the wagon behind the base of the staircase on the right side of the building and hustled up the steps to Magda's apartment.

"Hang on, little man," Laura said, rapping on the screen door.

"Yes," Magda said, opening the door just enough to peer out. "Oh, my gutness." She pulled the door wide open. "Velcome, is somethink wrong?

"I'm so sorry to barge in like this, but David is desperate for a bathroom."

Magda leaned toward David and pointed toward a door across the room. "Right through zat door, liebling."

Laura trotted after David to the bathroom. "Thank you so much," she said when they returned to the living room. "I don't think he could have made it home, and didn't want him to have an accident."

"You're velcome anytime. Vould you like some tea and cookies?"

"That would be lovely, thank you." Laura followed Magda into the kitchen, just a few feet to the left of the front door. "Can I help?" She was surprised at the difference in a woman she'd thought pleasant, but plain. Magda's unfettered curls framed a face that was wholesome and sweet, with hazel eyes that sparkled, and a lovely, warm smile.

"No, I haf got zis." She carried a small tray to the dining table. "Please, sit down und help yourself."

Laura led David to the table where Magda had placed a tray. She lifted him onto a chair and sat down next to him. "I didn't mean to put you out, but it's nice to spend time visiting. Sometimes it's hard to only have the children to talk to."

"But don't you talk with your husband?"

The question hit Laura like a blow. Everybody else in town knew the story. "My husband is wonderful to talk with, but he's in a hospital in Illinois."

Magda's hands flew to her mouth. "I'm so sorry. Vhat happened? Vhy is he so far avay?"

Laura brushed away tears that threatened to overflow. "He had a mental breakdown. The doctor called it shell shock from the war, but they don't know what to do. He's been away for over four months, and we have no idea when he'll be home." It was getting hard to maintain control of her emotions. She squeezed her hands tight together and took a deep breath. "We had a truck, but it broke down, so I have no way to go see him even if I could afford the gas. We have no phone so I can't call him."

Magda leaned toward Laura and patted her hand. "I vish I could help."

Laura straightened her shoulders and took a deep breath. "Thank you. I'm sorry, I usually don't let it get me down, especially in front of someone else. You've been through lots more than me, so I should stop feeling sorry for myself."

Magda handed David another cookie, "Vould you like a glass of milk?" He glanced at Laura, then nodded.

Magda continued, her voice soft. "I cannot imagine how difficult it must be for you. Vorryink about your husbant so far away, but shtill takink care of yourself and zee children," she said, scooting closer to Laura. "Vhen thinks seem too hard, I tell myself to only focus on vhat I'm doink right zen. And vhen zat task iss finished, I zink about zee next one. If my hands are busy vith somesink I can do, I'm not vorryink about future problems I cannot fix."

Both women stayed silent awhile, watching David and sipping their tea. They felt no need to fill the silence with conversation, comfortable with the one another's presence.

"More?" David lifted his empty plate.

"No, you don't need more," Laura said to David. "But you do need to thank Mrs. Cohen for your snack."

David's lower lip stuck out, but he put the plate down and said, "Thank you, Misscone."

The quiet spell was broken. Smiling at David's pronunciation, Laura stood and brushed his crumbs into her hand. Magda cleared the table and grinned each time she looked at the little boy.

"I'm so glat you came. Please come again, and brink zee ozer children. I know Helga vould love zat, and Harvey, my husband, likes havink company."

"It would be like an invasion with all four children, but maybe we can plan for one afternoon after school lets out."

The women hugged one another, then Laura carried David down the stairs, collected the wagon at the bottom, and headed home.

CHAPTER TWENTY

Bullies Are Cowards

"Thank goodness he still takes naps," Laura said to herself after she'd finished working outside with David at her side. Now that he was asleep, she had time to relax a bit and read her letters. She decided to save her sisters' letters until last, and opened the one from Barbara.

Laura's favorite memory of Barbara was when she and Glen got married. Barbara had been her Maid of Honor, and her best friend. It was hard to say goodbye when she and Glen left Tulsa for the Seminole oil boom. They'd never imagined it would be the last time they'd see Barbara for...fourteen years. "That was way too long. She'd write a long letter as soon as she finished reading Barbara's."

Laura smiled at Barbara's loopy, round handwriting. Her smile got bigger as she read.

...head over heels in love, and with an Army Sergeant from a family of military men. His name is Louis Canfield. Can you believe it?...

That was hard to imagine, but wonderful too. Barbara deserved someone to love her. She just hoped the guy was good enough and would treat her right

...Louis knows how much I love to dance and takes me to dances all the time. He does a mean boxstep, but we'll never win any dance contests like you and Glen did. The scuffed toes of my shoes will never be the same ...

Laura's smile widened at memories of weekends in Tulsa with Barbara and their friends. She and Glen played music and danced almost every weekend, and won many dance competitions.

As soon as Laura finished reading, she began to write her letter back. She found responding to most of Barbara's comments was easy. She wrote two full pages about the children. Soon she had only Glen to write about. This was so hard. How can she tell her what had happened? But Laura couldn't lie either. She didn't want to ruin Barbara's excitement about getting married when there was nothing she could do. Laura tapped the pencil eraser on the table, trying to find the perfect words. After many false starts, she wrote,

> *Glen is going through some tough things right now. He was so worried and afraid about the possibility of another war with all the news from Europe. When a young man died in a freak accident on the job site, he kind of lost it, and flashed back to Bobby's death. He's working with a doctor, though, so we're hopeful.*

She signed the letter and pushed the pencil away. Barbara and Glen had been so close, the only ones left in their family. Laura could almost hear Barbara cry out, demanding to know what was going on, terrified of something happening to her brother. If only Barbara was near by, so they could support each other and Glen through this mess. Laura feared Barbara would blame her in some way, just as she sometimes blamed herself, even though there was nothing more she could have done to help Glen.

"I draw, too," David said, reaching for the pencil.

Laura jumped and gasped. "You scared me," she said, pulling him into her lap. "I thought you were still sleeping, you sneaky little thing." She tickled his ribs, loving the sound of his giggles. "You can help me make cornbread and mashed turnips."

David wrinkled his face. "Turnips? I like turnips?"

"You'll love these, I promise." Laura turned a chair around and pulled it up to the kitchen counter for him to stand on. "You're my helper for chores this afternoon, starting with these." She dumped a bowl of turnips into the sink and turned the water on low. "You're in charge of washing them, then I'll do the peeling."

"Hi, Mama." Jimmy was first through the washroom door. "Raymond and Delbert got into a fight at lunch and Raymond won."

"No, I didn't," Raymond said. "I mean, I made him shut up, but we didn't fight."

June, her boots stowed under the bench and her coat hung on the hook by the door, pushed past her brothers and entered the kitchen. "Jimmy has it half right. Delbert started calling Helga names at our first recess and Raymond said he was ignorant and told him to shut up. Delbert put his fists up, but when he saw all three of us in front of Helga, ready for him, he backed down and walked off."

"Good for you. Bullies are cowards. I'm proud of you." Laura loved the happy smiles on the kids' faces. "Come on now, get to work on your homework before it's time to eat."

⌁

After she put David to bed for the night, Laura and the older children lounged in the living room, basking in the fire's warmth.

"Mama," June said, "Helga told me they left home so fast she didn't even get to say goodbye to anyone. They were on a big boat for days and days. She said it looked like fun at first, but the waves were so big the boat rocked all the time. Lots of people got sick, so it smelled awful. She said she never wants to go on a boat again."

Laura listened, sensing there might be questions from her daughter.

"She's nice, but seems so scared and sad," June said, playing with her fingernails. "She's really skittery, too. A couple of times kids yelled on the playground and she jumped liked they were after her. Lizzie and I asked about her trip here, and Helga wiped her eyes, sniffed, and looked down at the ground when she answered us. I asked if she was crying, but she shook her head no."

"Well, she's been through a pretty scary experience." Laura hugged June. "Having a friend to talk to is important, but she'll have to learn she can trust you. Give her time and she should start feeling safer in her new home."

June shrugged her shoulders and stared at her lap without responding, then Laura said, "I met Helga's mother today. She's very nice."

That got the boys' attention as well as June's. Laura told them all about how she and David had met Mrs. Cohen, and that they'd been invited to visit the family sometime.

The conversation slowed after that, so Laura shooed them off to bed. She retrieved the letter from Willa and curled up on the sofa. Willa's letters made Laura smile, no matter what the subject was. She was always surprised at the resiliency of the tiny, slender woman who had endured so much.

When the families met on the side of the road, Willa had been pregnant, but hadn't complained about the rough conditions. She and Isaac had lost their last baby hours after his birth, and were determined to save this one. Their excitement at the birth of a healthy, beautiful baby girl, Leah, sang from the pages of Willa's letters.

Four months later, Leah contracted measles and died. The family had been devastated, but they clung together in their sorrow, focusing on the memories they'd always treasure.

...Can you believe that Ruben is eighteen? He's a man now, and Isaac is teaching him accounting...

That was hard to believe, since Laura remembered Ruben as a gangly, tall, sweet-natured twelve-year-old. He'd charmed the children so much that Raymond had wanted to go with him.

... Isaac and I, just like you and Glen, listen to the news daily. Now we pray every single day that America doesn't get drawn in, or Ruben might end up in the military...

Lord, she hoped not. Glen was terrified about the possibility of another war and the deaths that would mean, but the idea of having a son old enough to go fight? That would kill her. And Ruben? He was one of the gentlest souls she'd ever known, unimaginable as a soldier.

Details of their daily life filled the rest of Willa's letter. Isaac, through the help of a friend they'd known in South Dakota, had found an accounting position. It didn't pay much, so he'd started helping small businesses with their bookkeeping. After two years, he'd formed his own small company and started teaching Ruben to help him. Willa did her part too, maintaining the office and answering the phone.

As always, Willa ended her letter by sending her love to everyone. Laura felt guilty for not writing about Glen before now, but had waited this long for something positive to say. Now, who knew when or if that might happen? She should write and explain what had transpired. Laura knew it was the right thing to do, but feared the sympathy she'd receive would break her down.

"Stop hiding and just get it done." Laura stood and headed for the kitchen. She'd write the letter right now before she could come up with more lame excuses.

By the time Laura finished addressing and sealing the envelope, the fire in the fireplace was a memory, with only embers remaining. It felt good to have shared with Willa, like a huge weight was off her shoulders. Her sisters' letters remained in her handbag, but Laura didn't have the energy to open them.

CHAPTER TWENTY-ONE

Somehow, We'll Make It Together

L aura didn't open her sisters' letters until the next day after the kids left for school and she finished the morning chores. She curled up on the couch with them, while David played at her feet with some blocks, two pots and a wooden spoon. Laura opened both envelopes, then read Lizbeth's letter first. She closed her eyes and said a silent prayer before reading Becca's, but the second letter only reinforced the words of the first. Martha, Ruth's mother-in-law, had been diagnosed with an advanced case of breast cancer.

It wasn't fair. Martha was such a kind, sweet woman. She and Jake had saved both Laura and Ruth from their pa. Ruth after she'd been beaten with a horsewhip until her back was ribboned with cuts, then Laura after she'd been raped. Thanks to Martha spiriting Laura away to her sister Emma's ranch, Laura had a safe place to live for five years. And now breast cancer. Becca said Martha hadn't felt well for a long time, but was always too busy to go to the doctor. She and Jake, with Ruth and Paul's help, had worked every day in their store after they'd let most of the employees go. She'd also been an amazing grandmother whenever Paul and Ruth needed a little time away from their three children.

Lizbeth said that Jake had insisted on her seeing their doctor after he'd watched his wife take patent medicines for weeks with no improvement. Now, after waiting so long, her only option was surgery. They'd have to take her to a specialist in Oklahoma City for the operation, but Martha's chances for recovery from the disease were poor.

"Mama?" David stood against Laura's knees, peering into her face. He reached up and touched the tip of his finger to a tear hanging from her chin and stared into her eyes.

Laura sniffed, wiped her eyes and pulled him into her lap. "Mama's fine, little man. My eyes are just watering." She tucked the letters into her pocket, and squeezed him hard.

David wiggled loose and got back down from the couch. "Too tight," he said.

"Okay." Laura tapped his nose and pointed to the pile of blocks on the floor. "Show me what you're building."

꙳

The letters remained hidden in Laura's pocket until the end of day, after the children were sleeping. The night was clear and cold. The crisp, still air was illuminated by a steady glow from the moon, and stars that pulsed with light and secret life. She wrapped herself in Glen's heavy coat and sat on the front porch glider, tucking her feet underneath her thighs. The papers crinkled as she moved.

"Oh, Glen, how I wish you were here. You'd love the sky tonight. I'd lean against you, cry a little if I needed to, and we'd talk about what was happening in the world and with our friends and family." She sighed, breathing the brisk air deep into her lungs. "You wouldn't have answers to all the problems, nobody could, but just sharing them would ease the pain and give me strength."

For the first time since he'd gone to the hospital, the thought that he might not return crept into her mind—unthinkable, impossible, unbearable, yet it might happen. How could she handle dealing with everything alone, just her and the children?

Laura shifted her body to her other side. She thought of the letters in her pocket and the fact that she had family, people who loved her and would want to help. All she had to do was move back to Ardmore, Oklahoma, and she'd have their support.

She remembered the last time she'd visited her sisters, so many years ago. She was living in the hotel with Barbara and several other girls. Ruth and Paul had sent her train tickets and Glen had taken her to the station. "Their little boys, Elliot and Aaron were just toddlers, so cute. They followed me around like puppies."

Laura continued talking out loud, with only the stars for an audience. "My goodness, they're grown now, nineteen and seventeen years old. And we've never even met their little sister, Maggie. It's hard to believe she's thirteen now."

Even with her eyes closed, Laura couldn't picture those two adorable little boys as young men and their baby sister a teenager.

Ruth and Paul had surprised Laura with a wonderful family dinner. Lizbeth and her husband, Roy, brought Becca and their newborn baby. "Lily smelled so sweet. That was the first time I'd ever held a baby that young." A faint breeze ruffled Laura's hair in the dark, an answer that was almost a soothing caress to go with the memories. "And now Lily is fifteen, almost a woman herself. And Becca, sweet Becca who had always lived with Lizbeth, married to a baker and mother of twins."

The need for her sisters caused an ache in Laura's chest, the pain of missing them almost unbearable. If she moved back to Ardmore they'd all be together again, able to share in one another's lives once more. "I'd have them, but I'd also have Pa in the same town. I never want my children near that disgusting, vicious excuse for a man." Laura remembered running into her pa on that same trip. She'd faced him down and felt good about it, but never wanted to go through that again. And who knew where her brother, Ben, was? Ruth said he'd grown into a duplicate of Pa, mistreating his wife and children. No telling when he might show up in Ardmore if Laura were there.

She pulled the coat tighter around her, burying her nose in the collar. There was still a slight scent of Glen remaining in the fabric, and she breathed it in. "No, I can't think about moving. Besides, there's no way I could move without begging for money, and my sisters are all dealing with their own family problems." She stopped moving and listened a moment, thinking she'd heard one of the children cry out.

"Must have been my imagination. Nothing out here but me talking to myself."

The evening was peaceful in the dark, under the night sky canopy. When Laura's legs fell asleep, she decided it was time to go to bed. "Good night stars. Thanks for the company." She walked inside, having made her decision. "No matter what, I've got to keep things as normal as possible for the children. Aurora is their home, and somehow, with or without Glen, we'll make it together."

CHAPTER TWENTY-TWO

Your Pa Isn't Here

Two Weeks Later, January 1939

Laura stepped outside, braced against the wind that almost ripped the lantern out of her hands as she closed the washroom door behind her. She held the slippery rubber material of the slicker hood tight under her chin, took a deep breath, then headed down the steps toward the barn. Thunder boomed as lightning split the sky overhead. Stinging rain drenched Laura, making it hard to breath, and the sharp smell of ozone tickled her nose. Hard drops pelted her face and bare hands and soaked the legs of her coveralls. Water funneled inside the tops of Glen's oversize boots, soaking her socks.

So much for a mild winter. Laura tromped as fast as she could through muddy rivulets coursing between the house and barn. Nasty weather all weekend was bad enough, but if it didn't let up in the next hour, she'd have to keep the kids home from school.

She eased the barn doors open enough to slip inside, and dropped the wooden cross-bar in place to keep them closed. She draped the dripping slicker across a bale of hay and hung the lantern on a hook above the first stall door. From there, she made her way down the center aisle to the cow holding pen on the left, and lit the lantern that rested on a shelf inside the pen door.

In minutes she had the first of their four cows secured with a clean bucket beneath her swollen udders. "Sorry about the cold hands, Sassy." Laura rested her forehead against the cow's warm body, focused on nothing but the rhythmic motion and the sound of the milk splashing in the bucket.

"Okay, Sassy, you're all done." Laura stood, patted the cow's flank, and lifted the bucket. She headed for the supply room where the milk cans were stored, but half-way there her feet flew out from under her. The milk can flipped upside down as she went down on her back, slid on the milky floor, and slammed her left arm into the doorframe.

Laura held her breath, afraid to move. "Please, God, don't let anything be broken," she whispered, squeezed her eyes shut, and started checking out her body. Her back hurt, from her shoulders to her tailbone, but her ribs felt okay. She wiggled her feet, her legs and hands, no problems. Laura turned to the right, freeing her throbbing left arm, then lifted herself first to her knees, then up on her feet. She stared down at the floor behind her and saw boot slide marks through a slimy cowpie.

"Oh no, I forgot to shovel that up." She remembered Pixie dropping the mess on her way back to the stall after being milked last night, but she'd been too tired to clean it up. Now, soaked to the skin with sticky milk and manure, it'd have to wait until she finished milking the other three cows and feeding all the animals.

"Ha." a snarky little voice in her head said. "Dumb excuse, since it'll take more time to clean up an even bigger mess now, and you ruined a bucket of milk."

"Oh, shut up." Laura hated to admit the voice—her conscience?—was right. As soon as the cows were milked and back in their stalls, she realized she didn't remember the last time she'd thoroughly cleaned the stalls. She filled the feeding troughs, refilled the water buckets, then examined the straw bedding. All three stalls looked the same. Tamped down straw, damp with manure and urine, not enough dry space for a cow to lie down and sleep. Ashamed and embarrassed, she apologized to the patient animals and promised that she'd clean everything that day, right after she fed the children breakfast.

How could I let things get this bad? Laura asked as she walked to the pigpen, her back and arm pulsing with every painful step. The neglect was the same for the pigs and chickens. She'd assigned some animal tasks to the children, but the ultimate responsibility was hers.

No, they'd agreed that the responsibility was Glen's. The angry retort popped into her mind unbidden, even when she tried to shove it away. That was part of their rental deal with this place. She took care of the house, garden, and children. He was supposed to handle the animals and work that was too heavy for her. He was sick, but she was stuck with the extra work, and that wasn't fair.

The wind whipped the slicker around Laura as she walked back to the house, chilling her wet body to the bone. At least the rain had stopped. That figured, she thought. Rain would have washed away some of the milk and manure that covered her. Now she'd have to clean everything in the washroom sink.

"Morning, Mama," June said. She stood in the door to the kitchen, holding David balanced on her hip.

Laura rinsed off Glen's boots and balanced them on the edges of the sink. The slicker, dripping clean water, hung from a wire suspended above the sink. Laura grabbed the towel hanging on the wall and dried her arms and hands.

Jimmy and Raymond crowded into the doorway with June. "Phew, Mama, you stink," Jimmy said, holding his nose.

"You've got cow poop all over the back of your coveralls," Raymond said. "Jimmy's right, you stink something awful."

"Thanks a lot." Laura turned to face them. "I've got to get out of these coveralls and clean them. June, put a pot of water on the stove. It should be boiling by the time I'm done."

As the kids closed the kitchen door, lightning lit up the clouds, followed in seconds by thunder that shook the house. Rain pounded against the roof and windows once again. The lights flickered, but stayed on.

"No school today," the kids' voices rang out.

Laura hung the coveralls with the slicker, put on her robe and headed to her bedroom to change. When she returned to the kitchen, the water had almost boiled away, but the children were out of sight. Irritation bubbled up inside, rising as fast and hot as the steam from the thin layer of water on the stove. She added more water to the pot, then marched out of the room.

She found the kids in their bedroom, bouncing on the bed and hitting one another with pillows. "What do you think you're doing?"

Four startled faces focused on her, then glanced at each other. "We're playing," June said. "We can't go to school, so we're playing."

Laura crossed her arms and tightened her lips. "Just because the weather's too bad for school doesn't mean you can slack off. Instead of setting the table for breakfast, you let water boil away in the pot. That could have ruined the pot or even started a fire." She gestured toward the tangled quilt and sheet on the bed. "You should have made your bed by now. You need to put away toys in the living room from last night." Laura stopped herself, took a deep calming breath. "Get yourselves dressed, make the bed, then come to the kitchen."

Laura was placing steaming bowls of oatmeal, topped with dried apple slices, on the table when the children arrived. They looked at her, then at each other, and sat down without a word.

"June, fill glasses of milk for everyone. Raymond, get the spoons."

Jimmy pointed at his bowl. "Mama, you know I don't like..."

"Not one more word about what you don't like, James Allen, or your breakfast goes to the pigs and you can go hungry." Laura pulled her chair out and sat, ignoring the stunned looks and silence.

"Mama, why are you mad at us?" June's voice was just above a whisper. "We didn't mean to do anything wrong."

Laura kneaded her forehead, took a breath, then leaned on her folded arms. "I know you didn't mean to do anything wrong, but all of us, and that includes me, have let something awful happen." She stared down, spooned oatmeal back and forth in her bowl, then faced them again. "Tell me, how would you like to sleep on a wet, dirty bed tonight, with no way to stay warm and dry?"

None of the children said a word, just glanced back and forth among themselves.

"That's what our poor animals have right now. I've given you guys the job of feeding them, but not one of you has done a thing about cleaning up after them. I was sick to my stomach this morning when I checked out the stalls, the pigpen, and the chicken coop. They're all filthy, downright nasty. Your papa would be so angry and disappointed with us." Laura's eyes skewered each child as she leaned forward. "If my sisters and I ever left an animal pen as dirty as what I saw this morning, our pa would have used his belt on us until we weren't able to sit for days. He was a cruel man and I'm not threatening you guys with beatings, but he was right about never letting the poor animals end up like what I saw this morning."

David's lower lip quivered. Laura stroked his forehead, calming away the tears she saw were near.

"But Mama, Pa always took care of the those chores," Raymond said.

"Yes, but your Pa isn't here." Laura stood and moved to the counter. Staring out the window at the wind-lashed trees, she said, "While he's gone, we have to do everything. I want all of you to stay inside today. Take care of David for me and clean up after yourselves. June, you and Raymond can make sandwiches for lunch and heat the leftover chicken soup in the refrigerator if I'm not finished in time for dinner. I'll be outside working and I don't want anybody bothering me. Unless somebody stops breathing or breaks a bone, work out any problems among yourselves. June is in charge if there are any arguments."

Laura turned round, stared at each wide-eyed child, then left the room.

CHAPTER TWENTY-THREE

I'm The Grown-Up

The wind and rain hadn't abated when Laura, once more clad in overalls, damp boots, and oversize slicker, opened the barn doors. This time, unlike earlier in the day, she secured them in place to light up the interior. She strode down the center aisle, stepping around Pixie's smeary pile, then opened and secured the door that led into the corral behind the barn. One by one she released the cows, shooed them out of the barn, and watched them head straight across the corral to the three-sided shelter on the other side of the pasture.

Laura stared at the smelly straw in the stall nearest the corral door. On clear days, the stuff could go straight to the garden, but today it went to the manure pile. She marched straight to the supply room, threw a pitchfork and shovel into the wheelbarrow, and pushed it to the closest stall. After shrugging off the slicker, she tossed it over the stall sidewall, then started forking the smelly bedding into the cart.

The work was mind-numbing. Laura's thoughts soon returned to the scene in the kitchen with the children. She remembered the look on their faces when she'd told them her pa would have whipped her for not doing her chores, and twice as hard for not taking proper care of the animals. He had no emotional attachment to them. To him, they were just sources of food or money. But that made them more important than anything. She could still see his belt and remember the terror that gripped her and her sisters whenever he started taking it off. He'd yell in a menacing tone as he pulled the wide, black leather belt out of the loops. The big, square brass buckle filled his palm, then disappeared when he wrapped the leather around his hand three times, leaving a long strip free to swing hard against tender backs and legs. If he thought they'd broken the rules, nobody was safe, not even toddlers. And according to Ruth, when their ma was alive, she hadn't dared try to stop him or he'd beat the children harder until she stopped interfering with his discipline, then he'd beat her as a lesson for them all.

Laura switched from the pitchfork to the shovel to scrape the remaining dirt and manure off the stall floor. She and her sisters had hated their pa for his brutal cruelty. No matter what, she'd never resort to physical punishment with her children.

When the first stall floor was clean, Laura pushed the heavy wheelbarrow out the corral door, turned left to the side fence and opened the gate into the ten-foot-square wooden manure holding area. She dumped the load, then headed back to the next stall.

Once again she lost herself in the mindless rhythm, and this time her thoughts turned to Glen's childhood. He'd told her he idolized his father, who worked hard to support his family. Then he died in an accident, leaving them with nothing—no savings, no insurance money, and no extended family to help them. In her visions of Glen's family life after his pa's death, she had seen them struggle to survive. She saw his pain and fear, and understood his mixed feelings for his father. He and his sister and brother tried to ease the pressure off their mother, but were always hungry and afraid, way too young to carry such heavy emotional burdens. Even as a child, Glen understood that it wasn't fair to blame his father for dying, but couldn't help hating him anyway for what his death did to the family.

Laura stopped after dumping the second load and sat down on a bale of hay, yelping in pain when the pressure hit her tailbone. "Doggone it, that hurts." She leaned forward, stretched her back, then rolled her shoulders and shook out her arms to loosen the knots in her muscles. She must be getting old. Her arm muscles were turning into jelly, and the bruise on her left arm felt swollen and sore.

"I shouldn't have bawled out the kids. It's my fault for not paying closer attention, I'm the grown-up." Guilt ate at her for the nasty conditions the animals had endured because of her inattention.

That snotty little voice popped up again. "Glen's a grown-up too, and the animal care is his job. Why did he fall apart when other soldiers didn't?"

"Stop it," she hissed. "You don't blame someone who's sick, even if it is in the head." She took a deep breath, determined to ignore the mean voice. "Stop complaining and get back to work," She said, "If you sit too long making excuses you might not get back up."

The nasty straw in the third and fourth stalls seemed to weigh much more than the first two, and took more than twice as long to shovel. Good thing she'd cleaned all four first before starting with the clean straw, or she might have given up halfway. At least fresh straw was much lighter and a heck of a lot more pleasant to work with. Cows down, pigs and chickens to go.

The pig's wooden enclosure was against the barn wall on the side away from the house, surrounded by a fenced area with the feeding trough and water tub against one side. Laura hated working in the pigpen. The hogs were escape artists and tough to catch if they slipped past her. She parked the wheelbarrow outside the fence and slipped through the gate.

Thick mud sucked at her boots at every step as she made her way to the dutch door on the front of the enclosure. Only the bottom half of the door was open so the pigs could get in and out, but were shielded from most of the wind and rain. She opened the top portion of the door and fastened it against the wall. "Sorry, girls, but you'll have to move if you want clean bedding." The pigs, curled together at the end of the room, warm and cozy in spite of the filthy condition of their bedding, showed no interest in relocating. "Great. I'll have to work around them."

With a frustrated sigh, Laura decided to scoop up all she could before prodding the hogs out of their nest. After two trips to the manure pile, the empty end of the shed was covered with a thick layer of dry straw. In minutes the pigs relocated and settled themselves.

"Not even a thank-you," Laura muttered as she attacked the vacated nest. She was exhausted, but knew the worst job was still waiting.

The far corner of the pen was a reeking soup of mud, pig poop, and urine. This was always Glen's job, and Laura resented having to do it. She slogged her way closer to the mess to plan her attack, almost stepping out of the oversize boots with each stride. She'd have to park the wheelbarrow outside of the fence and shovel the nasty stuff over the top board. If she wasn't careful, she'd end up either losing a boot or her balance.

By the time Laura locked the gate behind her for the last time, her entire body shook with exhaustion and anger. She was mad at the pigs for pooping so darn much. She was mad at the children for not being able to do more of the animal chores. She was mad at herself for letting things go so long. But most of all, she was furious at Glen.

"Why did you have to do it, Glen?" Laura yelled out loud, knowing no one could hear her over the storm. "You'd gotten your memory back. Sure, they were stalling instead of letting you come home right away, but look at you now. And look at what you've done to us."

Angry tears streaked her face, the tracks lost and mingled with the rain. "You've never been violent, ever, but you almost killed Gary, and he was nicer to you than anyone else at the hospital." Laura's hands grasped the wheelbarrow handles so hard her knuckles hurt in the icy wind. "I know you wanted to come home. And God knows we need you here. But now what?"

Once inside the chicken coop, Laura leaned back against the door and closed her eyes. Hot tears flooded her cheeks and silent sobs shook her body. Scenes from her visions flashed in her mind, bits and pieces about Glen—at the hospital, trying to persuade Dr. Vaughn to let him go, in his room with Gary hurt and helpless on the floor, then Glen bleeding and unconscious on the riverbank surrounded by his three captors.

Her anger seeped away, leaving confusion and fear and weariness beyond anything she remembered feeling before. Her legs were near collapse, so she laced her fingers through the chicken wire behind her to stay upright. She opened her eyes, forced herself to walk stiff-legged to the enclosed portion of the hen house and opened the door. All the chickens were roosting, bodies at rest tucked close together in lines, feet curled around long branches, settled for the night. She stared at them a few minutes, and realized the darkness wasn't just storm clouds, the sun was setting.

"So much for getting all the animal pens done today," she said. "Sorry, birds, but I'll get you taken care of tomorrow." She locked the coop and pushed the wheelbarrow back to the barn. The cows, udders full and uncomfortable, waited at the corral door. Her hands were so sore and stiff that it was hard to milk them, but at last she finished and bedded the cows down in nice clean straw.

"Sleep well, girls. See you in the morning." Laura trudged to the porch, a journey that seemed to last for miles, but the washroom light and warm air were a soothing balm to her battered spirit. She could hear whispers beyond the door into the kitchen, but it stayed closed while she removed and rinsed the boots, slicker, and her coveralls. At long last, clad only in a robe over her underwear, she stepped into the kitchen.

The table was set, milk glasses filled, bread and butter in the center, and bowls of soup at each place. "Hi, Mama. Are you hungry? We figured you would be after such a long day, so we waited for you," June said, her brothers at her sides.

"Good job. Thank you." Laura's voice was soft, but when she looked at each child, they wouldn't meet her gaze. She pulled her chair out from the table and dropped in place, then dragged David on her lap and spread her arms wide. "Come here. I need a hug."

The children rushed into her arms,
David squashed in the middle. "I'm sorry for
jumping on you this morning," Laura said. "It's
not your fault that I'm behind on so many
things." She leaned back a little to see their faces
better. "I need your help more than ever while
you papa's away, though. And I want you to
keep your eyes open and let me know when you
notice something that needs attention. The poor
animals rely on us, so be sure to remind me if
they need something. Okay?"

June, Raymond and Jimmy brought their
eyes up to meet Laura's. They each nodded in
reply, then leaned into her body again.

The children clung to her all evening,
piled on the sofa together. The storm ruined the
radio reception, so they watched the fire twist
and pop in the wind currents that whistled
down the flue. One by one, they fell asleep
curled together.

Laura couldn't seem to go to sleep, even
after the wind died down. The house was quiet,
and nothing stirred outside in the storm's wake.
Every muscle ached and cried out for sleep, but
her mind kept circling, trying to avoid the
decision she knew must be made. Find a new
place to live or handle everything by herself?
Counting on Glen coming home soon was
foolish, she knew, but the farm had been their

home for five years. She listened to the soft breathing of the four precious bodies snuggled against her. With Glen, or without him, she'd keep the promises they'd made one another years ago to keep their children safe, and not burden them with adult fears and problems.

CHAPTER TWENTY-FOUR

No Choice, No Going Back

The next morning, Saturday, January 1939

L aura's pulse seemed to beat faster with every step she took toward Mr. Woltz's house. He'd always been a kind, understanding landlord, but this meeting would be different. After an almost sleepless night, she'd faced the fact that it was impossible for her to handle all the work Glen had done, plus her own chores, and still care for the children. Somehow, some way, they had to move, and she had to find a job.

Doggone, it's cold. Laura hunched her shoulders and tucked her chin down into the wool scarf wrapped around her neck and face. The cloudless sky was brilliant blue, but the crisp air stung her nose and throat. The temperature had plummeted with no cloud cover to hold the heat. She wished she'd worn trousers and one of Glen's heavy sweaters instead of the day dress and long cloth coat. Even with the heavy cotton stockings, her feet and legs ached from the cold.

After what seemed like an endless trek, Laura reached Mr. Woltz's front door. She took one last deep breath and said a silent prayer before she knocked.

"Mrs. Webber, what a pleasant surprise," he said, ushering her inside with a slight bow, his slender body bending forward from his waist. The room was cozy and smelled of sweet tobacco.

"Goodness, it's cold." He motioned her toward a brown wing chair near the fireplace. "Please sit here where it's warm. May I take your coat and scarf?"

"Thank you so much." Laura settled on the chair, while Mr. Woltz hung her things on a coatrack. She thrust her palms toward the crackling fire and sighed. "That feels wonderful."

"Good," he said, settling into an overstuffed chair near Laura, a small table between them. "Now, my dear, what brings you out on such a chilly day."

Laura hesitated. She'd rehearsed this moment over and over while she walked, but now her mind was blank. "I, um, I needed to talk to you." She swallowed hard, twisting her hands in her lap. "Our family has been so happy living in your house ... but now that my husband has been ill ... I mean, the doctor's have been trying, but they have no idea when he'll be himself again."

Mr. Woltz leaned forward, elbows on his knees, and sighed.

The sympathetic look on his angular face was almost more than Laura could bear.

"I've tried my best to take care of everything by myself, but ..." She pressed her lips tight, determined not to let her voice betray her, then pinched the bridge of her nose to stop any potential tears from falling. She closed her eyes a moment. "I just can't do it by myself. You've been so good to us, but I'm going to have to move into town."

"I'm so sorry. You have a lovely family. Your husband is a fine man and has been a good friend." Mr Woltz leaned toward Laura and patted her shoulder. "Actually, I was plannng to come see you this week about the place."

Laura gasped, and her eyes opened wide. "Were you going to ask us to leave?"

"Well, yes, but not for anything you've done wrong." Mr. Woltz picked up a pipe that rested in an ashtray on the table, stuck it into the corner of his mouth and puffed the smoldering embers back to life. "You know my son and his wife lived in the house before you moved in? And that they moved to New Orleans to be near her family when they found out she was expecting?"

Laura nodded. "Yes, Glen told me their story."

"Well, they have two little boys now and are expecting another baby. They've asked me to move in with them." He slid the pipe from between his lips and looked around the room. "I love my home here, and folks in Aurora are like family." He raised his left hand and rubbed the back of his neck. "But I'm getting old, Mrs. Webber, and I'd like to get to know my grandchildren before I die. I've decided to sell out and move, and was trying to get up the gumption to tell you. It seems wrong to ask you to leave, but I hope you understand."

She reached out and touched his arm. "I do, and I think you're doing the right thing."

"Thank you. I guess we both feel better now," he said. "I've already told some people that I want to sell, so it shouldn't take long to find a buyer. You and your children are welcome to stay until it's sold, and I'll get you some help with the work around the place." He puffed on his pipe, then pointed the stem toward Laura. "I realize this is hard on your family, and must come as a shock. Please let me know how I can be of help."

"I will, and thank you. To tell the truth, I just decided last night. I didn't want to go since we love the place so much and I kept thinking I should hold on until Glen got better." Laura stopped and swallowed, hoping to stop the quiver she heard in her voice. "But no one knows when that'll happen." She stopped again, played with the clasp on her purse, then said, "I'm going to town next to talk to Mr. Niedermann."

"Great idea. He knows everything that's going on with everyone in town," Mr. Woltz said. "I'll check with some people too."

They said their goodbyes and promised to keep in close touch. Laura bundled up and headed towards town. As she walked, her gaze skittered from one thing to another, unable to hold on to anything. Good thing she'd decided to move, but now it was real. If he'd sprung his plans out of the blue, she'd have been stunned and scared. Now there was no choice, and no going back.

～⟨⟩～

Laura waved to Mr. Niedermann when she walked into the post office, but didn't get in line. She walked to the side table covered with postal supplies, crossed her arms, and stared at the FBI Wanted posters on the bulletin board.

"Recognize anyone?" Mr. Niedermann said a little later, after the last customer left. "I've never seen you so fascinated by our gallery of criminals."

"You never know. Collecting a reward would be nice." Laura found it hard to smile, and wondered how to start the conversation.

Mr. Niedermann glanced at the wall clock. "You know what? It's a little early, but I think I'll close for my lunch break. Let me put the sign up and lock the door, then we can talk in the back room."

Within five minutes Laura found herself in a tiny office with a desk, two chairs, a filing cabinet, and a table covered with stacks of papers. "Wow, so this is your private domain," Laura said, sitting on the chair across from his desk.

"That it is, my own little kingdom for the last twenty-three years." He removed a large dinner pail, thermos, and a glass from a narrow closet and sat down at his desk. He swept paperwork aside, pulled two thick sandwiches from the pail and filled the thermos lid and a glass with water from the thermos. "Mrs. Webber, I've known you for five years now, but I've never seen you looking more in need of a friend. Can you tell me what's going on?"

Laura's eyes widened, and she felt her eyebrows rise into her hairline. She started to speak, then stopped, slumped in the chair. "You're right. And thank you." She licked her lips and swallowed hard. "No one can tell me when Glen might be able to come home, and we can't keep waiting the way we are. And I just learned that Mr. Woltz is selling his property and relocating to New Orleans. That means I have to move and find some kind of job." She met Mr. Niedermann's eyes, then glanced down at her clasped hands. "I'll need a place in town so the kids can walk to school and I can be close to work. We don't have a car anymore, so being in town makes more sense." She glanced around the room, as if the words she needed were hidden on the walls, then sipped some water. "You know just about everybody in town. If you think of a place we could move to, or a place I could work evenings and nights, I'd be grateful. I haven't looked for a job or an apartment since Glen and I got married, so it's like starting all over."

"I'm so sorry, Mrs. Webber. I'll do my best to help. Give me a few days and I'll see what I can find."

"Thank you," Laura said. She swallowed a huge lump in her throat, determined not to cry. She blinked her eyes to clear them and squeezed her fingers tight together.

Mr. Niedermann waved off her thanks. "Happy to do it. You and your children are some of my favorite people. Next time you come by, I'll try to have something."

She left him to finish his lunch, then slipped out the back door and walked around the building. The cold took her breath away when she emerged from between two buildings. Laura hunched down into the scarf, staring at the ground. She wished she had a warm winter hat, maybe even some toasty winter boots.

Somehow she'd done it. She'd talked to both Mr. Woltz and Mr. Niedermann, explained what was happening and what she needed, in spite of being afraid and embarrassed. And both had understood and offered of help. Pride warmed her insides, pulled her shoulders back and straightened her spine.

Marching home on frozen feet, she reviewed the problems they'd have to overcome. They needed a place with a kitchen, a bathroom, and two bedrooms, but it had to be in town and it had to be cheap. The new place would have to be furnished, since all the furniture in the house except for a rocking chair and a cradle belonged to Mr. Woltz. Moving their stuff would be a challenge, since it would be impossible in a kid's wagon. If she had to hire a truck, it would make an awful dent in their dwindling savings.

Laura needed a job, but that posed other challenges. She hadn't worked in years, so would have to convince someone that she could learn fast and follow directions. She couldn't leave David alone during the day, so she'd either have to take him with her, or find a job during the evening or night when June and the boys could watch him.

The biggest problem would be supporting the children without stealing their childhoods. They'd have to deal with a new place, and watch her juggle home and work. Somehow she had to make sure they didn't see her exhausted or worried about money all the time. She was determined to keep her promise to Glen that their children would never suffer what he'd been through.

CHAPTER TWENTY-FIVE

We Don't Want To Move

Laura's mind raced much faster than her feet, so she was surprised to find herself climbing the porch steps at home. The children pulled her into the toasty living room, eager to tell her all about their day. They all spoke at once, too excited to wait.

"Mama, the kitchen's all clean."

"We made the bed and picked up our toys."

"We swept the floor and dusted everything in the entire house."

Laura let them lead her throughout the house as they pointed out their accomplishments. "You kids did an amazing job. Thank you so much."

The children's faces beamed with satisfaction, making Laura wish she praised them more often.

"Let me change out of these town clothes, then we can curl up in the living room by the fire and talk."

Soon they settled in a semi-circle on the rug in front of the fireplace, bare feet pointed toward the roaring fire. Laura let the children prattle on about everything from school to the work they'd done. It took time for them to run down, but after awhile June asked about Laura's trip to town.

"Well, my first stop was to see Mr. Woltz."

"I like Rudolf," Jimmy said. "I mean Mr. Woltz."

Laura shot him a horrified look. "Jimmy, you know better than calling an adult by their first name. That's disrespectful and just plain bad manners."

"But he told us to call him Rudolf."

Raymond chimed in fast. "He did say that, Mama, but I told him you'd tan our hides if we called him by his first name, so we didn't."

Laura's restrained chuckle came out as a snort. "Good for you Raymond, and you're right, I would." She ruffled Jimmy's hair. "And I'm glad you did the right thing."

"What did you talk to Mr. Woltz about?" June said.

"Well," Laura searched for the right words. "Do you remember your papa telling us that Mr. Woltz's daughter lives in New Orleans? Mr. Woltz misses her something awful. She and her husband have two little boys now, and are expecting another baby. They've asked Mr. Woltz to come live with them, and he's decided to go."

"It'll be weird not having him around. I wonder who'll move into his house," Raymond said.

"It won't be his house anymore, he's selling all his property. That means this house, too." Laura saw that the children didn't understand. "When he sells, we have to move out of this house into another place."

Three shocked faces stared back at her.

"But this is home. We don't want to move. Where would we go?" June said. Her brothers nodded along with her.

Laura's stomach clenched. She didn't want to argue because she agreed with the children's sentiments. "I love it here too, but we don't have any choice." Laura raised her hands to quiet the outcry. "Besides, it'll be much easier for us to live in town. You can walk to school in half the time, and we'll be closer for me to shop and do our errands."

"But Mama," June said, "Are there any empty houses in town where we can go?"

"Not really. I've asked Mr. Woltz and Mr. Niedermann to ask around for an apartment we can move into."

"I thought we didn't have any money? How can we pay for an apartment?" June said.

"We don't, Junebug." Laura gazed into each child's eyes, then continued. "That's the other thing. While Papa is away, I'll need to find some kind of job to keep us going. And since David is so little, that means I'll need to work in the afternoons or evenings. You big kids will have to watch him for me while I'm gone."

The discussion continued with the children coming up with more creative reasons why they had to stay put, and Laura explaining over and over that they had no options. The last question came when she tucked them in bed.

"Mama," Jimmy's soft voice reached her in the dark as she pulled the door closed. "How will Papa find us when he comes home?"

Back on the couch in a living room lit only by the glowing embers of the fireplace, Laura sat with her arms curled around her knees, feet tucked in tight against her thighs. She kept hearing the children's questions and seeing their expressions, and wished she had wiser, smarter answers for them. Or better yet, that none of the changes were necessary.

"Mama, can I talk to you?" June whispered from the hallway.

Laura was startled out of her thoughts. "Of course, honey, come here." She opened her arms, motioned for June to join her on the couch, then hugged her close. "I thought you were asleep. What did you want to talk about?"

"Promise you won't get mad?" June said, her voice quivering. "I know I shouldn't, but I saw that letter from the new hospital where Papa is. It was on your dresser when I went in to dust, so I read it."

Laura started to scold, but bit it back. "You're right, you shouldn't have read it. Is that what you want to talk about?"

June nodded, her face buried in Laura's shoulder. "That letter said Papa hurt somebody real bad. That he attacked someone and escaped, but then they caught him." June sat up and stared into Laura's eyes. "Papa never hurt anybody. Why did they say those mean things?"

Laura brushed June's hair out of her eyes, then lifted her chin. "Sweetheart, I'm afraid that Papa did do what they said. But the letter didn't mention why. I know the only thing in the world that could cause your papa to hurt someone would be if he was protecting us." It hurt to see the pain in June's eyes. "I believe Papa must have gotten his memory back and wanted to come home, but they wouldn't let him. He would have been scared, worried sick about us, and thought escaping was the only way."

"But they caught him and moved him farther away."

"That's right, honey." Laura thumbed tears away from June's eyes and kissed her forehead.

June sniffed and rubbed her eyes. "Mama, do you think they hurt Papa when they caught him?"

June had come up with one of those questions Laura had hoped to avoid. She always told the children the truth, but this was a hard one. "It's possible. It sounds like he fought to get away, so he might have been hurt when they tried to catch him."

June's lips trembled, and she dropped her head down against Laura's shoulder, burrowing until she was tight against her mama's body. Laura shifted her position until her spine pressed against the couch back, then curled her arms around her daughter. Each found solace from the other, and soon June's soft snore was the only sound in the room. Laura pulled an afghan off the back of the couch, spread it over them, and joined her daughter in sleep.

CHAPTER TWENTY-SIX

We'll Take It

February 1939

More than a week passed before the weather cleared enough for Laura, pulling David in the wagon, made her next trip to the post office. Mr. Niedermann tipped his chin at her and grinned when she entered the lobby, then focused his attention on the people in line.

"Down," David said, clambering out of the wagon.

"Stay by me," Laura said, grabbing him under the arms as he tried to run for the counter. She lifted him, ignoring his protests and attempts to twist away. His struggle turned into giggles as the woman in front of them turned around and started clapping and making faces at him.

"You need to bring him in more often to entertain the customers," Mr. Niedermann said, grinning at David when they reached the front of the line. He pulled the ashtray holding his cold pipe out of reach, and said. "Lots of mail, Mrs. Webber. It's been stacking up." He placed a rubberband wrapped pile on the counter.

"Thank you." Laura rifled through the stack, hoping against hope to find an envelope from the hospital. Disappointed, she tucked the mail inside her handbag, folded the flap over and snapped it closed. She glanced around the empty lobby, then said, "Have you heard anything about a place for us? I hate to be pushy, but Mr. Woltz says he thinks he has a buyer, which means we need to move pretty quick."

Mr. Niedermann sighed, running his hands up and down his green suspenders. "I wish I had great news, but I only know about one place. It's pretty rough, but the location's good, the rent's cheap, and the landlord's an honest man."

"That sounds fine. How do I contact him?"

"I'll let him know you're interested and see if I can set something up. Could you come in on Saturday? I'll try to make an appointment for you to meet with him that afternoon."

Laura agreed, plopped David back in the wagon and headed out the door. Two days to wait, then maybe they'd have a place. Rough but cheap didn't sound very inviting, but at least it would be a roof over their heads. She held on to that thought, telling herself she'd make it work no matter what.

"What if it's awful? Even worse, what if he doesn't like you or the kids? You could end up on the street with no place to go." The nasty little voice whispered in her mind, sending tendrils of fear coursing through her body.

Laura shook her head to shut the voice out, determined not to let fear take hold. She would get the apartment, and she would make it work.

They traveled about a block past Magda's place, when CLUNK—the wagon stopped dead and tilted forward, causing David to slide against the front edge.

"Go boom," David climbed out of the crippled wagon and threw his arms wide, a huge smile on his face.

"Sure did." Laura knelt down and examined the wagon. Both front wheels lay almost flat on the ground. She lifted it and saw that the axle had sheared away from one of the wheel assemblies. "Wow, looks like the only thing holding this poor thing together was rust and mud."

With David holding one hand and the wagon dangling from the other, Laura detoured to the general store where she got permission to discard the pitiful broken thing on their trash pile. It looked so sad, crumpled atop a heap of garbage. Laura stared at the wagon, remembering how excited the kids had been the day Glen had gotten it when they lived in South Dakota. So many years of family fun, now discarded. Another piece of their history gone.

"Oh, well, little man, we'll have to manage without it," she said, with a sigh.

At first, David was thrilled to alternate walking and running at Laura's side, but that didn't last long. After two blocks, he begged to be picked up. "That place in town better work out, little man. You're way too big for me to carry around."

"Excuse me, Mrs. Webber. Could you use a ride?"

Laura whipped around, "Mr. Woltz, you startled me." His dusty black farm truck idled next to her. She ducked her head to see through the window as Mr. Woltz leaned over and opened the passenger door.

Laura opened her mouth to reject his offer, then changed her mind. "Thank you so much." She climbed up on the seat and settled David in her lap. "The wheels fell off our old wagon, and this boy decided he didn't want to walk."

Mr. Woltz eased out into traffic, then shifted gears. "Happy to give you a lift." He cleared his throat and asked, "Have you found a new place yet? I signed the sale papers and don't want to leave you in a lurch. It'll take me about a month to wrap things up and leave."

"I think so. I'll find out this weekend," Laura said, knowing she'd have to take the place if it was offered, no matter what it was like.

"Good. If it'd help, I can send a couple of guys with a truck to help with the move when you're ready."

Laura nodded and thanked him, but the phrase, "we don't take charity," reverberated in her mind, along with memories of the threats that always came with it from her pa. Her favorite birthday memory, a trip to town with her oldest sister, was marred by Ruth's panicked response when Laura was offered a free piece of candy.

"Thank you, but we don't take charity," her sister had said, terrified that someone might tell their pa about Laura accepting a piece of penny candy.

Mr. Woltz insisted on dropping Laura and David at the foot of their front steps. "Don't forget to let me know when you're ready to move and I'll have a truck to help you." He yelled out the window as he drove away, waving at Laura and the children, who'd met them on the front porch.

"Do we have to move?" Jimmy said. "I like it here."

Raymond rolled his eyes. "We all like it here, dummy, but Mama told us we have to move, anyway."

"Don't call your brother names, Raymond," Laura snapped. "Jimmy, we all like it here, but we have no choice." She led her children into the house. "In fact, we might as well start sorting our things and packing what we can so we'll be ready."

Laura gave each child one of the boxes she'd gotten from the grocery store on her last trip, and told them to place all their toys and treasured trinkets inside.

She carried a couple of boxes into her bedroom and opened the top drawer of the dresser. Oh, God, how could she do this? Her throat threatened to close as she looked down at Glen's socks, underwear, and handkerchiefs on the right-hand side of the drawer. She lifted each item and placed it in the box, stroking the fabric as she stacked them in place. Guess it made sense to put all his things together, since there was no telling when he'd need them again.

Laura took a deep breath and shook her head to clear it. Might as well get all his things out now and pack them. She opened each dresser drawer, pulled Glen's stuff out and put them on the bed. She did the same thing with his nightstand drawer. After that, she pulled his shoes out from under his side of the bed and added them to the pile. By the time she cleared his personal things—wallet, watch, notepad, pen, coins, cufflinks and tie tack—off the dresser, she could feel her heart pounding.

She shouldn't have been doing this. Glen was supposed to be the head of the family. Planning a move and organizing the packing was always his job. Getting sick was one thing, but checking out of life and leaving this family alone was not the same thing. Everything that was happening was just plain not fair. If he'd waited instead of trying to escape like some kind of madman, and hurting somebody in the process, he'd be home by now.

By the time Laura added Glen's bathroom items to the stack on the bed, she was fuming. She ripped his clothes out of the armoire, threw them on top of the pile, then dropped to her knees next to the bed and buried her face in her hands.

Scalding tears slipped between her fingers, and a wail threatened to escape her clenched lips. Stop it! She held her breath so that no sound could break free, wiped the tears away and sniffed hard. No more of that. She cleared her throat and pulled her shoulders back. Glen was not here and no amount of crying or carrying on would change that. Their kids didn't need to see her break down, so she'd better paste a smile on her face and get to work.

Laura arrived at the post office before noon on Saturday morning. "Good morning, Mr. Niedermann," she said. "Were you able to talk to the man with the apartment?"

"I sure did, and he's anxious to meet you." Mr. Niedermann handed Laura a folded note and said, "The address is 98 Walnut Street, #3. It's the third floor. Mr. Johnson, Charlie, is a nice guy, but can't take care of his places like he used to."

"That's okay. What time does he want to meet?"

"He should be there within the hour."
The door opened and Mrs. Brighton walked in.

"Good day, Mrs. Webber. I so wish you and your children would join us for Sunday services tomorrow." She looked down her nose at David, who was trying to reach the stacks of papers on top of the table. "Our Sunday School would be wonderful for your children."

"Thank you, Mrs. Brighton, perhaps one day we will." Laura said, wishing the nosy old bat would leave her alone.

Mr. Niedermann patted Laura's shoulder and whispered. "Come by and let me know how it went after you meet with him."

Laura nodded, and headed for the door, holding her head high. The day was clear and sunny, but biting cold with a blustery wind. When she turned right on Walnut, she saw four three-story buildings in a row on the block, three of which were almost identical in their state of disrepair. The fourth building was attractive, with white paint and blue shutters and well-spaced stepping stones leading from the street to the narrow front porch, and the neat grass edged by tidy hedges.

The address she'd been given was in the middle of the other three. Rough wasn't the word for the place. Instead of fresh paint and neat shutters, the scabrous clapboard retained only streaks of gray paint. Most of the shutters looked like they hung on only because they lacked the energy to pull away from the walls and fall to the ground. The stepping stones were hard to see in the tall grass that surrounded them. Laura stared at the front of the building, unable to see inside through windows that were opaque with layers of grime, and hoped the interior would be better. She felt sick inside, knowing she had no choice. But what on earth was she doing to the children?

"Mrs. Webber?" The voice, thin and nasal sounding, came from right behind her.

Laura whirled around, surprised that she hadn't heard anyone approach. "Yes. Are you Mr. Johnson?"

"I am, but most everyone calls me Charlie." Mr. Johnson held out his hand, and nodded his head. His cotton white hair danced around below the frayed edge of a green knit hat.

When they shook, Laura's hand disappeared inside one twice as large as hers. His hand was big, but almost skeletal. Knobby knuckles and long bones were wrapped in rough, liver-spotted, cold skin. "It's nice to meet you, Charlie. Mr. Niedermann told me you have a place for rent. Thank you for seeing me on such short notice."

"Glad to do it, Mrs. Webber. He spoke right highly of you." Charlie coughed, then cleared his throat. "The place has been vacant for a long time. I've been meaning to clean it and fix it up, but haven't gotten around to it, what with the arthritis and all. But he said it might work for you."

Laura followed Charlie through the front door, and walked toward stairs on the left side of the narrow lobby. The steps, tucked between walls on either side, were lit by dim lights mounted in the ceiling of each landing. Following Charlie up the steep incline, she could see that his body was as thin and wiry as his hands. He looked like he'd been a big, strapping man years ago, but now his clothing hung on a body shrunk tight to his frame. When he leaned forward, she could see the bones of his spine outlined through his coat. His pant legs slid up with each step, revealing stick-thin calves above rumpled socks. Climbing the stairs was slow, since Charlie stopped often to rest for a few breaths.

Laura pressed her hands into the walls on either side, since there were no handrails. The walls were sticky and damp, and had wide, dark streaks painted by the sweat and dirt from countless hands bracing their way up and down the stairs. By the time they reached the third landing, she was breathing hard and dreading what might be behind the door. How in the heck was she going to carry things up and down these steep steps?

"Here we are." Charlie opened the door, flipped a light switch, and stepped aside for Laura to enter.

Laura's first impression of the room was dingy brown, depressing and dirty. They stood in one large room with a wood stove on a platform at the end of the room to the right of the door. The kitchen area was a few feet to the left of where they stood, and consisted of a dusty counter with a sink. A small refrigerator filled the space between the end of the counter and the wall at the end of the room. The tiny stove, with only two burners and a miniscule oven below, stood against the end of the counter closest to the door.

"The last tenant was a single man who didn't do much cooking." Charlie scratched the back of his neck, then walked to the refrigerator and opened the door. "Not a lot of space for a family, but..."

"We'll manage," Laura said, pushing the image of their beautiful kitchen away. She tried to keep her expression impassive, and hoped that her horror at the conditions didn't show on her face.

Charlie nodded, while leading her to the first of three narrow doors in the long wall across the room. "There are shelves in here where you can store your things." He opened the door and turned on the light, revealing a dark, musty smelling space draped with cobwebs.

He moved to the second door. "Here's the bathroom," he said.

Laura peeked inside and saw there was just enough room to stand between a sink mounted on the wall, the toilet, and a rust stained claw-foot tub. A torn shade covered half of the tiny window in the wall above the tub. She couldn't tell if it was supposed to be opaque or if layers of dirt made it so.

"This here's the bedroom." Charlie held the second door open, revealing a space that held a single bed with a stained mattress and a tall dresser. No armoire, but a row of hooks lined the wall.

Looks like she'd be sleeping on that couch in the living room. "That will be fine." she spoke out loud as she cringed inside. Laura stepped into the middle of the main room. A table with four chairs filled the corner across from the kitchen area. A low table stood in front of the couch, while upended crates were on either side of it. Two faded chairs with saggy seats sat at an angle across from the sofa between the stove and a door. The floor was a faded brown and yellow linoleum, with edges that curled away from the walls. Bare walls peeked through a patchwork of blank wallpaper sheets pasted to the surface. There was no proper ceiling, just rafters and the underside of the roof.

"Oh, yeah, almost forgot. There are washers in the basement and some extra storage space." Charlie waved back toward the door, still open to the hallway.

The stairs down into the basement were much worse than the others. They were attached to the wall on one side, with an unfinished, splintery wooden railing on the other. Laura noticed spider webbing draped in the corners, dust and little silk-wrapped bundles dotting the strands.

Charlie pointed to two washing machines with two deep washtubs between them. Three clotheslines stretched across the room, one with a set of wet sheets that dripped onto the floor, where the water ran into a rusty center drain. The room felt muggy and smelled moldy.

"You'll share the washers with the other folks in the building. Excuse me." He turned away and coughed, a raspy, phlegmy sound.

"Those big cabinets along the back wall are for storage. The other tenants are pretty nice, but you might want to put a padlock on yours."

"Good idea," Laura said.

"Let's head back upstairs," Charlie said. When they reached the stairs, he stopped and faced Laura. "Mrs. Webber, I'm sorry this place is such a mess. My missus used to keep everything clean and tidy, but since she got sick I haven't kept things up."

"I'm sorry to hear about your wife."

"Thank you. Doc Farnsworth says there's not much we can do. She gets lost if she goes outside by herself, and sometimes even forgets who I am. Our oldest daughter stays with us and cares for her."

"That must be awful hard on your family." Laura said. The words sounded inadequate, but were the only ones that came to her mind.

Charlie led the way into the lobby. "If you want the place, I won't charge any rent until the first of March. That way, you'll have a little over two weeks to get everything the way you want it."

"That's very fair. How much is the rent?" Laura cringed at the thought of all the work it would take to clean the place before she'd even consider moving their things.

"Well," Charlie scratched the back of his neck. "The other two pay twenty dollars per month, but since the third floor unit is tucked under the attic and isn't as nice, I'd say fifteen dollars. And since Mr. Niedermann referred you, I won't ask for a security deposit."

"Okay," Laura said. "What about utilities?"

"They're included."

"We'll take it." Laura shook Charlie's hand, grateful and horrified at the same time. "When would you like me to pay the first month's rent?"

They agreed to meet Tuesday morning at 10:00 to sign a rental agreement. Laura would pay the March rent and receive her key. Mind reeling, she headed for home.

CHAPTER TWENTY-SEVEN

So Much History

The children gathered around Laura when she got home, eager to know if she'd found them a new place to live. When she told them they'd be living in a tiny third-floor apartment, the whining began.

"I don't like stairs," June said, crossing her arms.

Raymond declared, "Me neither."

"Doesn't matter whether we like them or not, this place is the only vacant apartment I could find in town. You can complain all you want, but we'll be living there by the end of the month." Laura agreed with them, but was in no mood for arguing. She left them in a mutinous circle in the living room and marched into her bedroom to change out of her town clothes.

Laura tried to keep the mood light for the rest of the evening, avoiding talk about the apartment. She got out a box of dominoes, pieces from three different sets, and sat on the floor with the children. Each child got the same number of dominoes, then used them to create fanciful designs ranging from flat patterns on the floor to tall towers. They played until David put his head down and fell asleep surrounded by his dominoes.

"Looks like it's time to call it quits," Laura said, brushing David's hair away from his eyes. "That was fun."

She carried David to bed, and tucked the others in around him. She leaned over the bed for hugs and kisses, smoothed the quilt one last time, and headed for the door. "Good night, sleep tight..."

Only June was awake enough to mumble the last line, "Don't let the bedbugs bite."

Laura smiled, then shuddered. Bedbugs were funny in the silly verse, but real ones were horrible. What if that dirty apartment had bugs? That thought chased away any desire for sleep. There was so little time, and so much to do. The contents of the house wouldn't be hard to figure out, but what about the stuff in the other buildings? All the things that Glen used and took care of.

Once she knew the kids were asleep, Laura grabbed the lantern and headed to the garage. She never spent much time there, but it was full of tools and machinery. "Doggone, it's cold," she said, sprinting across the open area between the house and the garage door. Once inside, she closed the door behind her to keep the icy wind out, then placed the lantern on Glen's workbench. The flickering light created crazy moving shadows around the dusty tools that hung on the pegboard.

Laura flashed back to sweeter times, remembering standing next to Glen at the same workbench when he was repairing some piece of machinery. She'd watch him work and keep him company. They'd talk about anything and everything, laughing sometimes at silly jokes or stories. Sometimes they'd sing. She found herself smiling and tearing up at the same time.

Laura grabbed a wadded up handkerchief out of her coat pocket and blew her nose. Enough already, she thought, I've got to figure out what to do in here.

Where in the heck would she put the tools in the apartment? Perhaps in the basement, but the storage cabinet wasn't that big, and the canned food had to go there in the cool dark. With Glen gone, she'd better learn how to use tools since fixing things would fall on her. She recognized the hammer, crowbar, handsaw, drill, needle-nose pliers, adjustable wrench, a crescent wrench set, and a socket set. Recognized, but she had no idea what to do with a crescent wrench or a socket. The other items hanging from the wall were a mystery. Not a clue. She pulled down all the tools she thought she might use and piled them in a corner of the floor.

Laura's right hand fingers drummed on the workbench as she surveyed the garage interior and wondered what else she'd have to pack. No point in taking the spare tire or the gas cans. And they didn't need the partial case of oil. Maybe she could sell what they couldn't use to Mr. Giddings since he was a mechanic. He was Glen's friend and had paid a fair amount for the truck. Glen would just have to find a way to buy new things when he came home. And lord only knew when that would be.

"I'll need a bunch more boxes, at least two more just for the stuff in here. I've got to figure a way to carry them home."

Laura's shoulders slumped, and she dropped onto an old, sway-backed rolling chair, tilting her head back. No way all their stuff would fit into that awful, dirty apartment.

"I don't want to move either. The kids are right." She twisted the fabric of her trousers tight, fingers clenched so hard her knuckles turned white. "I'm tired of having to do everything. It's not fair." Laura's eyes began to burn and her throat hurt. She took several deep, shaky breaths and shook her hands out. "Stop it! Turning on the waterworks every time I turn around, what's wrong with me. Ruth always told us nobody said life had to be fair. I've got to quit feeling sorry for myself." Her only reply was the wind whistling around the building.

Blinking hard, Laura inspected the surrounding space, checking for anything she might have missed. Then she noticed Glen's bicycle, hanging on the back wall, hidden in shadows. She'd never learned to ride it, and Glen hadn't gotten around to teaching Raymond or Jimmy more than a couple of lessons each. She stepped closer, wiped cobwebs away from the pedals and chain, and stroked the dusty fender.

"So much history," she whispered. Glen's Uncle Dennis had given it to him when they'd left South Dakota. During the months they'd lived on the road in the truck, the bicycle had been Glen's main transportation whenever he went looking for work. And during the weeks they'd lived under a bridge, the truck stayed parked and the bicycle carried Glen to and from work every day. "No matter what, I can't leave this behind. In fact, it's time I learned to ride it and teach the children too."

☙❧

The next day Laura left David at home with the older children, and headed to town pushing a rusty, two-wheeled metal garden cart. She'd found it inside the gardening shed, filled with hoses and produce baskets. It wasn't pretty, and the wheels squeaked, but there was room for lots of boxes.

The grocery store manager, Mr. Jackson, was nice about promising her all the empty boxes she wanted. Instead of packing the boxes she already had, it might be smarter to make another trip today. The store would be closed tomorrow, and it was a lot easier to go to town without David.

After two trips into town for boxes, Laura was too tired to do much more that evening. But Sunday she enlisted help from the kids. "Today we're going to clean out the garage." She pointed to the stack of boxes stacked on the back porch. The boys pounced, grabbing as many as they could hold.

"Jimmy, don't try to carry too many boxes at once, honey. You can't see over the top."

"I can carry more," Raymond said, filling his arms.

Laura gave up trying to oversee who carried what. "Take all the boxes to the garage. We'll keep the empties in one place, then after everything there is packed, we can focus on the root cellar."

Minutes after everyone was in the garage, June lifted David into the biggest box, telling him it was his truck.

"Me drive, Mama, me drive," David shouted with a huge grin. He rocked back and forth, his hands in front whipping an imaginary steering wheel from side to side.

"Good thinking, June," Laura said. She pointed at the small pile of tools she'd piled together the night before. "Thanks. If you could put those tools in a box while you keep an eye on him, that would be a great help."

Laura lifted Jimmy up on the workbench, and told him to remove each tool from the pegboard and lay it on the flat surface. Raymond's job was to put them into a sturdy box resting on the floor.

"Just be careful, boys. Some of those tools are heavy, and some are sharp. I don't want either of you to hurt yourselves."

Rolled eyes and groans were the only response. Laura opened a tall cabinet at the end of the workbench and started sorting the contents.

"Can I help?" June said. "I packed the tools. David's fine, and watching him is boring." She peeked inside the cabinet at shelves full of all kinds of rags, jars, and bottles. "Can I pack these things?"

"How about I look through them first, then you can pack the things we'll be taking with us."

The garage was soon stripped, with several boxes and the bicycle against one wall, the garden cart full of items to be tossed on the trash pile. Half of the workbench was piled with useable items they were either selling or leaving behind. The boys carried the remaining empty boxes to the root cellar door on the side of the house, tired, but ready to tackle it the next day.

CHAPTER TWENTY-EIGHT

You Must Survive

Two Days Later, Tuesday, February 1939

"Why can't we stay home?" June begged. "Since you're going to town today, we could watch David. It'd be a lot easier for you without him."

"School is much more important than you making things easier for me," Laura said. "It's bad enough that you missed several days this year because of bad weather. Get your stuff so you're not late for school."

Raymond and Jimmy cast furtive glances at one another, then at June. Their agreement with her was clear.

June crossed her arms and thrust her chin out. "But Mama, we can help. You said there's a lot of work to do at the new place to get it ready. We can get lots done here while you're in town," she said. "It makes sense."

"If you three don't grab your books and head for school, a few good swats on your backsides will make even more sense." Laura pointed to the front door. "Now!"

～✠～

An hour later, as Laura and David made their way into town, he started drumming his feet on the inside of the garden cart and yelling. David wanted out because he couldn't see over the edge. At that point, June's argument about staying home to take care of him sounded pretty appealing. "David, stop it. I'll let you out when we get to the store."

"Laura? Is that you?"

Laura spun around, surprised to see Magda coming out of the shoe store. "Hi," she said. "Our old wagon broke down and I have to use this big clunky garden cart to get boxes from the store. David's not happy sitting below the edge."

Magda giggled at the sight of David sitting in the bottom of the cart, his back on one side and his legs sticking up on the other, his little body bent in a V shape. "I'm goink home now, so he could schtay wiz me vile you do your shoppink. Vould you like to visit after you're finished?"

"Are you sure? He can be a handful. But shopping would be a lot easier without him."

Magda bobbed her chin and reached for David. Holding hands, they set out for Magda's apartment, while Laura sauntered behind the squeaky cart in the opposite direction.

Mr. Jackson stopped sweeping the sidewalk in front of his store and waved when Laura approached. "Good Morning, Mrs. Webber," he said. "Mr. Woltz stopped in today and told me about selling his property and moving to New Orleans. No wonder you need boxes."

Laura nodded, not sure she liked having the whole town know her business, but resigned to the speedy way local news spread.

"I've got a whole stack, all broken down nice and neat, for you." Mr. Jackson led the way past the two cashiers, through the aisles, and into the back room. "This way you can carry a lot more at a time. All you need is a tapegun and some tape and they'll go back together, ready to fill up."

"Tapegun? Uh, I don't have one of those. How much do they cost?" The stack of flattened cardboard looked great, but depleting her funds for something she'd never use again didn't sound like a good idea.

Mr. Jackson chuckled. "Most folks don't, no problem. You're a good customer and I have a bunch of 'em." He loaded the garden cart with as many boxes as it could hold, then grabbed a tapegun with a full roll of tape and dropped it on top. "You can return it after the move."

Waving away Laura's thanks, he continued. "I know Charlie's place is awful small after living in Mr. Woltz's house, but he tries to do for his tenants. He used to do better when his wife helped, but now he spends most of his time taking care of her."

Laura felt her face flushing. Were there no secrets in this town at all?

Mr. Jackson walked Laura all the way to the front door. "I'll put aside a stack of boxes for next time."

"Thank you very much. I appreciate it," Laura said, wishing all the people in the store weren't listening and watching. Maybe they weren't, but it sure felt like it.

All the way to Magda's place the wheels seemed to screech, "Look at me, look at me." Laura kept her head down, not wanting to meet curious or sympathetic faces. As soon as she got home, those darn wheels were getting a good squirt of oil. Guess she'd better take that battered old oilcan they'd left on the garage workbench after all.

Laura parked the cart out of sight under Magda's stairs. Magda opened the door after a single knock.

"Come on in. David's been a perfect little angel."

Laura followed Magda to a couch which faced the fireplace at the end of the single room, separating it into living and dining areas. "Thank you so much for letting him stay," she said. "I'm glad he's been good, but don't let that fool you. He can be a terror at times."

"Mama, look," David crowed from his spot in the middle of the living room rug. He had three metal bowls in front of him, as well as a pile of clothespins, wooden thread spools and pieces of cardboard. He held a large mixing spoon and a spatula, and was mixing and moving the items around from the pile to the bowls and back again.

"Great job," Laura said, turning to Magda. "You're brilliant. He'll have more fun with those than any of his toys." Laura tilted her head and sniffed. "Something smells wonderful."

Magda jumped up and ran to the oven. "I vas varmink up a loaf of berches and forgot about it." She grabbed a dish towel and pulled the pan out of the oven.

Laura followed Magda into the kitchen. "Berches? I've never heard of that before." She looked at a golden-crusted, braided loaf with

270

covered with poppy seeds. "Beautiful, and it smells heavenly."

"It's a schpecial bread ve always made in Germany for Sabbaz. Harvey and Helga love it, so I made extra this week. Vould you like to try a piece?"

"I'd love to, but I don't want to take it away from your family." Laura stared at the fragrant loaf. "Did you braid the dough yourself? It looks hard."

Magda nodded. "Yes. My mother taught me how to braid dough for both berches and challah. I alvays add mashed potatoes to my berches to keep it moist." Magda picked up a sharp knife, sliced off two generous pieces, then handed one to Laura.

The two women settled back on the couch with their bread, where David joined them, begging for a piece. Laura pulled off a bite and put it into his open mouth. "This is delicious." She finished eating. "I'm embarrassed to say I've never tasted any Jewish foods. I have one wonderful Jewish friend, Willa Young, but since we met on the road, I've never been to her home in California. Are there any other Jews in Aurora?"

"Not zat I know of, but zere is a lovely synagogue in Schpringfield, and a group zat's vorking hard to save rabbis and zeir families from Europe. In fact, Rabbi Ernest Jacob and his vife, Annette, came from Germany a few monss

ago. ve've only been to service once zough, since
it's a long drive."

"Yes, it is." Laura paused, searching for
proper words. "Magda, my husband and I
listened to the news about Europe every evening
before he got sick. Glen's brother was shot and
died right next to him during a battle, so he was
terrified that another war would break out. The
things I've heard and read in the papers sound
awful. It's hard to imagine they could be true,
but since you're here now, I'd like to know
what's really happening. How bad are things in
Germany?"

"Vorse zan any stories you've heard,
vorse zan any nightmare you've had." Magda
cleared her throat and clasped her hands in her
lap. Her gaze shifted from Laura's face to a
carved wooden box on the table. She pointed at
it and said, "My mozer gave me zis box a year
before she died. I insisted on bringink it vith us
vhen ve escaped because it has ze only pictures
of my family." Magda caressed the edge of the
lid, then opened it. "Except for Harvey and
Helga, I don't know if I'll ever see any of zem
again."

"I'm so sorry," Laura said, swallowing to
clear her throat. "The box is gorgeous, and a
perfect place to keep treasured pictures."

"Zank you. It vas one of my mother's
most precious things."

A high-pitch squeal broke into the conversation, then evolved into a full-bodied laugh. Both women's attention whipped around to David. He was holding the big spoon, then raised it up and crashed it down on the edge of a piece of cardboard balanced on top of a spool, with a clothespin on top. The clothespin sailed through the air like a wooden cannon ball, right over David's head. He screeched again, mouth and eyes wide, and watched the projectile hit the wall.

"Oh no, David, don't do that." Laura looked at Magda, then back to David, and said, "You can't shoot things all over Mrs. Cohen's house."

Magda was in stitches, almost doubled over, at David's antics. "It's all right, Laura, he's one schmart little boy. And I love to see a child laugh like zat."

"Are you sure?"

"Yes. Helga used to play like zat vhen she vas little." Magda waved at David, then pulled the wooden box onto her lap. "In ze beginnink, Harvey and I were happy and carefree too, just like David."

She lifted the top picture out and showed it to Laura. "Here is my fazer and Harvey and I just after ve got married."

"You were so young and pretty." Laura studied the picture. "Your father didn't look too happy. Didn't he like Harvey?"

Magda touched her fingers to her father's image in the picture. "He liked Harvey, but didn't approve of our meeting on the steps after Synagogue service. He knew Harvey was American, and didn't vant me to become involved vith someone who'd eizer leave me and travel zousands of kilometers avay, or take me viz him avay from my father."

"But he didn't leave you."

"Harvey vas determined to marry me, but I vouldn't dream of marryink him vizout my fazer's approval. He vasn't just my fazer, he vas my rabbi, too."

"And..."

"And my fazer gave permission as long as Harvey agreed zat ve'd stay in Germany instead of goink to America." Magda beamed and smoothed out a wrinkle on the edge of the picture. "He was a smart man, and a good talker."

"Is that your parents in the next picture?" Laura touched the corner of the next photograph, which had a family, two adults and four children.

Magda put the first picture down on the table. "Yes, zat's our vhole family vhen I vas a very small girl." She pointed to the toddler sitting on the woman's lap. "Zat's me, the youngest, sitting on my mozer's lap."

"Such a nice family. Your mother was a beautiful woman." Laura leaned in for a closer look. "Where are they all now?"

Magda whispered, stroking the picture. "Zey are all dead. My sister died of pneumonia a year after zis was taken, since after the war there vas almost no medical care. My brozers died in the var, just a few monss apart." Magda peeked up at Laura, then back at the photo. "Mama died of a heart attack just veeks after learnink about my brozers. My fazer said she died of a broken heart. It just looked like a heart attack."

Laura rubbed Magda's back. "I'm so sorry, so very sorry. But what about your father?"

Magda put the picture down, wiped her eyes, and twisted her body toward Laura. "Zat came much later. Harvey and I lived with my fazer in his apartment above the furniture store. My fazer made sturdy, plain vooden furniture, and some with fancy carvinks like ze ones on zis box. Harvey vorked with him and over ze next years learned to make custom furniture, too." Magda stood, wiping her hands on her skirt. "Vould you like some vater? I need somethink to drink."

Laura glanced at David, still engrossed in his play and oblivious to their conversation, "Yes, thank you. May I help?"

Magda waved her offer away. When she sat back down, Magda put the pictures back in the box and faced Laura on the couch. "Ve vere happy togezer, and my fazer vas very happy vhen Helga vas born. Life in Germany vas very difficult after ze var, but ve vorked hard to build a future togezer and for our daughter. Zen zinks changed as Hitler started gaining power."

Laura could only nod and wait out Magda's long pause.

"At first, no one paid much attention to him. Ve vere sure our leaders in ze government vould put a schtop to his rantinks. But zey didn't, and zinks got worse and worse. Soon everyzink ze Germans suffered vas blamed on ze Jews. Violence was common, and nothink ever happened as long as ze victim was Jewish."

Magda stopped and drank half her glass of water. "My fazer was the one who started talkink about Harvey and me takink Helga to America. Ve didn't vant to leave him alone, and insisted zat ve vould only leave if he came, too. But my fazer vouldn't hear of leavink the members of our synagogue. Ze buildink was damaged in ze var, but he schtill held services and helped his people. He said he had to care for zem and vould not leave zem behind." Magda cleared her throat and wiped at her eyes.

Laura swallowed a lump in her throat, and wiped her eyes. "Your father sounds like an amazing man. I can't imagine how hard it must have been for you to leave him behind. How on earth did you decide to do that?"

"Ve fought many times over leavink, but tried to keep thinks as normal for Helga as possible. Zen ve couldn't hide the facts from her anymore vhen Jewish children vere no longer allowed to go to school, or to parks, or libraries. Zen came ze Nuremberg Laws on September of nineteen-zirty-five. 'Jews Unvelcome' signs vere all over. Germans vere not allowed to do business vith Jews, so most of Fazer's customers schtopped comink to the store. Soon after zat he was forced to sell the buildink and all the furnishings, includink our apartment and ze store, to a German for a very small price. Ve moved into a tiny place viz two ozer families on ze second floor of an old empty factory. My fazer and Harvey supported us by doink odd jobs. Leavink vas no longer an easy choice. Even zough Harvey was an American, ze embassy vouldn't help us escape."

Magda stopped again and closed her eyes. She took a deep breath. "Zen came November tenth, the second night of 'Kristallnacht'. Ze two ozer families had left durink ze day, afraid to remain in the city. Ve had hidden in ze basement and blocked ze door leadink up to ze ground floor."

Laura felt the room change around her. She still heard Magda speaking, but in her mind she was no longer in the room. Laura was caught up in a vision accompanied by Magda's words. She was an invisible entity in the room with Magda's family, watching everything that happened. Magda, Harvey, and Helga huddled together behind a mountain of packing crates across the room from a barred door. The room was dark, but she could still see them and sense them. The family was terrified, and the smell of desperate fear permeated the small room.

Laura knew that Magda's father had stayed upstairs alone, first concealing the hatch that led to the basement, then locking the doors and windows and hiding in a closet. She heard loud voices, cursing and laughing, in the street outside, and the sound of marching feet. There were also the sounds of gunfire, breaking glass, and screams of agony. Then she heard the windows in the room shatter, increasing the volume of the cacophony outside. Hammers pounded against the door. Loud metallic screeching pierced the air as the hinges gave way.

The scene changed and Laura saw five men, all wielding weapons, enter and destroy everything in their path. Furniture, cabinets, machinery, all fell under the hammer blows. The closet door couldn't protect Magda's father, who was dragged out and thrown to the floor. The men kicked and beat him until he no longer moved, while blood pooled around his body. Then they spit on him, booted him out of the way, and left.

"I was vorried sick about my fazer," Magda said, her voice clear, even as Laura's vision continued. "Harvey refused to check on him until ve could no longer hear any noise or footsteps from overhead. He told me zat my fazer had insisted on protectink ze door so ze Nazis vouldn't find me and Helga. My fazer and Harvey agreed, even knowink what might happen."

Laura heard Magda crying, but remained caught up in the vision. She saw Harvey open the door when he was sure it was safe. He and Magda made Helga close the door behind them, and promise not to come out or open the door until they returned. They climbed the stairs on silent feet and opened the hatch.

The room was dark, but stank of dust, blood, and urine. The moonlight shining in through the broken windows revealed a shadow on the floor a few feet away. Harvey and Magda knelt next to her father, and saw tiny bubbles break through the blood coating his broken face.

Harvey covered Magda's face to prevent her from screaming. "Not a sound, Magda. Not a sound." He breathed into her ear, not releasing her until she shuddered hard, then nodded.

"Papa, oh Papa, I love you," she whispered, afraid to touch him for fear of hurting him more.

"Go now, tonight." They saw the supreme effort it took for him to form those words. "You must protect Helga. You must survive." He licked his torn lips. "My son, you know the way. Tonight, don't wait."

One of Magda's father's eyes was buried in swollen flesh, but the other focused on his daughter's face. "I love you. You're the only one left. You must survive." Those words took the last of his strength.

Harvey wrapped his arms around Magda and pulled her away, back down toward the basement. Once there, they grabbed packed satchels from a corner, cleared the entrance to a hidden tunnel, and fled.

Laura's vision faded and she was back on the couch. Without a word, she opened her arms and wrapped them around a sobbing Magda.

CHAPTER TWENTY-NINE

Doggone Rats

The next day, Laura couldn't get Magda's story out of her head. The images she'd seen haunted her on the way home, and stayed with her all evening. She tried to push them away so the children wouldn't sense something was wrong, but Magda's intense suffering and the vivid flashes from Laura's vision tormented her. After the kids were asleep, Laura went to her bedroom and changed into her nightgown. She fell to her knees against the side of the bed and pounded her fists on the mattress.

"God, how can you let such unspeakable things happen? Magda's father was a good man.

He didn't deserve to die like that. And those awful men would've hurt Magda and Helga too, just because of their religion." Hot anger bubbled up, battling against the anguish that overwhelmed her. "Why should anybody believe in you when you let horrible things happen to kind, decent people?"

"Don't blame God. He created us but doesn't control what we do." The powerful voice fillied Laura's mind and vibrated throughout her body, without making a sound in the room.

"People make bad choices that cause awful things to happen, but those actions aren't directed by God."

"Ma?" Laura murmured, "Maybe you're right, but why do evil people seem so much stronger? They seem to get away with everything. It's not fair. Look at poor Glen, pushed beyond his limit and locked up for who knows how long. And what about Magda's family? And all the other people Hitler is killing and torturing? How can that be right? You always taught us there was a loving God somewhere, even when we saw how horrible Pa was to you, but I can't believe that anymore."

"That's enough." Ma's tone stopped Laura in her tracks, the same way her children stopped when she used the same voice. "You don't have to understand, no humans really can, but you've seen enough to know that we're always given the strength to go forward. Don't dishonor Magda by falling apart when she's working so hard to build a new life for her family. And don't dishonor Glen by giving up on the dreams you two shared for your children."

Laura started to reply, but stopped and took a deep breath. She stood and climbed into bed, closed her eyes and let the warmth and strength of her ma's presence surround and fill her, washing the rage away, and carry her off to sleep.

The next morning after the older children left for school, Laura counted out fifteen dollars from the mason jar. She reached up to put the jar back in the top cabinet, then changed her mind and pulled out another ten dollars. She'd better have extra money since she might need cleaning supplies for that awful place. Taking materials from the house wouldn't work very well using the garden cart, since she'd have David with her.

David bounced and waved his arms as soon as he saw Magda's building. When they reached the top of the stairs, he banged on the door with both hands

"Goot mornink," Magda said, opening the door. She leaned down, her dark curly hair shielding her face from Laura's view, and hugged David, not quite meeting Laura's eyes.

"I'm sorry for breakink down yesterday," she said.

"Are you kidding?" Laura grasped Magda's shoulders. "You don't need to apologize. In fact, I'm amazed at how you've survived and are building a new life here." Laura squeezed Magda's shoulders and stared into her eyes. "You're a strong woman, but whenever you need a shoulder to cry on, I'm here for you," Laura said. "And trust me, I do understand the need to fall apart and bawl sometimes."

Magda's lips trembled and her eyes glistened. "Thank you, but I vasn't brave or schtrong, just lucky ant a goot runner." She pointed to a stack of kitchen utensils and bowls, spools and clothespins on the living room rug. "David, look at all those things for you to play with."

"Thank you so much." Laura watched her son plop in the middle of the toys. "I hated the thought of him on that filthy floor in the apartment."

"Don't vorry about him, ve'll have fun togezer. And now's a goot time for you to go while he's busy," Magda whispered, embracing Laura in a tight hug before they walked to the door.

🦇

Everything looked the same when Laura arrived at the apartment building—peeling paint, uncut grass, grimy windows. How was this depressing place ever going to feel like a home?

"Morning, Mrs. Webber." Laura jumped at the sound of Charlie's voice behind her.

She spun around, the fingers on her right hand pressed against her chest. "Oh, my goodness, you startled me."

"I'm sorry." Charlie was dressed in the same frayed clothes and green knit cap he'd worn before. "I live a couple of blocks away, so I almost always walk. Let's get inside out of the cold."

As they reached the top step to the apartment building porch, the front door burst open. Two men, whose appearance marked them as brothers, shoved their way through. They were both short and round, with pale freckled skin and flaming red hair and mustaches. One of them was pushing the other in a wheelchair. "Morning, Charlie," the one pushing the chair said, as he maneuvered it through the door and locked the wheels when they reached the middle of the porch. "When are you going to do something about the basement? It's dim as a darned cave down there since two of the four lightbulbs are burned out. Yesterday I 'bout broke my neck trying to get some things out of our storage cabinet. And it smells like a moldy, old swamp."

"Sorry, Zeke," Charlie said, hanging his head. "I'll try to get new bulbs in and clean the place up this week."

"Charlie, you been promising to clean it up for over a month now." The brother in the chair pointed a crutch at the landlord. Laura noticed that he was missing his left leg below the knee. "We all feel bad about Pauline getting sick and all, but you've got to find somebody to take care of the maintenance around this place. The folks in the other buildings are complaining, too."

A flush crept up Charlie's face. He rubbed the back of his neck, glanced at Laura, then back at the brothers. "You're right. I'm sorry. I'll see what I can do." He shoved his hands in his pockets and turned toward Laura. "Laura, these gentlemen are your new first floor neighbors, Zeke and Lem Frasier. Zeke, Lem, this is Laura Webber. She and her four children are moving into the third-floor apartment."

Laura and the brothers bobbed their heads to one another. "Come on, Zeke, we need to get moving," Lem said.

"Okay, okay." Zeke reached for Lem's hand to help him stand up. "Nice meeting you, Mrs. Webber." As soon as Lem balanced on his crutches, Zeke pushed the chair down the porch steps, through the tall grass, all the way to the street. As soon as he parked the chair, Zeke bounded back to the porch.

He stayed at Lem's side, keeping a close watch on his slow walk with the crutches across the uneven, treacherous footing all the way to the chair. Once seated, Lem pulled the crutches across his lap and waved to Charlie and Laura. "Let's go, Zeke, we're already getting a late start."

Laura and Charlie watched Zeke shove Lem across the street at a fast clip.

"Lem lost his leg from gangrene after getting shot during the war," Charlie said. "Zeke's the oldest, and he's taken care of Lem from the day he came home from the hospital. Unless the weather is bad, they spend every day at the town square park with the other veterans, playing chess or cards. They're a little rough around the edges, but they're both good men."

Laura watched the brothers squabble as they moved down the street. "Typical brothers," she said, "picking at each other all the time, but still protective of one another."

One last glance after Zeke and Lem, then Laura turned back and followed Charlie through the front door and up the stairs. While they stopped at the second floor landing, waiting for him to catch his breath, Laura asked, "Who lives here?"

"Phoebe Zimmerman, an elderly widow lady, has lived here for over ten years. When her husband died, her son insisted she sell their house in Illinois and move here. He said he wanted to help take care of her, but his wife is the one that stops by with groceries every couple of weeks."

"What's Mrs. Zimmerman like?"

"She can be pretty testy, doesn't like change, and isn't very friendly. Course, she's deaf as a post which doesn't help." Charlie straightened up, then started climbing the last of the stairs.

Laura glanced back at Mrs. Zimmerman's door as she started up the stairs. Might be a good thing she was deaf, since there'd be four active children jumping around right above her head. Laura decided to try and make friends just to help keep peace in the building.

Charlie unlocked the apartment door, turned on the light, and led her inside to the kitchen table. Laura's lips tightened and she couldn't help grimacing. Everything she saw looked the same. Nothing had been touched. And that meant a trip to the store and hours of hard work before she could feel safe about having the children in the place.

They settled on scarred wooden chairs at the stained kitchen table. Charlie reached into his pocket and pulled out a paper and pencil. "Here's the rental agreement. I collect rents on the first of the month. Write your name here at the top and sign at the bottom." He pointed at the two places. "Fifteen dollars for March. I'm not charging for the days left in February, since Mr. Niedermann gave you such a good reference."

"Thank you." Laura signed the paper, then opened her pocketbook and pulled out her frayed coin purse. It was done. She'd secured a home for her children, but was heartsick at the conditions. If only there had been a different place available.

A soft squeak and a scurrying sound from the rafters above caught their attention. Laura's gaze whipped to the ceiling and spotted a huge brown rat that scampered the length of the beam toward the top of the wall, where he disappeared from sight.

"Doggone rats. Guess I need to bring you some traps." Charlie swallowed hard, his lips pinched tight.

Traps? That was a scary thought, almost worse than the rodents. Rats were filthy creatures and might bite a child during the night, and a rat trap could break a finger or toe. Both would be dangerous around an inquisitive toddler like David.

"I have to go to the store for stuff to clean with, so I can get them for you. That way I can set them out before bringing my children here." Laura handed her crumpled bills to Charlie.

"I'd appreciate that. Just tell Mr. Jackson I said to put it on my account." Charlie pushed himself upright. "Let's go to the basement so I can show you where things are. Could you get some lightbulbs, too?"

It took Charlie a long time to climb down three flights of stairs. When they arrived in the basement, Laura saw it was every bit as bad as Zeke had described—dim, dirty, sour smelling. She batted spiderwebs aside and headed for the washtubs and washing machines. One of the tubs had something she couldn't identify soaking in slimy grayish water that looked like it had been forgotten and left for days. She lifted a washer lid and saw slimy soap scum coating the inside, and figured the other one would be just as nasty.

Charlie waved his arm toward the other side of the room. "The storage area is at the end. One big closet and a row of shelves for each tenant. This one is yours." Charlie opened the double doors on the only unlocked unit, revealing more dusty webs and three lonely mason jars full of mold on the bottom shelf.

"Is there a ladder down here?" Laura turned around to take in the whole room, her arms tight around her torso. "That would be a big help for changing lightbulbs and placing traps on high beams."

"There are two ladders, both in that corner at the end of the storage area." He pointed, started to speak, then cleared his throat. "Mrs. Webber, I'm really sorry. I've never had someone move into a dirty apartment before. My Pauline always cleaned from top to bottom. She took care of the basements too, while I did the bigger maintenance jobs." He looked at Laura, then his gaze slid to the side.

"I don't feel right about the way things are, not at all." He reached into his pocket and pulled out the folded bills he'd taken from her earlier. "I know you're going to clean your place before you move in, and it's a big job. If I give your March rent back, would you consider cleaning the basement too? Heck, maybe you could keep the basement clean all the time in return for part of the rent every month." He held the rent money out in his hand. "What do you think?"

Laura stared at the money, wishing she didn't need it so much. "I think cleaning in place of rent this month would be a good deal for us both." Laura took the cash and tucked it into her coat pocket. "We can talk about next month when we know more what all the cleaning would entail."

CHAPTER THIRTY

Ugly And Depressing, But Clean

Laura composed a shopping list on her way to the store, feeling much better with the extra fifteen dollars in her pocket. Charlie's rat traps and lightbulbs for the basement, a broom and dustpan, string-mop, bucket, sponges and scrub brushes, rags, as many old newspapers as she could get, plus two gallons of Scrubbs Cloudy Ammonia.

When she reached the store, Mr. Jackson held the door open for her. "Mrs. Webber, good to see you again. Do you need more boxes?"

"Thank you," Laura said. "But today I need a long list of cleaning supplies. And

Charlie, Mr. Johnson, asked me to pick up some rat traps and lightbulbs and have them charged on his account."

Mr. Jackson pulled the door closed behind them. "Of course. Just remind me when you're ready to check out."

Finding everything in the store was easy, but she had to borrow a shopping cart to carry her purchases back to the apartment. After three trips upstairs, Laura was breathing hard and overwhelmed at the job that faced her. Where should she start? The nasty floor so that tomorrow David could walk around and sit down without getting coated with filth? Or the bathroom so the grimy fixtures were safe to use. How about cleaning the kitchen first just in case she or David needed a drink of water before heading home? Her skin crawled as she looked around, trying to decide what to attack first.

A soft, chittering sound from the wall under the sink caught her attention. "Guess I'd better set some rat traps before I start scrubbing anything." She knelt and found a chewed section of wall surrounding the pipe. She shivered with revulsion at the tooth marks and droppings. "Good thing Mr. Jackson suggested some steel wool and caulking compound to seal rat holes."

She stood and headed for the door. First she'd have to get the ladder from the basement to set one of the traps on the beam where they'd seen the rat earlier. Then she'd set a couple more traps where she found signs of rodent activity.

Laura placed four rat traps baited with peanut butter before she resumed working in the bathroom. The first trap was on the beam above the middle of the room, one was on the ridge above the wall where the beam rested, and two were in bottom cabinets where she'd found piles of rat droppings. Back in the bathroom, she listened for the sound of a snap while she created a plug for the rat hole. "Mr. Jackson said to pull off enough steel wool to fill the hole, and squirt caulk into the middle of the steel wool to fill it up." She repeated his directions out loud as she worked. "Next, I have to roll the stuff around until the caulk covers the steel wool, position it in the hole, and make sure it sticks to the wall." When the gummy mass was in place, Laura smoothed the surface with her fingers. "Not bad. Hope the darn rats wait until the caulk hardens."

Laura was surveying the dingy, but now clean bathroom, when she heard a loud crack and a thump in the main room. She turned to check the noise out and discovered a large brown rat caught in a trap. "Yuck." She picked the trap up, the rat body dangling from the other end. The trap had broken the rat's neck, so she lifted the trap bar and pulled the body out by the tail. "Oh, my word, that thing is about eight inches long, not counting the tail. Disgusting." She dropped it in the garbage, glad David wasn't with her. "One down and who knows how many more to go." She baited the trap again and put it back in place.

Laura's legs were shaking with exhaustion when she called it a day. But the bathroom was clean, the apartment floors had been scrubbed and rinsed until there was a slight shine in some places, and the windows were no longer opaque. She'd also plugged several more holes along the base of the walls.

She stood inside the door and surveyed the place one last time. "One more day, maybe two, and this place will be clean, ugly and depressing, but clean. Then I'll start on the basement."

When she reached the ground floor, Laura caught sight of the grocery shopping cart tucked under the stairs and groaned. She was worn out, but didn't want to disappoint Mr. Jackson. Only after she'd returned the cart could she head for Magda's building.

"Quit whining, woman, and get a move on." Laura sighed, summoned her last bit of energy, and headed for the store.

⌐╲┌

Laura's legs shook when she climbed Magda's stairs. She knocked on the door, grateful that there'd be no more steps to climb that day.

"Come in unt sit dowt." Magda beamed as she let Laura inside. "Vould you like a hot cup of tea? You look exhaustet."

"Mama," David crowed, then ran and wrapped his arms around Laura's legs.

Laura dropped onto the couch, pulled David up on her lap and kissed the top of his head. "A hot cup of tea sounds wonderful. Just what I need."

David cupped her face in his hands and turned her toward the rug. "Look what I made."

Laura stared at a jumble of utensils and other household items piled into a tower. "Wow, you've been busy." She grinned at Magda over David's head. "That's amazing."

"He's a sweetheart." Magda joined Laura on the couch and placed two steaming cups on the table in front of them. "So, how dit itt go viz zee landlort? Vas zee place ready for you?"

Laura shuddered, "Not at all. He hadn't done anything, and it was even worse than I remembered." She told Magda about everything that had happened. Magda drew back, eyes wide, when she heard about the rats.

"Rats are the worst," she said, pulling her shoulders up with a shiver. "One night, durink our escape from Germany, Helga vas bitten on her little finger. Harvey slapped his hant over her mouz to smozer her cry so our hidink place vouldn't be discoveret. All I could do vas pour a tiny bit of vater over zee vound and tie a piece of cloz over it. She still has a scar."

Helga burst through the door, slamming it behind her. "Hi, Mama, hello Mrs. Webber."

"Oh, my goodness, I didn't realize it was so late. David and I had better head home." Laura joined David on the floor. "Where would you like us to put these things?"

"Don't vorry, I'll take care of zem," Magda said. "Vould you like to brink him back tomorrow?"

"Thank you, but you've done so much already."

"He's fun to have arount, and you can vork much better vithout him under your feet."

"That's true, but he's a lot of work. It doesn't seem fair to impose on you like this."

Laura didn't argue too hard when Magda insisted, because she knew cleaning would be much easier without rambunctious David underfoot.

And so it was decided. Not only would David spend the day with Magda again, but June and the boys would come home with Helga and wait for Laura.

CHAPTER THIRTY-ONE

I Don't Like It Here

Saturday, February 25, 1939

Thanks to Magda's help with the children, Laura finished cleaning the basement right before noon on Friday. She was grimy from her cobwebby hair, to her arms and dress stained with dirt and cleaning residue, to her shoes damp with dirty water. Thoughts of a hot bath filled her mind all the way home, but scant minutes after David clambered out of the cart and climbed the front steps with Laura behind him, Mr. Woltz's car pulled into the driveway.

Her heart started racing, but she waved and swallowed hard, waiting for him to reach them. "Good afternoon, Mr. Woltz. How are you."

"I'm fine, Mrs. Webber. How are you and the children doing? I understand you're moving into one of Charlie Johnson's buildings."

"Yes, we are." Laura bit her lower lip, then noticed she was twisting her wedding ring round and round, so moved her hands to her sides.

Mr. Woltz nodded, took a deep breath and blew it out. "I'm glad. He's a good man." He paused and looked around. "The thing is, my buyer is eager to start moving on Wednesday, the first. Do you think you could move this weekend? I can have a truck and two men here tomorrow morning. They can help you finish packing, load all your things into the truck, and carry everything upstairs into your apartment." He cleared his throat and crossed his arms over his chest. "I hate to push you, but if you could manage, I'd really appreciate it."

"You mean tomorrow? You want us to leave tomorrow?" Laura's voice rose higher in disbelief. "We still have an awful lot to do, and were counting on three more days." She crossed her arms, but had a hard time mustering up the energy she needed.

Mr. Woltz leaned against the porch railing, and rubbed his chin. He opened his mouth to speak, stopped, and took a deep breath first. "I know, and I hate to ask. But the two men I hired to load everything won't be able to work on Sunday or Monday." He stopped and scratched at the back of his neck. "Like I said, they can help you pack and do all the heavy work of loading and unloading."

Laura's shoulders slumped. "I planned on cleaning the place top to bottom after we got our things out, but I can't do that if we have to finish moving tomorrow."

"Don't worry about that. You've always kept the place in great shape."

Laura felt overwhelmed with fatigue, her body and mind both ready to drop. "We'll be ready for them tomorrow, but please ask them to wait until noon." Laura's voice was firm. "And I appreciate your providing the help."

Mr. Woltz nodded, lowered his brow, then turned to step off the porch. When he reached the bottom of the stairs, he stopped and said, "Mrs. Webber, it's been a pleasure getting to know your family. I sure hope everything works out for you and your husband."

Laura stared at his car until it disappeared around the curve of the driveway, and tried to ignore the stinging in her eyes and the pressure in her throat.

Mr. Woltz's men arrived at noon, and by nightfall everything the family owned had been carried into the new apartment. Before the men left the apartment for the last time, they stacked a good supply of wood next to the pot-bellied stove. Laura was ashamed to have them see the tiny, dismal apartment, even though she'd spent days cleaning it, compared to the farm they'd lived in for five years.

When the moving men left, the family stood in the middle of the room staring at the mountain of boxes and loose items that filled the space. The children, who had come to the apartment for the first time with the last truck load, clustered together and stared at their mother.

"Where's the rest of the place?" June said, extending her arms toward the walls.

"Yeah, where are we supposed to play?" Raymond's voice cracked as he stood with clenched fists on his hips.

"I don't like it here. It's ugly and it smells funny." Jimmy stuck his lower lip out and crinkled up his nose.

"I know it's small, but we'll manage," Laura said. She pointed to the two rooms across from the front door. "The bathroom is on the left and the bedroom is on the right."

"Just one bedroom? Where are we going to sleep?" Raymond and June moved a step closer to each other, both with their jaws clenched and eyes narrowed.

"You guys sleep in the bedroom. I'll either sleep on the couch or unroll a mattress on the floor each night."

David's face swung back and forth between them, then he shifted his focus to the pile of goods on the floor. He grabbed an open box and started pulling towels and washcloths out and tossing them in a pile.

"David has the right idea," Laura said. "We need to start putting things away."

"I don't like it here." Raymond thrust his chin out and glared. "We need to go someplace else, someplace better."

"Me, neither," June said. "Papa would never make us stay here. He always found good places for us."

That was the last straw. Laura saw red and felt her control disappear. "Your papa isn't here. He tried to escape when the doctor wouldn't let him come home, and hurt a man real bad. He got himself locked up a long ways away, and we don't know if he'll ever get out. I don't want to hear anymore about what Papa would do." Laura was horrified at the words spewing from her mouth, but couldn't stop herself. "This place is it for us. We have no other choices, and it won't be easy. So stop whining and start helping me put all this stuff away."

Jimmy started crying, then sniffed hard to stay silent as he swiped his tears away. June and Raymond leaned closer to each other, but avoided eye contact with Laura.

Laura's anger disappeared. She wished she could pull the ugly words back. Why had she said those things? The kids are scared and hurting, why had she yelled and made it worse for them? She wanted to apologize to the children, take them in her arms and comfort them, but could see that the damage was done and didn't think they'd listen. The silence stretched out, filled with the children's anger. The anger peaked and slipped into pain, which showed in flushed faces, swollen eyes, and trembling lips.

Dropping down on the floor next to the pile, Laura opened her arms wide to her children. "I'm sorry, guys, so sorry. You're right, this is an awful place and I don't like it either. But we have no other place to go now that Mr. Woltz has sold his property." She felt her eyes begin to tear and rubbed them hard. Her voice shook. "Papa wouldn't like this place either, but since he's not here we have to hang on together and do the best we can. Remember when we were traveling on the road? He always said that as long as we had each other, nothing else mattered."

Was she getting through to them? Laura's control was slipping away. Then Jimmy threw himself into her arms, followed by June and Raymond. David couldn't be left out and squirmed into Laura's lap, right at the center of the family huddle. "I love you kids so much, more than anything in the world. Just hold on tight and we'll make it together, somehow."

The hug lasted a long time, ending only when David cracked his head into Raymond's chin while he tried to push higher in Laura's lap.

"Ow, you made me bite my tongue," Raymond screeched, cradling his chin in both hands.

June and Jimmy giggled at the sight of Raymond holding his chin while David rubbed the top of his head. Somehow the huddle turned into a wrestling and tickling match, which ended with everyone stretched out on the floor, breathless.

David plopped on top of Laura's stomach, announced, "I hungry," then bounced up and down.

"Oof," Laura gasped, catching David by his arms and moving him to the side. "David's right. It's time to take a break and have something to eat." She stood and moved to the counter and opened a box of cold items that hadn't fit into the tiny refrigerator. "We need to use up this salad stuff and the boiled eggs. There's also a package of opened bologna, some cheese, and a partial bottle of milk. The bread is starting to get dry, but a little mayonnaise will fix that."

In short order June found plates and utensils, Raymond pulled glasses out of a box and poured milk for everyone, and Jimmy corralled David and helped him up on a chair. "Here you go." Laura filled each plate. "Help me put the food away, then you can quit working for tonight. I'll get the bed made up, and that will be it for this evening."

✳

Laura sat and bounced on the mattress in the bedroom. She wondered how old the stained, nasty-looking thing was. The old mattresses they'd carried with them when they'd lived on the road had more life left in them than the one on the bed. Perfect, she thought. Laura dug through the pile until she freed the children's old mattress, then carried it to the bedroom. Pushing and pulling, she arranged it on top of the other mattress, and made up the bed with a sheet, two blankets, and their pillows. She bounced again, and was satisfied with the result.

The children pulled out a box of dominoes and settled on the floor near the stove to play. Laura stared at the couch, more loveseat than couch, sat and assessed it as a bed. It was no cleaner than the mattress had been. She muttered under her breath. "Sure don't want to put my face or hair down on this thing. I'd get a case of the crawlies even if there was nothing there. Guess I'll have to keep it covered with a blanket, whether I sleep on it or not."

She knelt beside the pile of boxes and searched for blankets, pulling them aside and stacking them next to her. She also pulled out the other rolled-up mattress, not at all sure whether she'd sleep on it or the short, lumpy, dirty couch. But using the mattress on the floor put her in easy reach of any rats that might come exploring at night.

The children were still playing with the dominoes when Laura interrupted them. "Time to quit. It's been a long day."

A chorus of groans and complaints followed.

"It's too early."

"I'm not tired."

"No fair."

Laura shook her finger at them, pointing to each in turn. "That's enough. June, uncross your arms and straighten that pouty face. Raymond, don't glance at your sister, you do as I say. And that goes for you too, Jimmy. I'm the head of this household, not your sister or brother."

David stared at her, then dropped the dominoes he was holding and rubbed his eyes.

"Come on, little man," Laura said, lifting him into her arms. "You need to go potty and change into your nightshirt."

By the time she got him ready and tucked in with the others, the mutiny had disappeared. She added another blanket on top and tucked them all in, since the heat from the stove didn't seem to do much to warm the bedroom. She slipped out the door and leaned against the wall, her eyes closed. Scant minutes later, rhythmic breathing and soft snores let her know the children had fallen asleep.

CHAPTER THIRTY-TWO

Growing Up So Fast

Laura pushed away from the wall and threaded her way to the other side of the room past the sofa, then dropped on the floor with her back against the rolled up, still tied mattress. The heat from the stove enveloped her. She pulled her knees up, wrapped her arms around them, and rested her cheek on top. The huge pile of their possessions filled her sight and mind. The amount of work that remained overwhelmed her, competing with a level of exhaustion that pervaded her very soul. Laura didn't know whether to cry, scream, or throw something. She ended up falling asleep instead.

She jerked awake, almost falling over on her side, heart racing in panic mode. Her lips and eyes were dry and burning from the stove heat, but she didn't see anything wrong. Laura peered at the stove, but the door was shut tight, preventing any stray embers from escaping.

"Perhaps a piece of wood popped and woke me," she mumbled, leaning back. "That thing throws a lot more heat than a fireplace." She'd have to make sure the kids didn't play too near it, or someone could get a nasty burn.

Laura stood and picked her way to the bedroom, needing assurance that the kids were safe. Just visible in the dim light from the living room, their four bodies filled the bed from edge to edge. David was tucked under June's chin, cuddled into her body, with Jimmy between him and Raymond. Jimmy rolled onto his back and threw both arms out, smacking June and Raymond in the head. They both shoved his arm off, but none of them woke up.

Laura stifled a laugh. Jimmy always liked to sleep spread out like a starfish. Sure enough, in seconds he spread-eagled again, before his sister and brother shoved his arms away. This time something caught her eye. She didn't know what, but something was different. Raymond and Jimmy were both on their sides, but June had shifted to her back, with the blanket pushed down to her waist.

Laura leaned in, legs pressed against the side of the bed, and tried to figure out what had caught her attention. Nothing. But when she lifted the edge of the blanket to cover June, she noticed the faintest swelling of budding breasts poking against her nightgown.

Her mind raced. That couldn't be happening. June was way too young. But Laura realized her daughter would turn eleven in three months. Laura shook her head and stared at her children. They were all growing up so fast, how could she have missed the signs? She tucked them in once again, and stumbled out of the bedroom.

No more question about where Laura would sleep from now on. The time had come for June to stop sleeping with her brothers, so she'd have to move to the couch. The children all needed more room. The old mattress on the floor would have to be Laura's bed. Not tonight though. She'd have one night with no worries about being in easy reach of vermin.

Sleep was slow in coming, but not because of wandering rodents. Laura's thoughts focused on her own body changes, back when she lived in the sod house where she grew up. Her ma had died when Laura was only three, leaving the role of mother to twelve-year-old Ruth, the oldest child, to fill. Laura didn't remember any special talk or support about what it meant to change from girl to woman, but all three of her older sisters talked a lot whenever their pa was in the fields. She'd learned what to expect by listening to them, but their discussions left glaring holes in her knowledge. Laura fell asleep near dawn, still wondering what she was supposed to say to her head-strong daughter.

⋙⋘

Breakfast the next morning was pan-fried toast with grape jelly and scrambled eggs, washed down with water. Laura only had dry toast and water. She stared at the piled-up belongings and imagined having the children help her put things away in the tiny space. The picture wasn't pretty, so she clapped her hands and announced "I've got an idea. You've worked so hard these last few days, we need a break. How about we bundle up and go spend the day in the park."

In no time, the older children were barreling down the stairs with Laura and David lagging behind. When they reached the park, Laura waved at Lem and Zeke, grouped around a chess game with three other men. She found an empty stone bench where she could keep an eye on the kids as they played tag and climbed on the war monuments throughout the park. They were great kids, but it would be much easier to make some order in the apartment without their help. She planned on getting the bulk of her work done after they went to bed. Uh, oh, thinking about putting them to bed reminded her she needed to have a talk with June. She'd also need an explanation for the boys about why June wouldn't be sleeping with them anymore.

Laura's thoughts roamed from the apartment to June's maturing body, then to her own childhood, all while watching her children. She noticed June stop playing freeze tag and start leading David away from the game to some shrubs around the base of a statue. Laura stood, started to shout at June, stopped, and ran to her instead. "June, what are you doing?"

June stopped, a puzzled look on her face. "David has to potty."

"Not here in the public park. There are too many people around. You'll have to take him home." Laura glanced around at the folks scattered about. "Can you find your way there and back?"

June rolled her eyes, nodded, picked David up and headed out of the park.

Laura returned to the bench after June reached the street. Raymond and Jimmy joined her to find out where they had gone, decided they needed to go too, and ran to catch up.

When the kids returned, Laura patted the seat next to her and said, "Thanks, Junebug. Sit with me for awhile. I need to talk to you."

June looked surprised, but perched on the edge of the bench.

"Last night when I checked on you kids, you were crowded as can be. I think it's time you all had more room. From now on you'll sleep on the sofa."

"We've always been crowded, and David needs to snuggle during the night. Can he sleep on the couch with me?"

"No, he'll have to cuddle with Jimmy."

June snorted. "Jimmy doesn't cuddle, he stretches. If David was next to him he'd get hit in the head and end up crying." June gazed at her feet, which swung back and forth. "Besides, I like curling up with him."

Laura took a deep breath. "Honey, David needs to learn to sleep without you. You're growing up now, so you can't sleep with your brothers any longer."

June's face flushed. She kept her face turned away but didn't say a word.

"June, the changes in your body are natural, a normal part of the process of becoming a woman. Nothing to be embarrassed about."

"All right, I get it," June hissed, "I'll sleep alone on the sofa."

Before Laura could say a word, June sprinted across the grass toward her brothers.

That night the kids, mellow from playing at the park, gathered at the table to make things with dominoes. Laura lifted David from his chair, sat down, and settled him on her lap.

"Today was fun. You guys deserved the break after all the work yesterday." She paused, kissed the top of David's head while searching for the perfect words. "You guys are all growing up so fast. In fact, you've gotten too big to share a bed anymore."

June glared at Laura, then stared down at her hands.

"June will be sleeping on the sofa from now on, so you boys will have more room."

"Yeah," Raymond crowed, "Maybe I won't be half falling off the bed now." He stared at David. "But David always cuddles with June. Will he be on the couch too? He doesn't take much room."

"No, you boys will all be together. Raymond, you should be in the middle to protect David from Jimmy during the night."

June was stone-faced all evening and never said a word. Laura thought the discussion was over until the children were ready for bed. Raymond and Jimmy cheered when they stretched out, but David cried when Laura wouldn't let him sleep with his sister.

June stalked to the sofa, ignoring his sobs. She arranged her blanket and pillow on the sofa, turned her back to the room and hid her face under her crossed arm.

Laura carried David to the boys' bed, tucked him next to Raymond, and patted his back. "You're a big boy now, sweetheart. You can wake June up in the morning."

When Laura found herself falling asleep on her feet, she gave up and bedded down on the mattress. The room was far from empty, but she'd made a big dent in the pile. Her last task was putting out fresh clothes for each child to wear in the morning. She kissed each of her babies as they slept before stretching out on her pallet. "Just like when I was a little girl," she whispered. "Sleeping on the floor, listening to the family breathing and stirring around me." She moved around and punched the pillow. "Never thought I'd be living like this again."

CHAPTER THIRTY-THREE

We Need Some Good News

"Mama, I can't wear this today. I wore it Friday." June shook the dress Laura had laid out for her in front of her mama's face, waking her from a fitful sleep.

"Oh no, I overslept." Laura stretched and jumped off her bed. "There's nothing wrong with that dress. Nobody will even notice.June took a deep breath and crossed her arms, a scowl on her face.

Laura ignored the impending temper storm, filled a pot with water and started the stove burner. "Not another word about that dress. If you can find something else to wear without making anyone late for school, I don't care."

June's mood was contagious. By the time everyone was clean and fed, Laura had had it with the bickering and sniping. She slammed an empty metal bowl against the table so hard the last spoon of oatmeal flew out onto the floor. "The next kid who says one whiney word is getting paddled. This is where we live now, like it or not, so deal with it. I don't want to hear about your clothes, your bedroom, or all the reasons why you shouldn't have to go to school." She looked from face-to-face, fists clenched on her hips. "Is that clear enough?"

No one said a word.

"Do you need me to walk you to school today, or do you know the way?"

Quick, horrified glances shot between the children, then June said, "We know the way. You don't need to come with us." They grabbed their book bags and ran out the door.

Still irritated, Laura cleared the table and started running water in a basin in the sink. Her movements were choppy and abrupt, so when David called for her to look at him, she snapped back, "I'm doing dishes. I don't have time right now."

David didn't say a word, but a few minutes later Laura turned to check out a curious clumping, sliding sound. There was David, wearing Glen's dress shoes, shuffling forward, one careful step after another. She giggled at the studious expression on his little face, an expression that changed to delight when he heard her laugh.

"Big shoes," he said, throwing his hands wide apart.

Laura tossed her dishcloth to the counter. "They sure are." She knelt and gathered him in tight for a hug.

He wiggled free, pointed at his feet, and said. "Papa big shoes." The laced tops of Glen's Sunday shoes almost hid David's scuffed, Buster Brown oxfords.

His words were a stab in the heart. Glen should be here to see this. Irritation drained away in the face of David's innocent smile, replaced by determination.

"Come on, little man, let's go for a walk." They'd stop by the post office just in case, but if there was still nothing from the hospital, she might have to visit Dr. Farnsworth and beg for help.

Laura changed into a day dress, hanging her sad looking house dress on a hook on the wall above her rolled-up mattress. She'd love to run errands in the same clothes she wore at home, but that'd never work. She could almost hear the whispers between folks in town about her change in status, which would be much worse if she appeared in public in a housedress.

David loved walking instead of riding in a cart. He ran between doorways and shop windows, grinning at every person he passed. His energy flagged just before they reached the post office, but revived the moment he spotted Mr. Niedermann.

Laura grabbed David before he could run straight to their friend. A man, who looked sort of familiar, was in front of them in line at the counter. When he turned around, Laura saw that the skin on his face and big, scarred hands was tan and leathery-looking. His weathered skin, combined with his overalls and billed cap with John Deere stitched on the front, identified him as a farmer.

"Morning, Mrs. Webber," he said, then touched his cap and turned back to finish his business.

Laura smiled and dipped her chin, wishing she remembered his name. Glen would have known. He was much better with names than she was.

When they reached the counter, Mr. Niedermann pulled out a single envelope for her. "Just one for you today," he said. "Sure hope it has good news."

Laura's pulse shot up when she saw the hospital logo at the top of the return address. "Me too, Mr. Niedermann, me too." She almost ripped it open on the spot, but didn't like being watched as she read it, even by a friend. Laura cleared her throat, stared at her name on the thick, creamy paper that shivered in her trembling hands. She took a deep breath, then tucked the letter inside her pocketbook. "Come on, David, we need to go." Laura thanked Mr. Niedermann, started to say she'd let him know what the hospital people said, but couldn't do it.

She wanted to run to the apartment, but ended up walking with David at her side about half the time, and carrying him the rest. It seemed to take forever before they finished climbing the stairs. She shooed David off to play, sat at the table and took the letter out of her handbag.

She squeezed her eyes shut tight and said a silent prayer. "Please, God, we need him home. Please, please, let this have some good news."

Laura picked the flap open and pulled the two pages out. She glanced at David to make sure he was okay, swallowed a huge lump, and began to read.

> Dear Mrs. Webber,
>
> As you are aware, your husband, Glen Webber, was committed to this institution after being declared criminally insane following his violent escape attempt. He attacked an orderly and caused very severe injuries which, had the man not had emergency surgery, might have been fatal.

When apprehended by a search team, Mr. Webber again resorted to violence, forcing the guards to take extreme measures to subdue him. Had he not been a patient of the Springfield Mental Hospital at the time, your husband would have been arrested and convicted of assault, or even attempted murder, and been sentenced to many years in prison. The judgement was made that, due to his mental illness, he would remain here until he was no longer a danger to himself or anyone else.

There is no easy answer as to when Mr. Webber might, if ever, be considered safe for release. This is not primarily a treatment facility. We house a large population of inmate patients, many of whom are violent. Our job is to protect society while offering what treatment and/or counseling we can to those inmates who show signs of responding. An inmate who seems to recover would still require observation for a lengthy period prior to being evaluated for release.

The final decision is made by a judge after reviewing the original criminal charge, the medical case summary, and recommendations from a neutral panel whose members have each interviewed the patient. As you can see, it is a long process which few inmates complete successfully.

In answer to your request to communicate with your husband's physician, there is no one single doctor handling his case. We have a small staff in comparison to the number of patients, so medical teams are responsible for groups of similar types of patients. We've found this system works best for everyone. You need to send all correspondence regarding Mr Webber to the Medical Administration Department, which designates the proper medical professional to address your concerns. Our protocols do not work well with telephone calls, so please confine your requests to mail.

In case you were considering a visit, we have very strict rules due to safety concerns. No children are allowed in the facility, and there are no exceptions to that rule. While we realize that regulation can create hardships for the family structure, we cannot guarantee safety for children. All potential adult visitors have to be cleared in advance. If you want to be on a list of accepted visitors for your husband, you will have to complete an application form and return it for review. If accepted, you have to schedule all visits well in advance. Please note that scheduling a visit does not guarantee that you will see your husband. Scheduled visits can be cancelled if the inmate is not in a condition to receive visitors. For that reason, it is wise when scheduling visits to allow an extra day or two in case it's needed.

We hope this letter answers your questions. If you need more information, please send your requests via letter as explained above.

Respectfully,

Alfred Beal, MD,
Director, Medical Administration

The pages fluttered to the table from Laura's nerveless fingers. Two phrases rang in her mind, "... when Mr. Webber might, if ever, be considered safe..." and "...process which few inmates complete successfully..." Losing hope felt like all the oxygen in the room had been sucked away, suffocating her in emptiness. Elbows braced on the table, she dropped her head into her hands, lacking the strength to hold it up without help. She didn't even have the energy to cry or vent her outrage at the unfairness of the situation. If only she could sink into an abyss with no sound or light and never come out.

A warm little hand patting her elbow roused Laura from her lethargy.

"Mama, look. Look at me."

Laura rubbed her eyes, then opened them and lifted her head. David was back in Glen's shoes, but had added one of Glen's work-shirts and best hat tilted way back so his eyes, twinkling with joy, were visible under the brim. She forced a grin and clapped her hands, since David was so happy with his outfit. "Wow, you look great. Where did you find those things?"

David pointed to an open box with an undershirt draped over the cardboard flap.

Was it wrong to save all of Glen's things if he wasn't coming home? They had so little space. No, she couldn't give up. Besides, having their papa's clothes and personal items near would help keep his memory alive for his children. It wouldn't be right to take hope away from them now, not when they'd lost so much already. Someday she'd have to answer tough questions, but not today.

Laura found enough strength to force her lips up into something that resembled a smile each time she looked at her happy son, then resumed the chore of emptying boxes and putting things away. The letter was back in her handbag, which she'd hidden under her mattress. Each time her thoughts bounced back to the letter she swallowed the pain and anger deep inside, promising herself she'd figure out what to do after the children were asleep. They were facing enough disruption in their lives without adding more.

By late afternoon, Laura had moved all of Glen's tools to the basement, together with the bicycle. She'd stacked boxes of his clothes and personal items against the wall behind the woodstove. A line of nails, angled up to function as hooks, holding the boys' shirts and pants lined the walls in the bedroom, while Laura and June's clothes were on similar hooks in the living room. Everyone's underwear and personal items were stored in boxes by their beds. Only the last of the kitchen items and mason jars of canned garden produce remained in the living room.

When the older children burst through the door, they marched to the table, dropped their book bags, and started complaining.

June was first and loudest. "Raymond got in trouble again for fighting, but it wasn't his fault."

"That teacher blamed me, but Delbert called us whacky crumbs." Raymond was indignant, his red face swollen on one side, with a bit of dried blood on his upper lip. "Then he said it was no wonder June plays with a dirty

Kraut Jew, since we're all dumb losers living in a dump."

Jimmy, wide-eyed, stood shoulder to shoulder with his big brother. "Raymond was real smooth, Mama, the way he popped Delbert before he knew what was coming."

Laura's shoulders drooped as she gazed from one set of eyes to another. "Even if this place is a bit of a dump, that doesn't mean you're dumb losers. You shouldn't fight," she said, "but I'm proud that you stuck together and defended yourselves."

"You and Papa, too," Raymond said. "Delbert said our pa was a crazy jailbird, and you were nothing but..."

"That's enough." Laura shook Raymond's shoulders, interrupting him, then leaned forward and cradled his face in her hands. "Delbert is an ignorant idiot."

June and Jimmy giggled, and repeated Laura's comment to each other.

"Don't you guys dare repeat that, even if we all know it's true. We have enough trouble already." Laura took a deep breath and closed her eyes, searching for the right words. "I'm so, so sorry that you guys have to go through all of this. It's not your fault that your papa got sick. It's not your fault that Mr. Woltz sold his property. And it's not your fault that this crummy apartment is the only place in town I could find for us to live." She felt equal parts anger and sorrow fighting for dominance inside. "Kids who tease and call you names for things beyond your control are just plain dumb and mean. But that doesn't mean you can punch them in school." A quick smirk between June and Raymond made her add, "or out of school either."

"So when can Raymond punch them?" Jimmy's question was serious, but everyone laughed anyway.

Laura kept the promise to herself through homework, dinner, and bedtime. When she felt the control on her emotions slipping away, she closed herself in the bathroom and started filling the tub. The sound of running water masked the keening sound that accompanied her tears.

CHAPTER THIRTY-FOUR

They'd Make It, Somehow

Laura immersed herself in the hot water, arms wrapped tight around her torso, and held her breath as long as she could. When she emerged from under the water, the tiny room was filled with steam that filmed the window and mirror. Laura felt hidden away from the world. She didn't know what she should do. Her emotions enveloped her like a fog, cycling from anger to sorrow to despair and back around. This whole mess was Glen's fault, right? Not being able to get past his brother's death was sort of understandable, but to recover his memory and attack someone was downright crazy. Sure, he missed them and wanted to get away, but there must have been a better way than almost killing a man.

Then when Laura's anger worked itself to a fever pitch, she remembered the tenderness on Glen's face on their wedding day, on the day June was born, and so many times afterwards when he watched their children doing ordinary things. He was an amazing father, and their children missed him. They needed him, and she couldn't take his place no matter how hard she tried.

And how was she supposed to manage without him? In addition to organizing and handling all the household responsibilities, Glen made her feel precious and powerful at the same time. She hadn't been in love when she married him, but his love and patience had won her heart and made her feel whole for the first time in her life. Now she was alone, and being alone with four children was terrifying. Being strong all the time for them wore her out, and the fear of failing the children haunted her every single day.

Laura shivered, and realized the water had grown cold. She pulled the plug from the drain, stood on shaky legs and grabbed the towel. Clean and dry, but covered with goosebumps, Laura pulled her nightgown on, wrapped a robe around her trembling body, then headed for the wood-stove.

Once parked by the stove, rotating to warm all sides of her body, Laura stared at June. Curled up on her right side at the nearest end of the sofa, blankets cocooned about June's body with only the top part of her head visible. Wisps of shiny, straight dark hair lay across her cheek and forehead. Laura wanted to smooth the strands away from June's face, but feared she might wake her. Poor June, her papa's girl from day one, had wrestled with Glen's absence for no reason she could accept or understand, with no way to bring him home. And now having to deal with the physical and emotional changes of puberty along with the teasing in school about her pa, the move, and her friendship with Helga. Laura wanted to pull June into her lap and rock her until all the pain and unhappiness went away, but those days were long gone.

June's breathing quickened and she rolled over on her other side. Just in case her gaze had made June uncomfortable on some level, Laura left the stove to check on the boys.

The bedroom was dim, lit by the faint light of the moon through the window and the feeble glow from the wood-stove through the door. Laura saw that Jimmy was in his usual spread-eagle position on one side of the bed, with Raymond on his back on the other side, and David curled up in the middle below Jimmy's outstretched arm. Even though it was cold, the boys had pushed the covers down to chest height for the older two and the top of David's head. She missed being able to hold and cuddle them like she had when they were babies.

Raymond muttered in his sleep, and turned to his side toward David. Laura thought long and lanky Raymond seemed to be growing into the family's fierce protector, and would be taller than Glen. His sandy hair was also like his papa's, as was his easy manner and way of studying everything around him. He tried hard to fill shoes much too big for an eight-year-old.

The boys were so different. Jimmy and David had her dark hair, although David's was wavy, while Jimmy's was straight like hers. Jimmy shadowed his big brother whenever he could, but was always ready to spend time with David. In fact, his patience with his baby brother was amazing.

Jimmy didn't say much, but his words revealed both his thoughtfulness and his sensitive side. Glen's absence hurt Jimmy, and Laura had caught him in tears more than once, crying all alone for his papa.

And David? What would the future hold for the happy little guy? He knew his papa was gone, knew which things in the boxes belonged to him, but how much did he remember? As time passed, would those memories fade until they disappeared? Glen adored all of his sons, and how sad it would be if David forgot him.

The cold floor was freezing Laura's feet, so she leaned over the bed and kissed each boy on his forehead. Then she returned to the living room where she unrolled the mattress, spread her blankets, and added a log to the stove. Once she was sure that the place would stay warm throughout the night, Laura curled up and fell asleep.

A loud snap woke her hours later. What the heck was that sound? She sat up and listened hard, but heard nothing but the faint hissing of the wood-stove and June's soft breathing. Could it have been a trap? She got up, pulled her robe on, stuffed her feet into slippers and headed to the kitchen area.

She opened the cabinet under the kitchen sink, since she always found fresh rat pellets there each morning. "Gotcha," she said under her breath. "What a mess." The steel bar on the trap had slammed tight on the big black rat's muzzle, right below the eyes. He was dead, but had bled a lot. Laura freed the body from the trap, then wrapped the carcass in newspaper. Once it was stowed deep inside the trash bucket, she went to work cleaning and bleaching the bloody cupboard floor.

"Mama, what are you doing?" June's voice, still thick with sleep, was muffled by the covers.

"Never mind, Junebug, you can sleep awhile longer." Wide awake, Laura added fresh wood to the embers and stoked the fire. She was much too wide awake to crawl back under her blankets. She decided to fix the children a special breakfast, hoping that this day would be better than the one before.

The smell of frying salt pork and scrambled eggs enticed the children out of sleep and to the table. There was just enough milk in the bottle for everyone to have half a glass. Each child also had one slice of pan-fried toast sprinkled with sugar and cinnamon. The three oldest children inhaled their breakfast, then got ready for school. They grabbed their bookbags, and ran out the door, leaving David and Laura at the table.

"Wish we could feast like this every morning." Laura watched David as he chewed the last bites of his toast. "You are the slowest eater I've ever seen. When you start school, I'll have to feed you breakfast before anyone else crawls out of bed or you'll never make it on time."

David grinned, as his sticky lips and fingers continued to work on the mangled bread. Laura cleared the table, placed the almost spotless plates in the sink, and opened the tiny refrigerator to take stock. "Looks like we need to make a trip to the grocery store, little man. That was the last of the eggs and milk, and we only have half a loaf of bread left."

The thought of dipping into their money for food made Laura anxious, but she pushed the fear away, determined not to let herself give in. She'd be careful, and they'd make it, somehow.

CHAPTER THIRTY-FIVE

We Have Bugs

Wednesday, March 29, 1939

Routine settled in, and the next few weeks passed in a hurry, most of the days blended together. One morning after the older children left for school, David yelled. "Mama, bugs, bugs!"

Laura whirled away from the kitchen counter and saw him sitting by the wall near the door, batting his hands against his face and body, screaming. She plopped down next to him and saw that he'd peeled a wide ribbon of paper away from the wall, freeing hundreds of bugs from inside. "Oh my word." She carried him away from the wall, put him on a chair and wiped dozens of bugs, many of them tiny bed bugs, off his skin. She could see lots of swollen red bite marks.

"Hold on, baby, I'll get something for those bites." Laura ran to the bathroom and dug through a wooden box under the sink. In seconds she grabbed the glass bottle of Dickenson's Witch Hazel and a dry wash cloth, then ran back to David. "Here, little man, this will help stop the stinging." She wet the corner of the cloth and dabbed it on all the red spots. "Try not to scratch. I've got to close off that hole in the paper so no more bugs get out."

Laura went back to the sink for a wet sponge, then dropped to the floor by the torn paper. She pressed the hanging strip back into place, then soaked it with the sponge until the paper stuck tight to the wall. "Now for the darn bugs." She smashed all the insects she could find crawling on the wall and floor, but cringed at the thought of the ones that were already out of sight. She didn't think any had gotten on her, but her skin felt squirmy everywhere.

Rats were bad enough, but the idea of thousands of bugs surrounding her kids, held back only by a layer of paper, was even worse. Laura took David down to the basement where she remembered seeing wallpaper supplies. She found an old roll of wallpaper tucked into a corner with a thick brush and a bucket of paste. She dragged them upstairs, then pulled the ladder up to the apartment. By the time the kids charged inside after school, every crease, crack, or hole in the walls had been covered with fresh sheets of paper. Laura didn't care if the results looked patchy, all that mattered was having an extra layer of protection between her family and the thousands of bugs on the other side.

"Bugs, lots of bugs," David said, holding up his arms to show his red spots.

June's eyebrows shot up to her hairline. "Bugs? We have bugs?"

Thanks a lot for that helpful announcement, Laura thought. "David tore a hole in the wallpaper and some bugs were behind it," she said in what she hoped was a soothing tone. "Don't worry. I fixed the hole and covered all the suspicious spots in the place. Nothing to worry about as long as you don't pull any of the wallpaper down."

"Yuck, I don't like bugs." Jimmy wrinkled his nose, then looked around the room. "Are you sure you got them all?"

Raymond tilted his head back and jerked his thumb toward his chest. "I'm not afraid of bugs. Don't worry, if any of you see a bug just let me know and I'll squish it. Problem over."

Laura hugged Raymond, hiding a grin, "Thanks, honey, I'll call you for every bug I see."

By the time dinner was ready, the bug conversation had quieted down. When Laura asked about school, June and Raymond shrugged. Jimmy stared at his plate. "Do people have to buy new clothes for Easter? What if somebody can't?"

Laura swallowed and put her utensils down, hunting for the best words. "Buying new outfits for Easter is kind of a tradition, but not something that people have to do. Nothing bad happens if they don't." She watched the three oldest glance at each other. "Where did that question come from?"

June raised her chin high. "Easter's just over a week away so all the girls are talking about their Easter outfits. They'll wear them to church the first time, then to school after Easter vacation." She stopped and waited for Laura to respond, then continued. "Papa took us to church sometimes. Are you going to take us on Easter? We have to have new clothes if we go."

"Why do people want new clothes for Easter anyway?" Raymond said. "I think that's dumb."

"It is not dumb. You'd better not say that at school or people will make fun of us even more." June thrust her chin at her brother, daring him to say more.

"I'm sorry you guys have been teased, that's not right." Laura took a deep breath and tapped the tines of her fork on the table. "Easter is about Jesus when he rose from the dead. New clothes and Easter eggs are not really part of the religious celebration, but both are symbols of new life and new beginnings, like Jesus." She wished Glen were here now. He was so much better explaining church things. He always seemed to know the right words. "Do you want to go to church for Easter?"

The children looked at each other. June, the spokesman for the group, said, "I think we better go. It would make things easier. But we can't go unless we have new clothes." The last sentence was a stern pronouncement, almost daring Laura to contradict her.

"I'll see what we can do." Laura hated the thought of disappointing the children, but Easter was awfully close. How in the world could she find a way to get new outfits? There was no money coming in at all, and very little time left.

CHAPTER THIRTY-SIX

Never Spoken To A Nun Before

The next day Laura took David to the grocery store, but her thoughts focused on finding a way to get Easter clothes for the kids.

"Whoa," Zeke pulled Lem back when Laura rounded an aisle and almost ran into the wheelchair. "You almost ran us down."

"Oh, my goodness. I'm so sorry." Laura checked to make sure Lem was unhurt. "I guess my mind was a hundred miles away."

Lem waved her apology aside. "It's okay, we're fine." Lem winked at David and said, "You need to be your mom's navigator."

David loved the attention and grinned with delight.

"What's on your mind that's got it so far away?" Zeke grabbed a five-pound bag of pinto beans and dropped it on top of the pile in Lem's lap.

"Easter. Well, Easter clothes for the kids, to tell the truth." Laura was surprised to hear herself answer the question. "It kind of snuck up, what with the move. I used to always make new clothes for them, but there's not enough time now."

"You oughta go to All Faith. Save scads of money there, and they've got lots of kid's stuff," Lem said.

"All Faith?" Laura cocked her head. She'd never heard that name before.

Zeke balanced a bar of Lifebuoy and a box of Oxydol on top of the beans. "Yeah, big thrift store on Pine, three blocks west of Elm. We shop there all the time." With that announcement, he pushed Lem past Laura toward the cashiers at the front of the store.

Thrift store? Laura had never shopped at a thrift store before, but knew lots of people who did. She'd grown up with home-made clothes, which were always passed down. She'd taken down, patched up, and modified garments until they weren't good enough for anything but rags, then taken them apart and used them for cleaning and dusting until they fell to pieces. Now that store-bought clothes were easier to get, she guessed it made sense that some would end up donated to thrift stores.

Laura and David walked to the apartment and put the food away, then headed for All Faith. They found it with no trouble, tucked between a barbershop and a shoe store. "Come on, David, let's see what we can find."

The interior of All Faith was clean and well-lit, with hanging racks of clothes scattered among tables piled high with clothing and all kinds of household items. David spotted an area along the right wall set apart by a bright red area rug. Children's toys and books were scattered on low tables surrounded by child-size chairs. He yanked his hand free and took off.

"David, no, those aren't yours," Laura said, in hot pursuit.

A soft chuckle came from the other side of the room. "It's alright, ma'am, that's the children's play area, so adults can shop without worrying about them."

Laura turned to the voice, startled to see it came from a woman wearing a habit. A nun? What was this place? "Thank you," she said, knowing her curiosity must be obvious.

The nun's smile was infectious, "I'm Sister Mary Rachel, one of the Sisters of Mercy

from the Blessed Trinity Catholic Church. Our
church works with both the Lutherans and the
Methodists to run this store, and I'm the
volunteer for today."

Sister Mary's face was framed by a white
wimple above her voluminous black habit. Her
eyes twinkled above a wide, warm smile. "Your
little boy is welcome to play with whatever he
wants in the children's area. Now, how can I
help you?"

Laura's eyebrows shot up and her jaw
dropped. She'd never spoken to a nun before,
and this amiable woman seemed so normal.
"Um, we just moved and I've been so focused
on getting settled that I forgot all about Easter.
My children reminded me, but I don't have time
to make clothes for them." She shrugged her
shoulders. "A neighbor told me about this place,
and I thought maybe I could find something."
Laura dipped her chin and rubbed the back of
her neck. Then she looked at David and cleared
her throat. "My husband is away. He's in a
hospital in Illinois. Money is awful tight, but I
hate to disappoint my children."

"Don't worry, you've come to the right
place. No need to feel embarrassed either. Tell
me about your children." Sister Mary Rachel's
voice, warm and soothing, calmed Laura as they
walked toward the back of the store.

"Well, my daughter June is almost
eleven, Raymond is eight, and Jimmy is seven."

"Your little guy is small, but looks like he's about two?"

Laura glanced at David, absorbed in play with some wooden cars. "He'll turn two in May."

Sister Mary Rachel pointed at two racks of hanging clothes. "Girls' clothes are on the left, and boys on the right. There are tables at the end with underwear and socks. All of our shoes are on shelves along the back of the store." She glanced at a big clock on the wall. "Uh, oh, I'm expecting a delivery in a few minutes. Help yourself, dear, and come find me in my office when you're ready."

"Thank you," Laura said, as the Sister turned away. "Wait. I'm sorry, but I didn't bring money for clothes. I'll have to go home first." Laura felt a flush creeping up her face.

"No need. Pick out what you want. Then we can figure out the cost together and I'll hold it for you until you're ready. And don't forget, we're here to help," Sister Mary Rachel said with a final wave as she disappeared through a door at the back of the store.

Laura checked on David again, then started searching through the stock. The price tags shocked her, since all the clothes looked clean and neat but were only a fraction of the cost for new things. Perhaps she could do this after all. The last time she'd bought clothes for the kids had been before school started. They needed shoes and at least one full outfit each.

"How are you doing?"

Laura jumped, startled by Sister Mary Rachel's voice at her side. "I think I went overboard, but if you can tell me what the total is for this stack, I can figure out what I can afford today and what I'll need to put back." She patted the clothing she'd piled together. "I know it's too much at once, but maybe I could get the rest later."

The Sister scooped everything up and marched toward the front of the store. "Let's see what you've got." She glanced at Laura pacing beside her, and said "Besides, we always give extra discounts for volume. And I like to round the totals out for easy bookkeeping."

Laura watched as the tags added up, squeezing her eyes shut at the total, $19.75. But before she uttered a word, Sister Mary Rachel said, "So, how about we call it an even ten dollars."

The words from her past screamed in her mind, We don't take charity! Somehow the sister must have read her mind, because she said. "Not one word about that discount, now. We have to move our inventory and we want to keep our prices affordable. You've got a lot of stuff here. Can you bring me ten dollars later today or tomorrow morning?"

"Yes ma'am, I'll be back as quick as I can," Laura said, ignoring the insistent "no charity" refrain in her head. "Come on, David."

Only the promise to return kept David from a full-blown tantrum on the way home. Laura pulled a five-dollar bill and five crumpled one-dollar bills out of the mason jar. She'd have to count the contents later, after the children were asleep. But in the meantime, the children would enjoy a special Easter and would not get bullied.

CHAPTER THIRTY-SEVEN

Ashes Seasoned By Failure

Easter Sunday, April 9th, 1939

The kids were excited about their new outfits. Laura had wanted to keep them hidden for a surprise, but decided it was safer to make sure everything fit. When the big day arrived, they left the apartment wearing new clothes and shoes from their skin out.

"Mama, are you wearing that dress?" June looked Laura up and down as they went through the front door. "I thought we'd all be in new outfits today."

Laura scooted David through the door and locked it behind them. "Doesn't matter to

352

me, Junebug. We're going to church, not a
fashion show."

June's furrowed brow showed her
dissatisfaction with that answer, but Laura's
expression didn't invite discussion.

During the eight-block walk to the First
Baptist Church, Laura's thoughts ping-ponged
back-and-forth between pride in her well-
behaved children and hope that she wouldn't
run into Mrs. Brighton. The pastor's wife was a
master at delivering sweet words laced with
subtle poison, all while wearing a self-righteous
smile. She reminded Laura of Glen's Aunt
Gladys, who'd lost every drop of compassion
and kindness in her soul when her twin sons
drowned in a tragic accident several years
before Laura met her. Gladys' mean-spirited
view of church and God had driven a wedge
between Laura and Glen. The final straw was
when she'd struck June and Raymond with tree
branches when they were only five and two,
leaving nasty, bruised welts on their tender
backs. Laura had insisted they leave Dennis and
Gladys's home to protect the children. She'd
been uncomfortable in churches ever since.

About an hour after they got home,
Laura was surprised to hear a knock on their
door. Surprise turned into complete shock when
she opened it. A well-dressed man and woman
stood on the landing. The man held a big box
with a white cloth draped over the top.

"Mrs. Webber?" The woman peered inside, where the children were clustered around Laura.

"Yes," Laura said. "What can I do for you?"

The man chuckled, and the woman said, "We'd like to do something for you. Pastor and Mrs. Brighton noticed you in church this morning, and asked us to add your name to our list of special Easter families. We've brought this whole cooked meal for you, everything from a ham with all the fixings to an apple pie."

Laura's breath seized up so tight it was hard to breathe. She wanted nothing more than to shut the door in these people's faces, but the excited murmur of the children's voices behind her made that impossible. "That's very kind of you." The barbed, wooden words clawed at Laura's throat as she stepped to the side, permitting the man to put the box on the table.

The children gathered around, inhaling the heady aroma of what smelled like a feast. "May we pray with you and your children?" The woman folded her hands in preparation, giving Laura a look that made it impossible to say no."

Laura dipped her chin and clasped her hands, willing her children to follow her lead. They did, and the blessing was short, but Laura didn't hear a word of it. She was lost in the memory of Glen telling her about a Christmas meal given to his family after his father had died. He had burned inside with shame at taking the food, but had been so hungry that he couldn't stop himself from eating. He'd told Laura that he'd vowed from that day on he'd never let his children be in the same position.

All her thoughts stayed locked inside while Laura thanked the couple and escorted them out. She set the table and let the children eat their fill, grateful that they enjoyed such a wonderful meal. But to her, every bite tasted like ashes seasoned by failure.

☙

The weather was beautiful all week, so Laura and the children spent part of each day at the park. "Go run while you can," she said when they arrived on Sunday afternoon. "Back to school tomorrow morning."

"And we get to dress up in our Easter clothes," June said, beaming.

"Only if you promise to be very, very careful and stay clean. No rough-housing in Easter clothes."

The boys acted like they hadn't heard the last words as they raced away. Laura figured they'd change their minds about dressing up rather than risk limiting their activities at recess. Sure enough, when she repeated the warning the next morning, they stuck to clothes they could play in.

"June, enough primping. It's time to go." Laura stepped into the bathroom and took the brush out of her daughter's hands. "You look lovely, but that won't cut any ice with your teacher if you end up being late."

After the children left, she grabbed a blanket and a bucket of things for David to play with, then led him down to the basement. "Okay, little man, let's get you settled so I can work." Hands on her hips, she surveyed the cavernous space, glad that no wet clothes hung from the clotheslines. "At least I don't have to duck under laundry today." Laura swept, wiped off counters and cabinets, and scrubbed the wash tubs and washing machines.

"Go potty," David announced, heading to the stairs.

"Don't you start up those stairs alone." Laura stowed the broom away, then gathered David's things. "At least you waited until I finished."

With David in tow, Laura repeated the process in Charlie's other two buildings. Her energy and David's patience were both gone by the time they finished and made their final trip up the stairs. She fixed peanut-butter and jelly sandwiches, then sent David to bed for a nap.

Doggone it, she was worn to a frazzle. Laura stretched her legs out on the sofa for a few minutes of rest while David slept. Cleaning those basements was hard work. It looked like some of the tenants were leaving their messes for her rather than picking up after themselves. She twisted around, sat on the edge of the couch, and rubbed the bottoms of her feet. Guess she shouldn't complain, since cleaning the basements covered their rent each month."

The thought of their finances sent her to the kitchen, where she reached into the top cabinet for the mason jar. She had long since closed the bank account, so the mason jar was it. Her pulse accelerated when she dumped the contents on the table and began counting. "That can't be right, I must have made a mistake," Laura whispered, then counted the wrinkled bills and stacks of sorted coins twice more, but the total was always the same. "How could we be down to $137.54? No rent or utilities to pay, where did it go?" She thought about all the trips for groceries, cleaning supplies, stamps, and paper and pencils for school. They never amounted to a lot, but added up. "I shouldn't have spent so much for Easter clothes."

Laura pressed her fingertips against her forehead. She had to find a way to bring in more money, or they wouldn't survive. David was too young to leave home alone, and she couldn't pay a babysitter. If Magda knew how desperate they were, she'd volunteer, but it wouldn't be right to take advantage of her.

Three sharp raps on the door surprised Laura. When she opened it, a young, blonde woman, dressed in a smart royal blue linen suit with a pencil skirt and jacket flared at the hips, waited on the other side.

"Hello, I'm Chloe Zimmerman. Mr. Charles Johnson suggested I introduce myself to you," the lady said. "My mother-in-law, Phoebe Zimmerman, lives below you on the second floor."

Laura stepped aside, "Please come in. How can I help you?"

"No, thank you, I'm really in a hurry. I need some assistance with her, and I thought, since you live right here..." The words tapered off. "Mr. Johnson said you might consider helping."

"What kind of help?"

"Laundry is the biggest thing. She can't get around anymore, but I don't have the time to do her laundry. Maybe tidy her place a bit, too." The lady glanced at her watch. "She's my husband's mother and he promised to care for her, but I'm always stuck with doing the work. It's not fair. So, would you help? We'd be happy to pay you."

"Um, Mrs. Zimmerman, I don't know what to say. Can I have a day or so to think about it?"

"Of course." Mrs. Zimmerman reached into her handbag and pulled out a tarnished key attached to an O-ring. "Here's a key to her apartment. Go check her place out, then let me know what you'd be willing to do. I'll be in town Wednesday, so I can stop by and see what you think."

Laura held out her hand for the key, not sure what to say.

"Great," Mrs. Zimmerman said. "I'll come see you in two days. Thank you so much." With that, she turned on her elegant heels and started back down the stairs.

Weird. Was she supposed to just walk in on her neighbor? What kind of woman handed a family-member's house key to a stranger without a second thought?

"Mama, who was that?" David's voice was still thick with sleep, but his eyes were focused on the door.

"Nobody special, sweetie." Laura dropped the key into her skirt pocket. She knelt down for a quick hug, breathing in the special scent of little boy, a mixture of baby sweat, shampoo, and dirt.

After a snack of crackers and cheese, David settled next to Laura on the sofa and watched her sew some buttons and mend a rip in Jimmy's torn pants. They had a scintillating discussion about, well, Laura wasn't sure what, but he was happy until the door burst open so hard the knob slammed into the wall.

June threw her book bag toward the table, not even noticing when it slid to the floor. "I'm never wearing this dress again," she said, tearing the buttons open as fast as she could. "And I'm not ever going back to school either. I'd rather die." She threw her Easter dress on the floor, then pulled her oldest dress from a hook and put it on. "Don't try to make me, Mama, I mean it." With that final pronouncement, she curled her body into the corner of the couch, tears coursing down her face.

Laura's heart ached for June. "Sounds like you had a pretty bad time. Why don't you tell me about it?"

June shook her head no, but Jimmy and Raymond, who'd followed her inside started explaining.

"Florence laughed at June and told everybody that she'd thrown that dress away two years ago." Raymond kept glancing between Laura and June as he started the story.

"Yeah, then all the girls started calling June a ragpicker," Jimmy said. "What's a ragpicker?"

"Oh, honey, I'm sorry." Laura tried to hug June, but was shrugged away. "A ragpicker is someone who collects and sells rags and second-hand things. It's a stupid insulting name, too. Most everybody is happy to have hand-me-downs since times have been tough for years."

"Florence's papa owns lots of buildings. She always has new things. All the girls want to be friends with her," June said, but kept her eyes down. "Even Lizzie called me names, just so Florence would like her."

"I'll bet Lizzie is ashamed of herself now, since you've been friends for such a long time." Laura smoothed June's hair away from her face. "What about Helga?"

"She stayed with me, but didn't say anything to the mean girls. They always pick on her anyway, so she's used to it." June raised her head, "Please, Mama, can't we throw the dress away?"

Laura wrapped her arms around June and held her tight. "I'll figure something out, Junebug, don't you worry."

CHAPTER THIRTY-EIGHT

I Get So Lonely

Tuesday, April 18, 1939

June tried hard to stay home the next morning. First, she pretended to sleep late, then she dawdled over breakfast and getting dressed, finishing up with dramatic coughs to prove she was sick and had a fever, but her entreaties fell on deaf ears. Laura forced her to follow her brothers out the door for school, ignoring the combination of an angry mouth and glistening eyes.

Poor baby, Laura stood at the door and listened as June stomped down the stairs. She'd hated forcing her, but was sure letting bullies win would only make things worse. She scooped up the dress June had left discarded on the bathroom floor. No way could they afford to throw it away, but she could make changes so no one would recognize it.

"Thank goodness for my sewing machine and Rit Dye," Laura said, examining the dress with a critical eye. "You'll be my helper, David, won't you."

David bobbed his head and jumped up and down, ready to go. "Let's get dressed first," Laura said, loving his enthusiasm. "Then we'll head for the store."

When Laura changed out of her house dress, she heard a clank when it hit the floor. She pulled the Zimmerman key out of the dress pocket, and transferred it to her handbag, tucking it next to the apartment key. "Let's go, little man, looks like we have three stops to make today . . . the store, the post office, and Mrs. Zimmerman's place."

David bounced next to Laura, swinging a small paper bag with each step. She had two letters tucked in her pocketbook, and two old newspapers from the store in her hand. She couldn't afford the paper each day, but old ones were available for a penny a copy while they lasted. David had wanted to carry something, so he got the bag with Rit Color Remover and Rit Dye in a pretty celery green color. "Hey, wild man, be careful with that bag," she said when David swung it over his head. "If those boxes break and spill powder all over, you'll be green and we'll both be in trouble."

When they reached the apartment building, Laura took the bag away from him so he could climb the steep steps on his hands and knees. "Go potty," she said when they were inside. "As soon as we clean you up a bit, we're going visiting."

Laura wasn't sure what to do when they stood in front of Mrs. Zimmerman's door. "Charlie told me Mrs. Zimmerman is deaf, but I'd better knock first. If she doesn't answer, guess I can use the key and introduce myself. I'll have to explain why I'm here anyway, but what if she gets mad and tells me to leave?" Laura rubbed her fingers over the sharp edges of the key and tried to decide.

"What?" David said, staring from Laura to the door knob and back.

"Nothing, honey, Mama's talking to herself." Laura rapped the door hard, waited and listened. No response. She waited a few more moments, then knocked again, four hard, sharp blows.

"Who's there?" The voice sounded frail and shaky.

"Mrs. Zimmerman, I'm Laura Webber, your upstairs neighbor. I'd like to talk to you."

"Um, what? I can't hear you." The weak voice was accompanied by a thud-shuffle shuffle, thud-shuffle shuffle sound.

"I'm Laura Webber, your upstairs neighbor. May I come in?"

"Who?"

This was getting nowhere. Laura inserted the key into the keyhole and opened the door. Poking her head inside around the door frame, she saw Mrs. Zimmerman leaning on a cane, her feet encased in shapeless beige knit slippers, a few feet away from the door.

"Mrs. Zimmerman? Your daughter-in-law gave me a key and asked me to check on you." David slipped around Laura's legs, stopping right in front of their neighbor. "Hi," he said with a wave and a grin.

Mrs. Zimmerman's attention shifted from Laura to David. Her cloudy eyes focused on him, and a smile appeared. "My goodness, you are a cutie, aren't you?" She reached out and patted the top of his head with a hand so thin and pale, the skin was almost translucent.

"Thank you, but he can be a handful," Laura said, still holding the door part way open. "May we come inside and visit?"

"Please come in. It's nice to have company." Mrs. Zimmerman turned and made her way across the room, leaning on the cane, then shuffling forward with great care. Once seated on a high-backed, well padded chair covered in blue corduroy, she gestured toward a matching sofa next to her. "Would you like some cookies?" I have some in the cabinet over the sink, if you don't mind getting them."

"That's very kind of you. David is always ready for a cookie." Laura made sure David was settled on the sofa, then walked to the kitchen area. This was a perfect opportunity to check things out. She opened the cupboard and found a glass cookie jar with a few stale looking cookies inside. A tea-towel was spread out on the counter next to the sink with a few clean dishes on top, including a sauce pan and lid. The sink had additional bowls, plates, glasses and spoons in greasy-looking cold water. Empty cans were lined up on the other side of the sink, identified by the labels as chicken noodle soup, green beans, and pears. The lids were still attached by thin strips of tin. She glanced under the sink and found a full trash box surrounded by tiny piles of droppings.

"Sorry to be so slow, but here are the cookies." Laura placed a small plate on the table between Mrs. Zimmerman's chair and the sofa. "It's very sweet of you to share with us."

David glanced at Laura, then grabbed a chocolate chip cookie with both hands. Mrs. Zimmerman smiled at him, but didn't respond to Laura's words.

"May I get David a glass of water to go with the cookie, Mrs. Zimmerman?" This time Laura raised her voice.

"Good idea." Mrs. Zimmerman grabbed the handle of her cane and leaned forward.

Laura patted Mrs. Zimmerman's shoulder, leaning close to be heard. "I can get it. Would you like something to drink as well?"

"Thank you, dear."

Laura filled a glass partway with water for David, then inspected the contents of the tiny refrigerator. She poured out a quart jar of sour milk and a small pitcher of orange juice with spots of mold. The three eggs looked okay, but the vegetables were all wilted. Half a stick of butter, and a partial container of grape jelly were all that remained. She filled another glass of water, peeking in the last cupboard as the faucet ran. All she saw were multiple cans of soup and vegetables, plus a partial loaf of bread.

"Here you go, be careful." Laura placed glasses in front of David and Mrs. Zimmerman. They both used two hands to hold their glasses.

She watched her son and neighbor as they smiled, enthralled with each other. Both looked so vulnerable and innocent. Mrs. Zimmerman's gray hair was matted in the back, but stuck out on top and around her face like errant blades of grass. Her skin was covered with fine wrinkles like ancient parchment, the color fading into the washed-out pink of her nightgown. Her smile revealed teeth in desperate need of brushing, while the sour scent from her body made it clear neither she nor her clothing had been washed in a very long time.

How on earth could someone let their mother live in such squalor? This poor woman wasn't mean or unpleasant. She needed human company and basic care. "Mrs. Zimmerman, can David and I come visit you more often? He'd love it, and I could help you a little, if you didn't mind."

"What did you say? Sometimes I have trouble hearing."

Laura repeated herself two more times before she was understood.

Mrs. Zimmerman clasped her hands to her chest. "Would you? That would be lovely. Come anytime." She looked down at David, then back up at Laura. "I get so lonely sometimes."

Laura couldn't resist leaning in to give Mrs. Zimmerman a gentle hug when she and David stood up to leave. David hugged his new friend, too. "Careful now, don't squeeze too hard," she told him.

Mrs. Zimmerman reached for her cane, ready to escort them to the door. "That's okay, we can let ourselves out and lock the door. You stay comfortable." Laura patted Mrs. Zimmerman's cold hands, then retrieved a quilt from the sofa and draped it around her thin, hunched shoulders.

"We'll be back soon."

Once back upstairs, David headed straight to bed for his nap, while Laura focused her attention on June's dress. She decided to strip the color first, then dye it green. The rounded Peter Pan collar could be changed to one with pointed ends, she could eliminate the sash tie, and change the buttons. She had some sandy colored grosgrain ribbon to add a bow in front at the neckline, then edge the puff sleeves and circle the waistline. Brass buttons from her button box could replace the fabric ones and complete the transformation.

"Good thing that boy sleeps like a rock," Laura muttered to herself as she slipped out the front door with the dress. "I'll put this in the basement with the Rit stuff until I can sneak away later to start working on it. Neither of my boys can keep a secret. We don't need them blabbing at school."

CHAPTER THIRTY-NINE

Pretty Is As Pretty Does

"Beans and cornbread again?" June stood near the table, hands on her hips, and looked to Raymond for back-up. "And not even any butter or honey to go with it?"

"I like beans," Jimmy said. When June glared at him, he added, "But I want something different, too."

"So do I," Laura snapped. "But we all have to eat what I can put on the table and be grateful for it." She stared at June and Raymond. "Truth is, we're darn lucky to even have beans and cornbread. I don't want to hear another complaint about food. We have to cut expenses to the bone as it is after all we spent on

Easter clothes." Laura could feel herself ramping up. She bit her lip hard to stop the flow of angry words that threatened to spill out of her mouth. She paused, then said. "I get tired of having the same old things, too, but I don't have any choice and neither do you."

No more discussion took place during dinner, but each child ate two full bowls of beans and their fill of the bread. Laura took her time emptying one small bowl and ate just a sliver of cornbread. She might not be able to provide much variety, but no way would her children go to bed hungry.

Once the children were asleep, Laura tiptoed out the door and hurried down to the basement. "Thank goodness I replaced all the lights down here." Laura mumbled under her breath, headed for the storage cabinet where she'd stashed the Rit bag and the dress. "I'd have broken my neck on those stairs in the dark." She opened the top of the washing machine nearest the stairs and started filling it with hot water. The steam wafted around her face as she opened the color remover and sprinkled the powder in the washer. She waited until it dissolved, dropped the dress in and watched the agitator turn and tumble the fabric. "Should be done in about twenty minutes. Sure hope it works." Laura put the lid back on and climbed up the steep stairs. "If I dye it tomorrow and start sewing the next day, June should be able to wear her new dress in two days tops."

Before the children woke the next morning, Laura ran to the basement to check on the dress. Still damp, but at least all the color was gone. "Fantastic. That white is so nice and even, the dye should set real well tonight."

"Mrs. Webber, are you home?" The words followed hard knocks on the door.

"Coming," Laura hollered from the bathroom where she was on her knees in front of the tub, wiping Bon Ami cleanser off her hands. She'd been so caught up in housework that she'd forgotten about Chloe Zimmerman's plan to come by. "Good afternoon, Mrs. Zimmerman. Sorry it took me a few minutes to get to the door."

Mrs. Zimmerman sniffed as she entered the apartment, pulled her arms in tight and hugged her purse close under her elbow. "Did you find time to visit my mother-in-law and look around her apartment?"

Laura had never felt so dowdy in front of someone in her life. Her housedress was stained and damp from the work she'd been doing, her hands were red and chapped, and strands of her hair hung loose from the bun she'd secured that morning. "Yes, I looked around yesterday when David and I visited her." She paused, trying to find the right words to convey the awful state the elderly Mrs. Zimmerman was in without offending this woman. A little extra money would help a lot. "She seemed so lonely, and the apartment needs a good airing out and thorough cleaning. It also looked like she's in dire need of food and supplies." Laura bit her tongue, wanting to say much more.

"Well, my husband and I visit her whenever we can, but his job is very demanding, and I spend a lot of time working with local charities. I can arrange an open account with Mr. Jackson's store, even delivery service for her purchases. We'd like you to handle the cleaning and laundry for her, if you're interested."

"I'm interested. I'll have to care for her around my family's needs, but I'm sure it can be done." Laura hesitated, rubbing her damp palms down the sides of her dress. "What did you have in mind for payment? She's a sweet lady, but caring for her will be a lot of work."

"Well, my husband said he'll pay five dollars a week, which works out to about two hours a day, five days a week. Will that be satisfactory for you?"

"I think so. If you can set things up with Mr. Jackson, I'll make a list of what she needs this afternoon."

"Good, that's settled." Mrs. Zimmerman reached behind her and opened the door. "Tomorrow's Friday, my regular day for luncheon with the Aurora Women's Auxiliary. I'll stop by after we meet and bring you three dollars for this week. Then I'll stop by each Friday and pay you." She stepped outside and headed down the stairs without a backward glance.

Laura stared out the door, wishing she didn't need money. No way she'd work for that rude woman, otherwise. She whirled around, almost falling over David. "Whoa, little man. You almost tripped me."

He pointed at the door. "Pretty lady."

Laura grimaced. "Pretty is as pretty does, sunshine, so she's not very pretty at all." She scooted him toward where he'd been playing, and headed back to the bathroom. "I've got to finish cleaning, then you and I will go downstairs to see Mrs. Zimmerman."

Once again, Laura had to use the key to let them into the apartment. This time they found Mrs. Zimmerman asleep on a chair, mouth gaping open, each exhale a soft snore.

"David, no." Laura's sharp whisper stopped him from running toward his new friend. "Let her sleep. Come sit at the table and have a cookie while I make some notes." She settled him in place with two cookies and orders to stay still, and began taking inventory of the kitchen and bathroom.

"No wonder she's so tiny. A bird could starve to death in this place." Laura slapped the paper and pencil on the table. "And this apartment needs a thorough scrubbing from top to bottom. I can't imagine her daughter-in-law doing that kind of work, so no telling how long it's been since the last cleaning."

"A bird?" David looked around. "I like birds."

"No sweetie, no birds here." Laura patted his arm. "I'm talking to myself again."

The sound of Mrs. Zimmerman clearing her throat sent Laura to her side. "Hi, we've come to visit again." Laura shouted next to her ear, then watched awareness creep into cloudy eyes.

"So nice to see you." Mrs. Zimmerman rocked forward, reaching for the cane that leaned at her side.

Loud thumps, accompanied by noisy talking and laughter, approached the landing. "Be right back." Laura hurried to the door and opened it as her children started up the next flight of stairs. "Hold on, there's someone I want you to meet."

She herded them into the apartment, where they joined David in front of the blue chair. "Mrs. Zimmerman, I'd like you to meet my other children." Each child dipped their chin in turn. "Since I'll be helping you from now on, you'll be seeing them, too."

After the introductions, Laura sent all four children upstairs to wait for her. She finished her inventory, warmed a bowl of canned stew and placed it on the table, then left.

The kids were curious about their elderly neighbor, but irritated to get only cold sandwiches, canned fruit cocktail, and milk for dinner.

"Last night I fixed you a hot meal and heard nothing but complaints. I'm going to help care for Mrs. Zimmerman to earn a little extra money for us, so I won't have as much time to cook." Laura's words were sharper than she intended because they were laced with guilt.

After the children fell asleep, Laura crept down to the basement to dye June's dress. Once the powder dissolved in hot water, she filled the machine half-full and added the garment. Since it took a full wash cycle to complete the dye process, she sat in an old metal chair with her eyes closed, head resting against the wall. "I sure hope this works. Poor June, those rotten, spoiled girls gave her such a hard time."

Laura jerked awake, shocked to find that the washer had long since finished the cycle. She fed the dress through the ringer, then shook it out and hung it on the line. She crossed her fingers and hoped it would look as good in the morning sunshine as it did under the ceiling lightbulb. Dragging herself up the stairs, Laura wanted nothing more than sleep.

The apartment was quiet and dark when she entered, lit only by moonlight through the window. She sat down at the table, kicked off her shoes, then stretched her ankles and toes. Her eyes focused on sheets of paper she'd tossed to the middle of the table, one with Mrs. Zimmerman's food and supply inventory, and the other a list of urgent cleaning chores. Tomorrow she'd see the arrogant daughter-in-law to review the notes and make the first shopping trip for her neighbor. Tomorrow she also needed to sweep and dust the three basements, make a decent dinner for her family, and start working on June's dress after the kids went to bed.

That was a lot of tasks for one day, but no way around any of them. She hoped she wouldn't regret accepting the job of helping Mrs. Zimmerman. They were in desperate need of income, so somehow she'd have to make it work, no matter what.

CHAPTER FORTY

The Scent of Cake Perfumed The Air
Monday, May 22, 1939

L aura and the daughter-in-law's, she couldn't bring herself to call the woman anything else, first Friday meeting set the tone for them all. Laura outlined Mrs. Zimmerman's needs, got an approval for the shopping list, then received her three dollar payment in cash. Mrs. Zimmerman made no lingering comments or suggestions, just a rapid departure because of the pressing needs of her busy schedule.

Laura and David spent an hour or so downstairs every morning after breakfast.

Sometimes one or more of the other children would join them on the weekends, since Laura couldn't stand leaving Mrs. Zimmerman alone for two full days. She devoted many extra hours to her care, including doing laundry, shopping for food and supplies, and random visits just to make sure Mrs. Zimmerman was safe in her home. Laura knew she deserved a raise to cover the additional hours, but didn't ask because she feared risking the only income she had.

June's Easter dress project was only a partial success. The alterations to the dress were lovely, but couldn't reverse the damage to June's school reputation and relationships with the other girls. Her former best friend, Lizzie, hurt June the most trying to cement her friendship with Florence, the primary tormentor, by taunting June all the time. Only Helga, a fellow outcast, remained steadfast at June's side. It hurt Laura's heart to see her daughter trudge off to school, miserable, each morning, when she'd loved school before. Understanding the cause for June's pain and her frequent outbursts of temper didn't make them any easier to handle. Raymond and Jimmy didn't understand why June was so moody, so spats between them were much more frequent than usual.

"Spoon?" David's little hand shot toward the mixing spoon resting in the bowl on the tiny kitchen counter.

"Go to the table and I'll give you the spoon and bowl." Laura popped the sheet cake pan and a tin cup of batter into the oven and set the wind-up kitchen timer. "It's your birthday cake, little man, so you get the spoon and the bowl all to yourself."

David scrambled down from the chair where he'd watched Laura prepare the batter. Seconds later, ensconced at his place at the table, he stared at the bowl and spoon filmed with creamy batter. Not taking any chances that Laura might change her mind, he grabbed the spoon and started licking.

Laura ruffled his hair, then kissed the top of his head. "Enjoy, sweetheart. Tomorrow you turn two, not a baby any longer." She watched him savor every sweet drop that reached his mouth, while ignoring the drips that ran down his fingers and streaked the lower part of his face.

"I done." David licked all the way up the spoon handle, tossed it into the metal bowl, then started climbing down from the chair.

"Oh, no, you're not." Laura swooped in with a wet rag. "Don't you dare move until we get you cleaned up."

The sweet scent of fresh cake still perfumed the air when the children came home from school. "I want a piece," Raymond said. "That smells good."

"My cake." David ran to the counter, putting his body between the cooling dessert and his brothers and sister.

"It's David's birthday tomorrow, so no cake until we celebrate with Magda's family tomorrow." She removed a big, covered pot from the refrigerator and set it on the back burner of the stove. When this chicken soup heats up, we'll have dinner. If you're all good tonight, you can share the icing spoon and bowl after I decorate the cake."

"What's this?" June pointed to the warm tin cup filled with cake.

"That's for Mrs. Zimmerman. She can't handle stairs, so David and I will deliver it in the morning. That way she can be part of his birthday celebration."

The promise of a party with the Cohen family kept the mood cheerful and upbeat all evening. David, almost giddy with excitement, dropped off to sleep with a grin. June was the last still awake, curled up on the sofa, watching Laura put the dishes away. "David sure is happy about his birthday." June rolled onto her back, head resting on her crossed arms. "Mine's coming soon, just over a week away."

"Yes, it is." Laura slipped the damp dish towel over the oven handle, then joined June on the sofa. She lifted June's feet onto her lap, rested her head against the couch back and her bare feet on the table. "Eleven years old. Can't hardly believe it."

"Me, either." June appeared deep in thought. "Only two more years and I'll be a teenager."

"Please, time's passing fast enough without talking about that."

"Okay," June said. "But can you make me a chocolate birthday cake? With chocolate icing. I know we can't afford a present, but I love chocolate. And pink candles. Pink is my new favorite color."

Laura grimaced inside, knowing she'd have to buy a tin of cocoa and try to find some pink candles. "I'll do my best, Junebug."

The next morning, after the older children left for school, Laura and David headed downstairs to Mrs. Zimmerman's apartment. Laura carried the tin cup, decorated with colored frosting just like the big one, then handed it to David when they reached her door.

"Mizerman, Mizerman," he sang out as soon as they were inside the door. "It's my birthday. We brought you cake." Holding the cup in outstretched arms, he ran straight to her. She took the cake and set it on the table by her chair for later, then wrapped her arms around him. He prattled on and on while she clapped her hands and smiled, both delighted with the other's company.

While David and Mrs. Zimmerman entertained one another, Laura stripped the bed and remade it, then tied all the dirty laundry inside one of the sheets and put the bundle by the front door. She pulled the garbage container out from under the kitchen cabinet and dumped the contents into a paper grocery bag, together with trash retrieved from throughout the apartment. Her last chore was cleaning the kitchen.

"David, stay here while I run to the basement." Laura, confident he wouldn't miss her, pushed the laundry and trash outside and locked the door behind her. She carried the garbage while kicking the tied bundle of laundry in front of her all the way down the stairs. Laura left the dirty clothes by the washers and dumped the trash into a large bin. She hoped the washers would be empty when they got back from the park, or it'd be a very long evening.

"You made it, come on in." June pulled Helga through the door and over to the sofa. Magda and Harvey followed the girls inside, but turned toward the kitchen area.

Laura welcomed them, but was pushed aside by David. "Come see my cake." He led them to the table, climbed up on a chair, and pointed to the green lettering on the white icing. "See my name? I two." He held up two fingers, almost dancing with excitement.

Magda hugged him tight. "Yes you are. Gettink bigger every day."

Since David was so wound up, Laura lit the two candles and everyone sang Happy Birthday. "Blow out the candles and make a wish." She blew with him just to make sure. "Okay, it's time for cake." Laura placed generous pieces on saucers and plates, handing out spoons and forks with them. The adults sat at the table, while the children perched on the sofa and at the coffee table.

"Can we play outside? Sitting in here is boring." Raymond finished his cake first and headed for the door, Jimmy on his heels.

"Why don't we head to the park? That way the kids can run and play, and you ladies can gossip to your heart's content." Harvey winked at Raymond. "I can stop and get the soccer ball from our place if you'd like."

They made the trip to the park in record time. Laura and Magda relaxed on a bench, leaning back against the edge of a picnic table. A basket with two jars of water and the remains of the cake sat behind them.

Harvey's soccer ball was a hit, making him the center of continuous games with the boys. June and Magda played when they first arrived, but soon switched to walking around, talking and giggling.

"Your Harvey is wonderful with the boys," Laura said. "And such energy. He's running right along with them. I would've dropped by now."

Magda giggled. "He'll feel old tonight." She watched Harvey zig zag around the boys. "Vee alvays talked about havink lots of children because vee bozh love zem, but now? Poor Helga schtill has nightmares. Vee tried to protect her vhen we left, but she saw and heard awful zinks she can't forget."

Laura wrapped her arm around Magda's shoulder and hugged her. "I'm so sorry. I wish there was something we could do to help." Laura rubbed Magda's back. "I'm just grateful that Helga and June have each other."

Magda's smile flickered, then disappeared. "It isn't just vorry about Helga, vee are so afraid for our friends and family schtill in Germany. My cousin, Solomon Weiss, sent us letters every couple of veeks since vee escaped. He always let us know vhat was happenink. Lots of people, entire families of Jews, are being rounded up and taken avay by the *Schutzstaffel,* you call them the SS. No one knows for sure, but rumors say zey're goink to big camps, and zat no one ever comes back."

Laura's breath caught as she searched for words. She squeezed Magda's fingers instead.

"Vee haven't heard from Solomon in almost two monzs. Harvey's written to him, but. . ." Magda's lower lip trembled. She took a deep breath and continued. "Ve're so scared for him."

Both women rearranged their faces into smiles when they saw Harvey and the boys coming their way. June and Magda lagged behind. Tired out, Harvey and the kids drank the last of the water and finished the cake.

"You boys wore me out," Harvey said. "I need to go home and hit the sack." He winked at Magda and Laura. "Are you ladies ready to leave?"

In minutes, the basket was packed and everyone was ready, tired but contented. By the time they reached the edge of the park, David had reached his limit. "I tired, Mama. Carry me." He was sweaty and covered with dust.

"Little man, we'll go slow, but you have to walk this time." Laura stepped around his body, ignoring the upraised arms. "I've got the basket, honey, and can't carry you, too."

David took a deep breath, but before he could let out a wail, Harvey swept him up on his shoulders. "Give your mama a break, birthday boy." The threatened cry turned into a delighted squeal.

"You don't have to carry him," Laura said. "You've worn yourself to a frazzle keeping up with kids today." Harvey just grinned, holding David's grubby knees on his shoulders.

David rode all the way to Harvey and Magda's building, then hugged the three Cohens when they parted ways. Renewed by the ride, he held tight to Jimmy's hand the rest of the way home.

~⊶~

Once the kids were asleep, Laura was ready to finish a lovely day with a hot bath before bed. She shut herself into the bathroom and perched on the side of the tub. After leaning down and pushing the plug into the drain, she remembered the laundry stacked next to the washing machines. She tried to come up with a fantastic excuse to wait until morning, but failed. Groaning, she stuffed her tired feet into slippers and headed downstairs.

When both washers were churning away, Laura pulled a wooden box in front of a dusty overstuffed chair and sat. She rested her feet on the box, closed her eyes and wiggled around, hoping to nap a little during the washer cycles.

Pain in Laura's neck and shoulder woke her up. "What the heck?" Disoriented and cramped from sleeping in the chair, it took her a few moments to remember where she was. The washers were cold, with wet fabric wrapped in tight, stiff ropes around the agitators. "I must have slept for an awful long time." She fed the wet bedding through the wringer, where it dropped into a basket. She repeated the process with the contents of the second machine, then grabbed a bag of clothespins. Her arms felt leaden by the time she finished hanging all the wet clothes.

"Boy, I sure wished we lived on the ground floor right about now," Laura whispered, pulling herself up the first flight of stairs. By the time she dragged her exhausted body through the door, all thoughts of a hot bath disappeared, pushed aside by the need for sleep.

CHAPTER FORTY-ONE

What I Wouldn't Give For A Nap

"Mama, are you sick?" June shook Laura awake the next morning. Laura jerked her head up, grimacing when a sharp pain lanced through her neck and the side of her face. "No, of course not. I must have slept wrong." She climbed to her feet and glanced at the clock. "Oh, my word, I overslept. Wake your brothers up while I get breakfast started."

Crazy chaos reigned, but the kids left on time for school. After the door slammed behind them, Laura sank into a chair next to David, who was making designs in the syrup on his plate. "Can't believe they made it, and without a single argument." Laura shook her head and winced. In spite of moving around and stretching, the side of her head and neck still ached. She rubbed her temples, surprised that her skin felt warm and damp. She'd better not be getting sick, she had way too much to do.

Laura picked up David's breakfast dishes and carried them to the sink. "Come on, little man, we've got a full day ahead of us." She felt woozy, but figured it was because she hadn't eaten. The kids had finished all the pancakes she'd cooked. No time to make more for herself. She finished June's glass of milk, instead.

Laura gathered their laundry and tied it in bundles. She needed to do it today, after putting it off since Monday. David was in high spirits, eager to help push one of the piles downstairs. "I do it by myself," he insisted, shoving her hands away.

Laura gave in, positioning herself and the first bundle a few steps below him. "Okay, go ahead and push it," she said, ready to catch him if he slipped. Of all the days for him to assert his independence, it had to be the one day she felt terrible and needed to hurry.

It took much longer to reach the basement than usual, but David was so proud of himself that Laura couldn't scold him. "Great job, but I need to do the rest. Go play." She waved him to the shelf that held some boxes and blocks. Cleaning around the hanging laundry slowed her down, but at least she was able to start two loads in the washers. She checked Mrs. Zimmerman's hanging laundry, but it hadn't dried, which meant another trip in the afternoon.

By the time they finished cleaning the other basements, hung up her first two loads of wet clothes and started washing two more, she was dragging. David led the way upstairs, still full of energy and eager to see Mrs. Zimmerman. "Whoa, boy." Laura scooped him away from the second floor apartment door. "I need a break first and you need a bite of lunch."

"Mizerman needs lunch, too," David said, trying to reach for the doorknob.

"Yes, and we'll help her in a little while." She pulled him toward the last flight of stairs and started climbing.

Thirty minutes later, Laura stood at Mrs. Zimmerman's door once again, David bouncing up and down beside her. When the key clicked the lock open, he pushed past her calling out, "Mizerman, I here."

Glass hit the floor with a crash. "Oh no," Mrs. Zimmerman cried. "You scared me. Now look what I've done." She stood next to the kitchen counter, a broken milk bottle at her feet, milk puddling around her slippers.

"Don't move." Laura wrapped her arm around frail shoulders and guided Mrs. Zimmerman to her favorite chair. "I'm sorry we startled you, but David's been anxious to see you." She motioned her wide-eyed son forward. "It was an accident. You two visit and I'll take care of the mess."

Laura made sure Mrs. Zimmerman hadn't cut herself, then cleaned the wet, milk-smeared soles of her slippers. After she picked up the glass, she had to clean the spill area and the sticky footprints between the kitchen and chair, before she tackled the routine bathroom and kitchen chores. David stayed next to the chair, making silly faces and gestures that kept Mrs. Zimmerman clapping and laughing the entire time Laura worked.

After what seemed like hours, she wrung out the cleaning rag for the last time and hung it over the edge of the tub to dry. She stretched, leaned back, and wished the aspirin she'd taken earlier had helped more. She ached all over and her right ear pulsed with pain. "What I wouldn't give for a nap," Laura whispered to herself. "But that's not gonna happen."

The lure of a short nap drew Laura up the stairs, but the clatter of the older children's shoes behind her on the steps drove the dream away. All three talked at once, almost shouting, the sound like nails piercing her forehead. Laura held the door open for the kids and said,

"Enough, please. I can't understand when you all talk at once. Put your stuff away and change clothes, then you can talk one at a time."

June finished first and rushed to Laura's side on the sofa. "It wasn't Jimmy's fault. He was in the nurse's office and had no idea someone took his things."

Raymond joined them by the sofa and said, "It was Nathan's fault, he's Delbert's brother. Actually, it's Delbert's fault because Nathan always does what he says, and he has it in for me and June." Raymond wrapped his arm around Jimmy, who had joined the others. "Delbert's scared of us, so he sicced Nathan on Jimmy."

Jimmy's face, bruised and swollen from his forehead to below his eyes, had a comma of dried blood below one nostril. "I'm sorry, Mama, the nurse made me lay down. I sneaked out and ran back to the playground when she left, but I was too late."

"Stop." Laura thrust her palms out. "Jimmy, what happened to your face? And what in the world are you talking about being too late?"

"It was that Nathan..." Laura's glare stopped June mid-sentence.

"The tetherball hit me in the face," Jimmy said. "It knocked me down and really hurt." His glance cut to Raymond at his side. "I wasn't playing, just walked by the pole when the ball whipped around and hit me." Jimmy sniffed and stared at his feet. "The yard teacher helped me up and walked me to the nurse's office, but I forgot to grab my lunchbox and library book. My class got to check books out in the library today, and when it was time for lunch, I took mine with me to share with Tommy and Willie."

"It wasn't his fault. Some kids told me they heard Delbert bragging about Nathan swinging the tetherball into Jimmy's face and then throwing his lunchbox and book in the trash while he was with the nurse." The words tumbled out of Raymond's mouth as fast as he could speak.

Laura took a deep breath, smoothed Jimmy's hair back, then cradled his face in her hands.

"So, first you were attacked and knocked to the ground, and then when the nurse tended to your face, someone stole your lunchbox and library book?"

Tears pooled in Jimmy's eyes as he bobbed his head.

"And you two thought I'd be mad at him for letting his things get stolen?" Laura said to Raymond and June. Laura closed her eyes a moment. "The only person I'm mad at is the one that hurt Jimmy. If he was in reach, I'd take a switch to him and his nasty parents for not teaching their bratty children how to behave."

The kids looked shocked at her words, then grinned. "The principal should make his parents pay for your things, but I'll bet there weren't any witnesses to prove he did it. We'll find a way to replace them, even if it isn't fair."

Dinner was fast and simple, peas, turnips, and fried bologna with ketchup. The kids were subdued, but Jimmy stayed close to Laura all evening instead of playing with the others. "Jimmy, would you help me get Mrs. Zimmerman's laundry from the basement?"

"Sure." he jumped to his feet and headed to the door.

All the clotheslines in the basement were full, and Laura still needed to hang her own two loads from the washers. Laura stood next to the line with Mrs. Zimmerman's sheets. "I'll pull the clothespins off, you be ready to take the clean clothes and put them on the table for folding." Soon they both sat on chairs next to the table, ready for Laura to fold. "Thanks for your help, honey. Now, how about telling me what's bothering you?"

Jimmy shrugged and looked at his lap.

"I know there's more, you've been looking at me all night ready to bust out with something." Laura lifted his chin. "Please tell me. I won't be mad. I promise."

Jimmy cleared his throat, glancing all around the room before meeting her eyes. "Remember I told you I went to the nurse? She cleaned my face and put an ice pack on it, then told me to rest a little while in the room behind where the office lady, Miss Abbott, sits. I heard them talking about what happened to me." Jimmy swallowed and hunched his shoulders. "Miss Abbott said she wasn't surprised we get picked on, since everybody in town knows Papa is crazy and a dangerous criminal." He bagan to speak faster as if the words tasted bad in his mouth. "The nurse said he wasn't crazy, just shell-shocked from the war. But Miss Abbott said that was proof of a weak mind, since the war was a long time ago and he should have gotten over it by now."

"What a hateful, nasty thing to say." Laura's nostrils flared and her lips tightened. "She doesn't know what she's talking about."

"But you said Papa hurt someone, and that's why they're keeping him locked up."

"Yes, but he just wanted to come home."

Jimmy climbed down from the chair and wrapped his arms around Laura. "Do you think they'll ever let him go? I miss Papa so much."

"I don't know, honey. I just don't know." Laura soothed Jimmy with her voice and touch, but inside she seethed. What she wouldn't give to tell those two biddies off. How dare they talk about her family with her injured son just a few feet away? What did they know about a soldier's suffering after fighting in war? Her energy fueled by anger, Laura finished doing laundry in record time.

CHAPTER FORTY-TWO

I Can't Lose My Hearing

Thursday, June 1, 1939

Once again Magda and Laura sat on a park bench, leaned back against the table, and watched their families play in the park. June's birthday was the occasion, and the children had finished every chocolate cake crumb before they left to play.

Magda tilted her head toward Laura. "How are you feelink? You look kind of peaked."

"I'm trying hard not to spoil the party, but this earache is killing me."

Magda patted Laura's back. "I'm so sorry. Earaches are the worst. Have you tried varm oil to ease the pain?"

"Yes, but it hasn't helped much," Laura said. "By bedtime, I'm hurting so bad it's almost impossible to fall asleep. I just want to rip it off." A slight breeze stirred the warm air, causing her to cup her right hand over the infected ear to block out the pain. "What about you? Have you heard from your cousin Solomon?"

"Yes, but I'm even more vorried. He was one of many Jews rounded up in Pankow, the section of Berlin ve're from. Unlike most of zem, he believed ze rumors about mass murders and death camps. He escaped at the train station with four ozer men vhen the guards' veren't lookink."

"Where did they go? Is he still in Germany?"

"The Nazis caught zree of the men and schot them. Solomon and one ozer man made it to the forest and got away."

"Oh, my goodness? Where are they now?"

Magda's chin trembled, "I don't know. Zey headed to Hamburg to get on a schip out of Germany, but the ozer fellow, Hans, was captured and killed by Nazis. Zey'd bought tickets on a schip headed for Cuba, but Solomon escaped. He mailed a letter after he left the port, but ve don't know vhere he is now. "

June's excited shout broke into their conversation. "Mama, Helga brought jacks and her papa says he'll play with us." June and Helga ran toward the table. Harvey jogged with David on his shoulders. Raymond and Jimmy ran alongside.

"Harvey plays jacks?" Laura's eyebrows rose toward her hairline. "Never met a man who could play jacks."

Magda chuckled. "He plays better zan me. Beats Helga most of the time, too. He makes up crazy rounds zat get us laughink every time." Magda cleared the table, shoving everything into Laura's picnic basket.

Harvey sat on one side of the table, with a boy on each side. Laura and Magda sat across from them, with David in the middle. June and Helga sat cross-legged on top of the table, one on each end.

"Are you two ready to get beaten?" Harvey said, jacks in one hand and the ball in the other.

"No way," June said. "Helga is the best jacks player in school."

Helga rolled her eyes. "Who do you think taught me how to play?"

"Let's play ... tongue touch." Harvey shook the jacks and looked back and forth between the two giggling girls. He put one jack piece down and said, "Throw the ball, grab the jack, stick out your tongue and touch it with the jacks, then catch the ball." He demonstrated the technique, sticking his tongue out as far as it would go. "If you're afraid to touch the jacks, you can touch your thumb instead, but it doesn't count if we can't see your tongue sticking all the way out."

David couldn't stop giggling, and together with his brothers, stuck his tongue out every time it was Harvey's turn. Magda and Laura cheered both girls as they played, but kept their tongues inside their mouths. Harvey beat the girls, but they claimed the giggling slowed them down.

The silly game was the perfect end to June's birthday celebration. Everyone's spirits were high on the way home. Since the next day was the last day of the school term, the children didn't even fuss when it was time for bed.

It took Laura a lot longer to fall asleep. She opened all the windows to catch any stray breezes, in hopes of cooling the cramped space. She was tired, but when she put her head down on her towel covered pillow, the pressure and pain increased in her ear no matter which side she had down. In desperation, she heated some oil and used an eyedropper to fill her infected ear canal. With her good ear on the pillow to give the oil a chance to work, the warmth helped, but the awful pressure and fullness made her wish she could claw deep inside her head and rip it open.

A few hours later, something crawled on Laura's cheek, intruding into her restless sleep. She slapped at the wiggling sensation and was shocked into full wakefulness when she encountered a line of thick, foul-smelling liquid coursing over her cheek. She sat up, grabbed the towel to wipe the disgusting stuff off her skin, and discovered that the pain was gone.

"Oh thank god, it's burst." She ran to the bathroom to clean up, careful to stay quiet and not wake the children. Once back on her mattress, she slipped into the best sleep she'd had in weeks.

〜🦇〜

Laura woke up to June shaking her shoulder. She sat up and heard June say, "Mama, are you okay? I've been yelling and yelling at you. It's late and we're all up already."

"I'm sorry. Guess I was sleeping really hard," Laura said. She stood and gave June a quick hug. "You guys get yourselves ready and I'll fix something quick to eat. You don't need lunches since today's a short day."

While Laura made her way to the basement to start cleaning, she kept thinking about how June had shaken her awake. Why hadn't she heard June calling? She'd never been so deep asleep before that they'd needed to shake her. Could her hearing have been affected? And if so, would it repair itself?

David headed straight to his favorite corner to play while Laura grabbed the broom and dustpan. Once he was absorbed in his play, she moved to the folding table, pressed her right hand tight against her ear, and rapped her left knuckles on the table. The taps were sharp and clear. She covered the left ear and tried it again, but heard nothing. Her heart raced, and her stomach rolled. "Oh, no, I can't lose my hearing. Please, God, haven't I lost enough? Not my hearing, too," she whispered.

CHAPTER FORTY-THREE

Divorce Him

July 1939

"Sure wish we were still on the farm," Laura said to herself in the mirror. The kids weren't awake yet, but beads of sweat already lined her hairline and upper lip. She rubbed cold water on her face and neck, then brushed her teeth and hair. "Caring for animals and a garden was hard, but at least we spent lots of time outside. Now the overgrown bit of grass out front is all the kids have."

Laura padded into the kitchen area, stepping around the chipped, circular base of a big fan that stood in the center of the room. When she turned it on, the circular face swung back and forth between the open bedroom door to the sofa where June slept. It was loud, but the moving air would make the place more comfortable.

What could she make for breakfast? No milk, eggs, or bacon, and just a tiny amount of butter was left. Looked like toast and honey, plus the last of their canned applesauce. Tomorrow's shopping list would be a long one, and would cost more than the five dollars she'd get for tending to Mrs. Zimmerman. She tried so hard to not spend more on food than she earned, but almost never made it.

"Morning, Mama." June stood in front of the fan, arms extended and eyes closed as her nightgown ballooned in the rushing air. "Can I spend the day with Helga? Mrs. Cohen says I'm always welcome."

"After lunch. While David and I are downstairs helping Mrs. Zimmerman, you and your brothers need to strip the beds and take all the dirty clothes down to the basement by the washing machines. After that, the three of you can sweep, dust, and take the trash to the dumpster out back."

"But it's summer vacation." June's complaint was loud and insistent. "We worked hard all year in school. It's not fair to make us work even more, now."

Raymond and Jimmy slipped out of the bedroom to June's side.

"I can add to the list if you want to keep talking back," Laura said. "You don't have animal chores or gardening now, but I can come up with more cleaning if you want to keep talking."

Raymond and Jimmy stepped away from June, as if to distance themselves from Laura's threat. "We didn't say anything," Raymond said, while Jimmy nodded at his side. David drifted out of the bedroom to join his brothers.

"Smart boys. After breakfast I want you to help June with the list of chores I gave her. When they're done, you're free to play all afternoon."

After finishing with Mrs. Zimmerman and releasing the children to join their friends, Laura changed into a day dress and headed for the post office. David skipped beside her, enjoying the adventure. No mail, and Mr. Niedermann was deep in conversation with someone about adding to their stamp collection. When they pushed the door open to leave, Laura took David's hand and changed directions. "This way, big guy. We're going to take a few minutes and see if Dr. Farnsworth is in his office. I need some answers."

No one was in the waiting room at the doctor's office, so Laura marched up to the desk where an unfamiliar nurse was sitting. "Good morning, ma'am, I'm Mrs. Webber. Is Dr. Farnsworth available?"

"Good morning, I'm Miss Bolton. Do you have an appointment?"

"No, but if I could just have a few minutes of his time. I have a couple of questions."

The nurse pursed her lips and peered over her glasses. "When the doctor is working on paperwork in his office, he doesn't like to be disturbed. Can you tell me what this is about?"

Laura cast about for a subject, not wanting to explain anything about Glen to this woman. "I've lost the hearing in my right ear after a nasty infection, and wonder if it will come back."

Miss Bolton sighed, poked her pencil into the tight bun at the nape of her neck, then heaved her considerable bulk out of the chair. "I'll check with him. Please wait here."

When Miss Bolton returned, her cheeks were flushed and her lips formed a thin line. "Come on back. He'll see you now."

Dr. Farnsworth examined Laura's ear, then leaned back in his chair. "Looks like your eardrum burst from the pressure of a middle ear infection. Left a pretty bad tear. Plus there's scarring indicative of perforations from past ear infections."

Laura nodded. "I've had ear infections before, but this one was the worst."

Dr. Farnsworth tented his fingers on the desk and leaned forward. "If you'd come in, I'd have prescribed antibiotics to help it heal and reduce the pain. No need to suffer like you did."

Laura shrugged. "With Glen gone, there's no extra money for medicine. I used a little warm oil for pain. Scared me when so much puss came out, I've never seen it that bad before." She played with her handbag flap. "All the other times my ear felt fuzzy afterwards, but this time I can't hear anything on that side."

"That's because the ear drum is in very bad shape. Most of the time, hearing loss disappears when the ear heals in a couple of months, but if yours doesn't, we'll have to consider surgery to repair it and restore your hearing." Dr. Farnsworth paused and cocked his head. "You're not taking good care of yourself, Mrs. Webber. You've lost a lot of weight since I've seen you last. Your body can't fight off infections unless you take better care of it."

Laura's shoulders slumped, and she gazed at her hands. Feeding her children took every cent she could find, so paying for surgery was out of the question. "Thanks, I'll let you know how it goes during the next few weeks."

She took a deep breath and straightened up. "May I ask you another question?" Without waiting for an answer, she continued. "I know you're not involved with his care any longer, but could you check on Glen's status? I haven't received any information at all, and don't know how he's being treated. And if he doesn't improve, it sounds like they'll never let him go."

Dr. Farnsworth spread his hands wide apart and leaned forward. "Mrs. Webber, I told you before, I had no influence with the mental hospital where he was, and even less than none with the institution for the criminally insane." He took a deep breath, shook his head, and blew the air out. "I hate to say it, but the chance of him getting out is almost zero."

Laura jerked back. "Don't say that. There must be something I...we...can do. Glen isn't a bad man. We need him."

Dr. Farnsworth slapped the desk, then pointed one finger straight at her. "The best thing you can do for yourself and your children is to move on. No way would your husband want you living the way you are, focused on nothing but waiting day after day. Divorce him and build a new life for yourself and the children."

Angry, discouraged and disillusioned, Laura grabbed David and bolted out of the doctor's office. Before they made it out the front door, however, Miss Bolton, called out and presented them with a bill for two dollars. Laura's fingers shook as she yanked two limp bills out of her coin purse.

She slammed the door behind her, irate and ashamed for wasting money on advice she couldn't use instead of paying for food they needed.

Laura's feet carried her of their own volition, while her mind kept replaying Dr. Farnsworth's horrible comments.

Her anger simmered higher and higher, so when she and David arrived at the apartment steps, Laura changed her mind. "I can't stand the thought of being cooped up in there." She looked down at David and ruffled his hair. "What do you say, little man? Shall we go to visit Mrs. Cohen instead?"

Magda looked surprised to find Laura and David at her door, but smiled and invited them in. "Iss zere a problem? Helga and June aren't back, yet."

"Oh, no, not at all. After visiting Dr. Farnsworth, I just plain didn't want to go back to that darn apartment. Guess you might say I'm playing hooky from work."

"Goot for you. Sit, I'll get some lemonade." Helga motioned David toward the box in a corner of the living room where she kept things for him to play with, then filled two glasses from a pitcher in the refrigerator.

Both women relaxed, sipped the cold lemonade, and watched David empty the box. Magda turned her attention from David to Laura.

"Are you okay? You look tired. Is your ear still hurtink?"

"What?" Laura turned toward Magda, seated on her right.

Magda repeated her questions, raising her voice a bit.

"It stopped hurting after the infection drained, but I can't hear out of it at all. And Dr. Farnsworth wasn't hopeful about a full recovery."

Magda shook her head. "Let's hope he's wronk and pray for ze best outcome." She tilted her head and stared at Laura's face. "Is zere somethink else? Your eyes are kind of puffy and red."

"No, I'm fine. Maybe a little tired." Laura's smile felt forced as she tried to reassure her friend. "What about you? Have you ever heard anything more about your cousin Solomon?"

Magda blinked twice, and her mouth started trembling. "Oh Laura, I don't know vhat to think, vhether I should be celebratink his good fortune in missink the ship in Hamburg or terrified about vhere he might be now."

Laura listened to the amazing, tragic story as it poured out. According to the news reports, the ship that Solomon had missed in Hamburg, bound for Cuba was full of Jews trying to escape Germany. Over nine hundred people, from singles to large families with children, had paid for Cuban visas, but then been denied entry when they arrived at the island. From there, the ship, the M.S. St. Louis, sailed to Miami, Florida, and then on to a port in Canada, where they were refused entry. Neither the United States or the Canadian governments wanted to establish a policy of accepting refugees. With nowhere to go, the captain turned the ship around and headed back to Europe. Holland, France, Great Britain, and Belgium each took around two hundred of the passengers. The rest were returned to Germany, where Magda feared they would be sent to concentration camps to die.

"My heart breaks for zose poor people, to have such hopes for the future only to have zem taken away. If Solomon had gotten on board, vould he have been one of the lucky ones? Zere has been no vord from him, so ve don't know if he's still alive. I vant to hope, but it's so hard."

Laura wrapped her arms around Magda and rocked her. There were no words that could help, but she hoped her touch was comforting. Magda relaxed with her head against Laura's shoulder, then took a deep breath and pulled away. "I'm sorry to fall apart. I'm lucky zat my family is safe, but sometimes I feel so guilty about all my friends and relatives schtill under Nazi control." She picked up their empty glasses, and glanced at the clock on the wall. "Gootness, look what time it is. I'm fixink a roast for dinner, but if I don't get it started, it von't be ready when Harvey gets home."

414

"I'd better get going." Laura called out to David and told him to put things away. "It was good to see you," she said to Magda.

David didn't want to go home, but once out of the apartment he skipped, jumped, and ran in circles at her side. She wished she had his energy, but was too old and tired. She kept a smile on her face for him though, not wanting to spoil his obvious joy.

Laura felt bad for Magda, and ashamed that her own troubles seemed overwhelming when her friend faced life and death issues. Dr. Farnsworth's words kept replaying in her mind, making her angry all over again. She'd feared his prognosis for her hearing, but hadn't expected him to lecture her on being so thin. Take better care of herself? Hah! Easy for him to say. He wasn't trying to feed four hungry kids on five dollars a week.

And her health wasn't the worst of it. His cold suggestion that she give up on Glen and divorce him had caught her off guard. There had to be something she could do. And even if Glen didn't come home, what made Dr. Farnsworth think she would give up on Glen and cut him out of their lives?

CHAPTER FORTY-FOUR

The Woman Was Now At Peace

Two weeks later, Sunday, July 22, 1939

Laura woke up earlier than usual, with damp sheets twisted around her sweaty legs. It was dark outside, but already heating up. She didn't turn on the fan for fear of waking the children, but opened the windows wide. The air smelled clean and sweet after rain during the night, but was already heavy with moisture.

By the time Laura fed everyone breakfast and was ready to head downstairs, the noisy fan blew a humid wind around the room and out the windows. The windows were only open a couple of inches, because the old, rotten screens provided no protection against David falling out.

"David, I want you to stay and play with your brothers this morning while I go downstairs. I need to hurry if we're going to spend the afternoon in the park."

Laura ignored his complaints and rushed down the stairs. As always, she knocked first just in case, then used the key to let herself into Mrs. Zimmerman's place. "It's awful in here, too hot and stuffy for anyone." She opened the windows wide to catch any air movement, wishing there was a fan to cool things down. Next, she headed toward the bedroom to wake Mrs. Zimmerman, surprised that she was still sleeping.

The minute Laura entered the bedroom, a sour, musty odor filled her nose. "Uh, oh, I'd better wake her and get her cleaned up," she said, turning toward the window and throwing it wide open. She stepped to the side of the bed and placed her hand on Mrs. Zimmerman's shoulder. Laura gasped and jerked her hand back. "Oh, no, oh, no." She didn't want to believe what her touch told her. She placed her fingers against the delicate, blue-veined forehead that was so familiar. Cool, flaccid skin under Laura's touch confirmed the truth she tried to deny. Staring down at the sweet, still face, two thoughts filled her mind. First, that the woman was now at peace, and second, gratitude that she'd insisted on David not coming with her.

Laura pulled the sheet up and smoothed it over her friend's face, then went to the kitchen to retrieve the piece of paper with the daughter-in-law's number from under the cookie jar. "Sure hope somebody's home. They might be in church since it's Sunday." She glanced back at the bedroom, wishing there was more she could do, then left the apartment.

"Can we go now?" Jimmy ran to Laura as soon as she entered.

"Not yet." Laura rushed past the children, grabbed her purse from the table, and turned back toward the door. "I'll be back in a little while. Stay here and don't fight."

"What's wrong?" June's voice sounded scared. "Why do you need your purse for Mrs. Zimmerman?"

Laura stopped, realizing there was no reason to rush for their neighbor. She took a deep breath and sat down at the table. "Kids, Mrs. Zimmerman passed away during the night and I need to contact her family."

"She died? Is she still in her house?" Raymond's gaze dropped to the floor as if wondering where she was below him.

"Yes, she's in her bed."

"That's so sad. She was a nice lady," June said. "When will they take her away?"

"Is Mizerman going away? I don't want her to go away." David's lip trembled. "Mizerman is my friend."

Laura pulled David into her lap. The other children gathered around her, solemn in the face of David's sudden silent tears.

"Mrs. Zimmerman was a very sweet lady who lived a long, happy life." She hoped what she was saying was true. Probably was, except for the lonely years she spent trapped in the apartment all alone. "She loved having you kids visit her, and always asked about how you were doing. And David, you made her happy every single time you went with me to see her." She paused and kissed the top of David's head. "But her body was tired, and she didn't wake up this morning. Now I have to call her son to let him know."

Ever practical, June said, "Are you going out to the telephone in your housedress? I thought you said ladies never did that."

"You know what, you're right. I'll change first."

Laura reached Mr. Zimmerman right after he and his wife came home from church. He was polite on the phone and promised to call Knight's Funeral Parlor right away. He asked if she could let them into the apartment when they came for his mother. He said Laura didn't need to stay downstairs. He'd send them to her door first to make it easy. When she agreed, he said he'd come by later that day after he finished making all the funeral arrangements.

Laura walked home in a daze, stunned by Mr. Zimmerman's attitude. Sure, he'd known his mother was old and in ill health. Her death couldn't have been a big surprise, but there hadn't been a hint of emotion in his voice. And he didn't even want to come see her before she was taken away. Laura didn't mind showing the funeral parlor people into the apartment so they could collect the body, but it seemed so cold to not have anyone from her family there.

Laura opened her front door, shocked to see Magda and Helga sitting on the sofa. "Hi. When did you two get here?"

"Just a little vhile ago. Ve got vorried vhen you and ze children didn't schow up at the park." Magda's voice was soft with sympathy. "I'm so sorry to hear about your neighbor. Vhat can ve do to help?"

Laura's throat hurt with swallowed pain as she sat down and let herself relax. "I'm okay, but I sure don't understand some people. Her son isn't even coming over to see her, just sending people from Knight's to collect her body. He said he'd come here sometime this evening to see me after he makes all the arrangements." She shook her head in disbelief. "When we talked, I didn't hear any emotion in

420

his voice at all." She sighed, staring at her lap, then looked up. "I'm sorry about our day in the park, but I have no idea how long I'll have to wait."

"Zen let me take ze children to the park. Helga and June can help me look after David, and ze boys can have a goot time runnink around and playing ball. I'll take zem home vith us vhen it's time for Harvey to arrive from vork, and you can collect zem vhen you're finished here."

"Oh, Magda, that would be wonderful. It's an awful lot for you to take on, but if you're sure."

Magda and the children hugged Laura and were gone in minutes, leaving her to wait for the people from the funeral parlor. She couldn't bear waiting in the empty apartment, and didn't feel right going back down to Mrs. Zimmerman's place until they arrived. She compromised and took a newspaper to the lobby and curled up on a bench to read.

"Excuse me, ma'am. I'm from Knight's Funeral Parlor and I'm looking for Mrs. Zimmerman's apartment." The man speaking was tall and thin, dressed in a black suit with a white shirt, black tie, and shiny black shoes.

Laura introduced herself and led the man and his assistant, carrying a gurney between them, up the stairs. Laura pointed toward the bedroom, but couldn't bear watching them do their job. After they left, she locked the door and went to her apartment to wait for the son to show up. Laura couldn't help wondering if he'd shed tears for his mother yet.

Mr. Zimmerman surprised her when he came inside. Laura had formed a mental picture of what he'd look like, and was shocked when she opened the door to his knock. Tall, just under six feet, average build, but with a well-padded, paunchy middle. His face was round and soft with a receding hairline, accented by heavy framed glasses that slid down his narrow, red-veined nose.

"Mrs. Webber, I presume?" He said, in a breathy and somewhat high-pitched voice. "Thank you for your assistance today. I made all the arrangements for the funeral next week, and even found time to let the landlord know he can take possession of the apartment by the end of the month." He stopped to clear his throat, then reached into his pocket and extracted a leather wallet. "My mother was very fond of you, and appreciated your helping her. I know this is just Sunday, but I'd like to pay you through the end of the week, and a bonus for the excellent job you did." He opened the wallet and pulled two five-dollar bills free from a thick wad of cash. "Also, if you'd tidy the place up for the landlord, since we rented it fully furnished, I'd appreciate it. Please feel free to take the food from the cabinets and the refrigerator. You can have any of her things you find, or donate them to a charity if you wish. I'll tell the landlord he can get the keys from you." He placed a key, twin to the one she had for his mother's apartment, on her table.

"But don't you want her personal items? I know she had an album of photographs that meant the world to her. I thought you'd want to keep that."

"Not necessary. That album just has copies of pictures that we gave her. We don't need them. There isn't anything we need or want. Help yourself or donate as you wish." He put his wallet back in his pocket and turned toward the door. "Thank you for your good work with my mother. I trust this takes care of everything." He opened the door and stepped outside. "Good day, Mrs. Webber," he said, and proceeded down the stairs without a backward glance.

That evening, after the children fell asleep, Laura sat at the table in the dark. She held the two keys, sliding them through her fingers, remembering the first time she'd used one to enter Mrs. Zimmerman's apartment. She'd accepted the position for the extra money, but ended up caring for a dear friend. The children were taking the loss hard, too, since they'd all learned to love the fragile old woman. Worries about the loss of the income tried to wiggle inside her mind, but Laura shut those thoughts off, determined to focus only on honoring Mrs. Zimmerman for this one night.

CHAPTER FORTY-FIVE

Nothing Left

The second floor apartment felt different when Laura entered the next morning, after once again sending the children to spend the day with Magda and Helga. She left the door open behind her, placed an empty milk carton on the table, then opened the windows all the way for fresh air. The place still felt stuffy, hot, and empty. "Just one day and it feels so different," Laura said out loud to herself, trying to fill what felt like an unfillable void. She turned in a circle, looking from the sofa with afghans draped over the back to the chair hollowed out from constant use, to the little table with tissues and reading glasses.

Everything looked so sad, like the life had been sucked out of each piece.

"I'm wasting time. Better get started." She opened the refrigerator and transferred everything to the table for sorting. Eggs, milk, butter, cottage cheese, ketchup, lettuce, tomatoes, bacon, hamburger, and a bowl of fried chicken sealed with foil. Many of the items untouched since their purchase on Friday. The freezer yielded two cartons of ice cream and loose ice cubes in a metal bowl. "This stuff will take a couple of trips. We'll have to eat some of it today since it won't all fit in our refrigerator." The words seemed to fall on the floor, with no living ears to receive them from Laura's lips.

It took several trips upstairs to transfer all of the food and supplies from the kitchen and bathroom. When all the useable materials had been moved, Laura started stacking Mrs. Zimmerman's personal items on the table. Soon her bedding, towels, dishes, books, clothing, shoes, and all her other miscellaneous possessions were piled high. "What to do with this stuff? It's not right to toss it out, and we can't use it." Then the answer popped into her head...All Faith Thrift Store. Laura grabbed her handbag and rushed out.

After two trips with a loaded cart loaned by All Faith, Laura was back at the table in the empty apartment. "I guess I'm done. Nothing left to do." Laura leaned her head back and closed her eyes for a few minutes, but the emptiness pressed around her. She stood up, closed all the windows, wrote the landlord, Charlie Johnson's, name on a piece of paper from her pocketbook, then placed the two keys on top of it in the middle of the table. She whispered a last goodbye to Mrs. Zimmerman, left the apartment, and pulled the door closed behind her.

꙳

Laura and the children enjoyed a feast of cold fried chicken, salad, and ice-cream, after an impromptu prayer thanking Mrs. Zimmerman. The meal put them in a pensive mood, so they spent the rest of the evening sharing family stories and memories. After the last glass of water, visit to the bathroom, and good night hug, the children settled in their beds and Laura curled up in the chair near the stove to listen to the night sounds through the open window. The evening had been sweet, but now the realities facing her began to force their way into her mind.

The ten dollars she'd received from Mrs. Zimmerman's son and the ten dollar coupon Sister Mary Rachel had given her for the donation were the last income she could count on receiving. There were only a very few things she could cut back on to save money. She already bought only day-old bread. The vegetables, fruit, and meat she purchased were from the store specials bins, which held items that were almost ready to be pulled from the shelves and tossed. She could switch to oleomargarine instead of butter, even if nobody liked it. Same thing with powdered milk. Those changes wouldn't make much difference though, which meant she had to think of ways to bring in additional money since the mason jar money was almost gone. She could care for someone like Mrs. Zimmerman, but if they were very far away it wouldn't be practical, even if they agreed that she could take David to work with her. Piecework, like taking in laundry or sewing, would be hard to find and couldn't be counted on for a steady income until she built a reputation and steady clientele. No telling how long that would take. She could sell something, but didn't have any jewelry or expensive things to offer.

Laura's thoughts turned to the boxes of Glen's tools, some of them specialized for machine and auto repair. How could she find out what they were worth and avoid being cheated? But most of all, how could she even consider selling tools he'd need when he came home? Somehow, in the midst of whirling, contradictory thoughts, Laura fell asleep and began dreaming.

The dream began with Glen's face at their wedding as he looked at her and recited his vows. His eyes shone, and his voice was soft and hoarse at the same time. She remembered knowing how much he loved her and promising herself that, even though she didn't love him the same way, he was such a good man and wonderful friend that she'd do everything in her power to make him happy. The scene changed to their wedding night when his lust was tempered by gentleness at her fearful hesitation, even though she'd never told him why she was afraid. The next picture of his face, full of incredible awe and love as he gazed down at his newborn daughter in his arms. The scenes began to flicker by, faster and faster—the birth of his sons, the silly way he played with the children, all the little towns they traveled through when they lived on the road, the weeks they lived under a bridge. Then the scene froze. Glen's face was front and center, his head thrown back, mouth open in a full-throated laugh, eyes shining. Behind him Laura could see the farm living room full of neighbors dancing and singing. Glen's face changed in slow motion until he was looking straight at her, lips together with just the barest hint of a sad smile, eyes full of tenderness. The background changed as well, until the happy dancers at the farm became the robotic men shuffling around the room at the hospital. Glen's face was still the focus, but he began to fade until only the shambling men remained. Then they disappeared as well.

430

Laura woke up, calling "Don't go, Glen, please don't leave me." Tears poured down her face as she recalled every scene, feeling more alone than ever before. She moved from the uncomfortable chair to the mattress, remembering with a pang that it was the mattress she and Glen had shared, spooned together through the nights with his strong arms wrapped around her.

She opened her mind, calling out to him, begging for a connection, wondering if he'd sent the dream. Instead she sensed only static, much like a radio when the signal had been interrupted by an electrical storm.

"Oh, ma," she whispered, "Is this the end for us? Is there nothing left of my Glen?"

No answer came, but she fell asleep feeling loving arms wrapped around her, holding her in a warm embrace, surrounded by the sound of a soothing, familiar lullaby from her childhood.

Acknowledgments

This book could not have been written without
the help of my mother, June Azevedo. Her
stories about growing up helped me create the
emotional framework for the fictionalized
characters and events. She told me about her
mother's incredible strength, and how she
stepped up when her father began losing touch
with reality. Mom remembers the time they
spent on a lovely farm. She remembers the
awful day her father was taken away, never to
return. Mom also told me how much it hurt to
leave the farm when her mother, the real Laura,
wasn't able to handle all the work alone.

      I also have to thank many writers in the
Sacramento community for their support,
patience, and guidance. The superb critique
group led by Gini Grossenbacher helped me

every step of the way, including Judy Pierce, and Sandra Heaton who toiled over my work each month. Special thanks to Judith Vaughn, an author and retired neurologist, who helped make sure my hospital scenes were realistic. Other special people, both writers and beta readers, who kept me going with their skills, humor, and kind words, included Michelle Hamilton, Norma Jean Thornton, and Marlene Meincke.

Writing can play havoc on home life but I am blessed with a marvelous husband, Stan Darrow, and daughter, Sheryl Wilson. They put up with my lack of attention while I agonized over the manuscript and loved me anyway.

Thank you all.

About the Author

I've been passionate about three things my whole life: reading, flying, and animals.

I was one of those kids who walked down the halls holding an open book, glancing up to keep from running into people or walls. I no longer read walking down the street, but I do manage to read a few sentences on my Kindle at red lights. Reading is as important to me as breathing, and one of my greatest joys now as an author is getting to know other writers. What could be more awesome than reading a fantastic book and being friends with the writer?

Thanks to a marvelous husband who knows how much I love flying, I've been up in a hot air balloon, a two-man helicopter, a glider, and an open cockpit bi-plane. He even encouraged me to get my private pilot's license, and sympathized when I had to quit during the economy crash in 2008. Every minute in the air was amazing, and today I'd go up in anything, with anyone willing to take me, anytime, and anywhere. No wonder one of my writing idols is Richard Bach, pilot and author of Jonathan Livingston Seagull and my favorite book ever, Illusions, The Adventures of a Reluctant Messiah.

My love of animals made me want to be a veterinarian, but I fell in love and married during my first year of college. In spite of dropping out, I still made a contribution to animal welfare by raising 514 bottle-fed kittens, working an all-volunteer cat spay and neuter clinic every month for 20 years, and writing books about animal rescue.

I believe that a supportive family is key to a happy life and am blessed with an understanding husband who has been my best friend and life partner for 54 years thus far.

Sacramento, California has been home for most of my life. Stan and I live next door to my parents, and share our home with our cats Gracie, Portia, Bonnie, Becca, and Ash. We now also have four chickens, Bernice Williams, Goldie Girl, Anna Banana, and Miss Cluck, that fertilize and cultivate our garden while taking care of insects throughout the yard.

My philosophy of life is simple. If you find harmony within, you can make a difference to the people around you. That in turn spreads out and makes a difference in the world. Life just gets better each year as long as you keep dreaming and loving.

One of the best thing in life for a writer is hearing from readers. I'd love to hear your comments, questions, or suggestions. You can find me on my website, https://www.sharonsdarrow.com, on Facebook at https://www.facebook.com/SamatiPress, or email me at sharon@samatipress.com.

I hope you enjoyed Desperate Choices, Book Three in the Laura's Dash series. If you'd like to learn more about what happened before, here are the first chapters from Book One, She Survives, and Book Two, Strive and Protect.

She Survives

CHAPTER ONE

Hardscrabble Birth

August 1903,
Five miles outside of Ardmore, Oklahoma

"Look, Jon, ain't she pretty?"

"She? She? Another damn girl? What's the matter with you, woman. Five young'uns so far, and only one boy. And him the last a'fore this'n, so he's no use to me on the farm for years." Jon turned away from the bed with a disgusted expression and headed toward the open door. "Pretty? Hellfire, just another useless mouth to feed."

Vera watched her husband shove five-year-old Becca aside as he pushed past his four older children to get through the doorway. He went straight to the wagon, jumped up on the wooden bench, and grabbed the reins.

"Miz Dobbs, aint you 'bout ready to head home?" he yelled.

The youngsters, clustered around the

open door in the sweltering August midday sun, stared at Vera and Miz Dobbs. They were careful to not look back at their father, hoping he wouldn't focus his attention on them. Ruth, the oldest, made sure Lizbeth and Becca stayed just outside the threshold where Miz Dobbs had told them to remain. She held Ben, just turned three, by the hand to keep him from rushing through the door.

Miz Dobbs patted Vera's arm and shook her head. "I got to go, Miss Vera. Mr. Cavanaugh sounds mighty impatient. You and the baby'll be just fine."

"I know. Thanks for your help. Can't imagine having to birth a baby without you." Vera squeezed the midwife's hand.

Miz Dobbs started to turn away, then looked back and whispered. "Miss Vera, you know your baby was born with a caul on her head. Ain't never seen part of the birth sack stuck to a baby's head like a hat before, but I've heard some folks believe that's a sign that the baby's born with the second sight. Least ways, that's what my gram told me. Do you want to keep the caul?" "I'd love to keep it for Laura when she's grown, but Mr. Cavanaugh wouldn't like it. Would you keep it?" "Yes, ma'am, I'll be proud to keep it for you." Miz Dobbs smiled, packed a collection of bottles, jars, and rags back into her battered leather bag, then hurried out the door.

As soon as she settled herself on the wagon bench, Jon slapped the horse's back hard with the reins. The horse lunged forward into the harness, jerking the wagon onto the rutted road.

Vera waited until the sound of hooves faded in the distance, then pressed her lips against the baby's damp hair. "It's alright, sweet Laura, it's alright. Mama loves you."

Vera stroked the baby's forehead, remembering how she'd looked at birth with the glistening white membrane stuck tight to her tiny head, covering her eyebrows, hair and ears. Poor little one. There should be a ceremony to guide your path and protect you, with all the clan members taking part. "What will it mean for you, my sweet Laura?" Vera whispered in her ear. She knew Laura's life path would be hard, no doubt of that, but she'd also have strength, luck, and special gifts of the spirit. "No tellin' what kinds of gifts they'll be."

Unable to resist their imploring looks, Vera raised her right arm and waved the other children, still waiting in the doorway, to come over to her bed. "Come on now, time to meet your new baby sister."

They rushed forward, jostled for the best

positions as they gathered around the bed, stroking the baby's face and arms, holding her tiny hands, and assuring themselves that their ma was alright.

"That's enough for now," Vera said, after each child

had a turn with the baby, "I'm awful tired. Ruth, will you fix something to eat for supper? And please close the curtain so the baby and I can sleep."

Ruth nodded, then herded the little ones away from the bed. She closed off the area by pulling together two blankets suspended from a rope stretched from wall to wall just below the muslin-covered ceiling. Something moving on top of the muslin above the bed caught her eye, a clear sign that some type of vermin had fallen through the sod and been caught by the cloth. Wooden pegs, pounded diagonally into the angle between ceiling and plaster-covered sod walls, kept the fabric taut. Ruth could see that Ma would need to replace the muslin soon since it had torn away from some of the pegs and sagged in many places from the weight of the dirt and small creatures it held.

Vera cuddled her daughter's soft, warm body against her breasts. She listened to the faint, whispery sounds of the baby's breathing, then drifted off to sleep, newborn in her arms, both exhausted from the rigors of birth.

Hours later, Vera woke to the sound of her husband stumbling to his side of the bed. She kept her eyes closed and her breathing regular, hoping he'd think she was still asleep. He stank of alcohol and sweat, cursing in the darkness as he pulled off his boots, overalls and shirt, then dropped on the bed and shoved his legs under the covers, still dressed in his dirty long-johns.

Vera heard the children stirring, disturbed by the sounds their father made, before they slipped back into sleep on their straw pallets just a few feet from her bed. Jon's heavy, rhythmic snores let her know when he was asleep, so she could climb out of bed with baby Laura in her arms.

Vera knew the baby needed to nurse but didn't want Laura to wake up enough to cry. Moving in slow motion to avoid making any noise, Vera sat down in an old wooden rocker near the foot of the bed and brought the baby to her breast. Little Laura rooted around for a moment before she latched on and suckled with greed, working her tiny, contented fingers against her mother's skin. As she rocked, soothed by the quiet perfection of the moment,

Vera began to sing the Cherokee Morning
Song, an ancient melody passed down from
one generation to another, just as she
remembered hearing it when she was little. She
loved the words, but the meaning—I am of
the Great Spirit, Ho, It is so, It is so—was even
more precious.

We N' De Ya Ho, We
N' De Ya Ho
We N' De Ya, We N'
De Ya Ho, Ho Ho Ho
He Ya Ho, He Ya Ho
Ya Ya Yaaa

She thought only Laura could hear the
words, but she was wrong. All of a sudden,
her body snapped forward propelled by a
hard slap to the back of her head. "I tole you
about talkin' Cherokee in my house. If'n I
hear it again, I'll knock you clean out'a that
chair."

Jon's voice was low, more like a
menacing growl than speech. The threat was
real as demonstrated by the force of the blow,
the promise of more violence clear.

Vera didn't make a sound, nor did she
turn to look at her husband. She could sense
his presence as he stood behind the chair,

looming over her. Squeezing her eyes closed against the pain radiating from the back of her head, she fought against the urge to react. She stayed still, her head bowed forward over her daughter's body, then resumed rocking and nursing after she felt Jon move away from behind her. Within minutes, Vera heard a liquid torrent as he used the thunder-jug from under their bed, then the noisy creaking when he lowered his body back onto the rope mattress. The pungent urine odor stung Vera's nose as she sat, waiting, until his snores once again filled the sod house. Only then did Vera let the tears run from her eyes while she changed Laura's diaper and rocked her back to sleep.

Vera stayed in the chair a long time, rocking and stroking Laura's warm little body, because she didn't want to climb back into bed next to her husband. How could I have thought he was a good man? If only I'd taken more time to get to know him. There's worse things than being alone.

Jon had first introduced himself at a church picnic. As Vera helped the other women set out bowls of food on long wooden tables, she noticed him watching her from where he stood with two other men. She felt his eyes on her throughout the afternoon, but he didn't speak to her until people started leaving.

"Hello miss, I'm Jon Cavanaugh," he'd said. "You're the schoolteacher, ain't you?"

"Yes, I'm Vera Miller." They talked a long time, seated on wooden benches in the churchyard. She told him about her students, and he told her about purchasing a homestead.

Vera enjoyed talking to Jon and considered him a handsome man. He was tall with dark brown, wavy hair, deep blue eyes, a dark complexion, big, strong looking hands, and a muscular, powerful build. He also had a scar running from just below his right eye to the base of his ear. The scar was pale, a wide, raised welt standing out against his dark skin. Vera tried not to stare, but couldn't help wondering what had happened to him.

Jon was courteous but didn't smile as they talked.

One week after they met, Jon caught Vera at school after her students had all left. He wasted little time before getting to the point of his visit, a marriage proposal. He explained that he needed a wife to help him work his homestead, and she needed a husband. They were both strong, young, and living away from their families. They were also

God-fearing, so should share the same ideals about the commandments to marry and raise children. Vera, after a day to think about it, accepted. It seemed like a reasonable decision based on sound ideals, a good match for them both.

Vera remembered her wedding day and wished she could go back and change things. No fancy clothes, flowers, or music, just standing in front of a preacher early in the morning. After saying "I do," she'd watched Jon nod to the parson, then lead the way outside to his wagon, piled high with their belongings. No kiss, no hugs, not even any soft words.

Reaching Jon's homestead had taken all day, and the condition of the place when they arrived was much more primitive than Vera had expected. No house at all, just a crude, three-sided lean-to built into the side of a small hill. She hadn't said a word, though, just followed her new husband's lead, helping him transfer the wagon contents inside and then trying to create some order. When the wagon was empty, Jon put the horse and wagon into the barn which was in much better condition than the lean-to, while Vera started a fire and began to prepare supper. Vera hadn't known what to expect when the sunlight faded, and the darkness drove them inside by the fire. She'd hung a blanket over a rope stretched across the length of the open side of the lean-to, providing them with shelter from the night. When she'd finished, Jon had reached for her without a single word, pulling her toward their bed against the wall. Vera sat down on the thin straw mattress next to him, then was shoved flat on her back and taken like an animal in the field. Vera hadn't fought or protested, understanding it was her duty as a wife to submit to her husband.

Jon wasn't a talkative man, but during long hours trapped together during their first winter, they'd talked about their family histories.

Vera's parents had died in a fire the year before she'd started teaching, only six months after her brother had gotten married and moved away to be with his wife's family. Vera couldn't rebuild the burned buildings or work her father's farm by herself. No clan members lived nearby, and the tribal reservation was miles away. Teaching in a nearby town was her only choice. The previous teacher had married and moved away, so the School Board was happy to accept her. Her education at a Christian off-reservation day school was sufficient for her to teach elementary school students.

Jon's mother had died giving birth to him, her fourth baby. His father had neither the time nor patience to deal with a baby, so he hired a newly freed slave, Millie, to take care of the home and the children, and to serve as a wet nurse. Jon's father had grown up with slaves in the family, so he treated Millie the same way. Jon had one sister, the second oldest child, whom Millie taught about women's work and about a woman's place. Jon's father was a firm believer in punishing youngsters who disobeyed him, using either a razor-strap or riding crop. The scar on Jon's face came from his father's whip, when Jon had tried to turn away once to escape punishment, a lesson he'd never forgotten. When Jon's pa died, the oldest son inherited everything, forcing Jon, his other brother, and their sister to leave and find their own way.

Vera's thoughts were interrupted when Laura started fussing against her shoulder. The motion of the rocker and comforting touch of Vera's hands on her back soothed the baby to sleep. Vera kissed the top of her head. If only they'd talked about family and raisin' young'uns earlier. Never would have married a man with no softness or love inside him. Wasting time looking back though, no way to change things now. Got to get some sleep.

Vera carried the sleeping baby back to the bed, tucked the warm little body tight against her side, and was soon dreaming, breathing in the sweet smell of her baby's breath.

Vera and baby Laura were together almost all the time for the first few weeks, a cloth sling holding the baby tight to Vera's body. Laura slept to the soothing sounds of her mother's breathing and heartbeat, comforted by the warmth of her mother's voice and body, and the familiar scent of her skin. When Vera needed a few moments without the sling, she would hand the baby to Ruth, always reminding her to hold baby Laura with care.

"I know, Ma, I know how to hold her." Ruth would roll her eyes each time and reply. "I'm nine now, you don't need to remind me every time." The baby took only seconds to settle into Ruth's thin arms, so different from Vera's rounded body. "See, she likes me holdin' her."

"She sure does, Ruth." Vera smiled as she replied, enjoying the sweet picture of her daughters together. "She knows you and loves you already."

Of course, whenever Ruth helped Vera with baby Laura, both Lizbeth and Becca clamored for their turns.

"Ruth, you've had her long enough, it's my turn now." Lizbeth always whined. "I'm seven, nearly big as you. Let me have her."

"Me, too. If Lizbeth gets a turn, I do, too." five-year- old Becca would chime in.

Ruth knew it was up to her to handle the two girls' requests. "You can both have a turn, but you gotta sit down first," she'd say, positioning baby Laura into one small lap after another.

Vera never worried about the baby with Ruth in charge. She loved watching and listening to her daughters care for baby Laura, their love for her clear even while they squabbled with each other for their turns. Vera also loved seeing how content the baby was with her older sisters whether Laura was sleeping or watching them with wide open eyes.

"Ruth is quite a little mother," Vera said one day, as she sat rocking and sewing. It was much too hot to work inside, so she'd dragged the rocker and a basket of mending outside and placed them in the shade next to the front of the house. Ruth sat near her, caring for baby Laura. Lizbeth, Becca and

Ben played hide and seek, running and giggling, in and out of the barn.

Ma and Pa would've loved them so much. Vera sighed as she watched her children. Near fourteen years and she still missed 'em every single day.

"Ma," Ruth asked, breaking into Vera's thoughts. "Laura is such a pretty baby. What was I like as a baby?"

"You were the happiest of all my babies. Didn't cry, just made little noises right after you were born. Miz Dobbs didn't even have to slap your bottom."

Happy with that answer, Ruth turned her attention back to Laura.

Vera's thoughts drifted back to the day Ruth was one week old. She'd never forget that day, never till the day she died. Vera sat in the same rocking chair where she sat now, bursting with happiness, holding her baby daughter. She'd been singing softly to the sleeping infant, the same song she liked to sing to Laura, when Jon walked over to her.

"What's that song? Didn't sound like no reg'lar words I ever heard," he'd said.

"Just a lullaby my uncle taught me when I was young. Men sing the lullabies in Cherokee culture," Vera answered.

"Cherokee? Your uncle's a Cherokee? You

tellin' me you're a damned half-breed?"

Vera stood up and placed the baby into her basket.

"No, I'm not a half-breed, I'm full blood Cherokee." Jon's slap split Vera's lip and knocked her down.

His hands were fisted at his sides as he stood staring at her on the ground, his entire body stiff with rage. "You tricked me into marryin' a dirty Indian? You lyin' whore."

Vera had tried explaining that she'd never hidden anything. It wasn't her fault he'd never seen an Indian teacher before, or an Indian woman who wore her hair up. It wasn't her fault that the Christian name she'd been given by parents educated off the reservation had confused him. He'd never asked, and she'd assumed he knew and didn't care. But her words had no effect. "Iffen anybody in town ever finds out about you bein' a Indian, I'll never live it down. And now my own blood daughter isa stinkin' half-breed? So help me God if this gets out I'll beat you to death myself." Jon's words, spoken in cadence with his fists striking her face and body, left no doubt he meant what he said.

That day was the first time Vera had been beaten. She'd never been hit before, but from then on, she had to endure both her husband's contempt and his thoughtless violence.

Shaking her head, Vera brought her attention back to the present. The past was over. She couldn't change it. Just got to protect the young'uns best as she could.

Vera kept a smile pasted on her face, not wanting her facial expression to invite questions about her thoughts. She watched Ruth handle all three of her younger sisters, moving the baby from lap to lap without ever losing her patience.

Ben, her only son, showed little interest in the baby. It made Vera sad, but she understood. He was three years old and already trying to follow his father's instructions to "be a man." Although his face and body still had the soft contours of babyhood, he almost never let her hold him anymore. And on those rare occasions when he came to her for comfort, he'd pull away if his pa came near them.

Poor Ben. He'd do anything to get attention from his pa. But if he got hurt, all he'd hear was "Stop that cryin'. Men don't cry." If he got caught havin' fun playin' with his sisters, Jon would yell at him, "What's the matter with you, boy, playin' sissy games with girls." And the rare times his pa'd see him huggin' her, Jon'd tell him to "stop bein' a baby."

Sometimes Ben would poke at baby Laura as she rested on one of his sister's laps, but he seldom talked to her or asked to hold her.

And Jon's relationship with the baby? He demanded respect and obedience from his children, not considering affection of any value. Vera took care to keep baby Laura out of his way, knowing it was

safer for both of them.

Strive and Protect

CHAPTER ONE

Betrayal

November, 1923

L aura was excited throughout dinner, eager
to see the highest rated movie of the year.
She skipped rather than strolled at Bruce's
side when they finished eating and headed
toward the Argosy. Bruce had parked the car, a
shiny black Buick Touring Car convertible, and
his most prized possession, a block away from
the cafe.

The theater's large marque announced
The Covered Wagon, in huge letters. The names
J. Warren Kerrigan and Lois Wilson, stars of the
film, appeared right below the title in smaller
letters. Bruce gave their tickets to the usher at
the door, then led Laura into the opulent
interior.

Laura's low-heeled shoes sank into thick
maroon carpeting. Heavy tapestries hung on the
walls between glass cases containing posters for
upcoming feature films, and muffled the

whispered conversations around her. Soon they settled in plush seats, waiting for the heavy curtains to rise. She was glad the interior was dim after being surrounded by pretty women that made her feel almost dowdy by comparison. They wore shimmering silk and satin, accented by fur wraps and feather bedecked hats. Her forest green wool frock with pale gold at the cuffs, collar, and narrow band accenting the dropped waist above narrow pleats seemed ordinary by comparison. Her patterned black stockings and cloche hat sporting a pale gold bow couldn't compare to sleek, silken hosiery and high fashion hats.

Laura took a shallow breath -- all she could manage with the tight brassiere that compressed her chest -- and gazed at the heavy velvet curtains. She resolved to think only of the movie and the handsome man next to her.

Laura's attention never wavered from the film, entranced from the movie title to the closing credits. She loved movies and the magnificent music and sound effects produced by the magnificent Wurlitzer theater organ. Her fingers danced over imaginary keys along with the organist seated at the gold and black console in the orchestra pit.

"That was the bees knees. No wonder it's the most popular movie around." Laura and

Bruce maneuvered through the dense crowd. "Thank you so much for bringing me. Tonight has been the best evening ever."

"You're welcome." Bruce placed his arm around Laura's slim waist, holding her close even though she stiffened at his touch. At last, they got out of the theater and headed for the car.

"Let's find a quiet place to talk. I've got something important to ask you."

Laura's mood changed from excitement to worry in an instant. She cared about Bruce very much—in fact, sometimes she thought she might be in love with him—but his tone sounded serious. She stayed quiet until they got back into the car, listening for any clues to what was on his mind. Bruce chattered about the movie, paying no attention to Laura's distracted responses. He parked the car near St. Thomas Catholic Church, then led Laura to a secluded bench under the trees on the park-like grounds.

"It's so peaceful here," Laura said, settling on a bench. She shivered a little, wondering what was coming.

"Yes, and perfect for us," Bruce said. "Hey, don't look so serious. I've got an exciting idea."

Laura tried to control her rapid breathing, waiting to hear what he had to say.

"What are you doing for Thanksgiving?"
Bruce said.

"Uh, just having dinner in the dining
hall, I guess," she said, a little surprised by the
question. "Nothing special. The YWCA has a lot
of rules, but we're not required to eat there. I
could skip the Thanksgiving dinner if you want
me to."

"Well, my family celebration should be
over by three."

The family celebration? Is he inviting me
to join them?

Bruce continued talking. "What would
you say about us going to Oklahoma City for
the weekend? If we left at three thirty, we could
get there Thursday night, and then come back
Sunday evening. I'll get us a room in the best
hotel in town. We can do whatever you want for
two whole, wonderful days." Bruce pulled her to
him.

Laura shoved him away, not sure she
understood what he'd said. "What? Are you
asking me to join you for Thanksgiving dinner
and then take a trip?"

"Wish I could, but my parents are old-
fashioned. I've told them how much I care
about you, but Mother
hung up on her society rules. She'd never be
able to see

past you being half Indian."

"How can you say you care about me? It sounds like your mother isn't the only one hung up on stupid society rules."

Bruce reached for her hand but Laura stayed out of range. "It's not just that. My father's most important goal is having me take over the bank when he's ready to retire, but he insists that I have to find a wife with the perfect pedigree or he won't pass it on to me."

Laura stood and stepped away from the bench, shaking her head in shocked disbelief.

"Don't be like that, doll. I'm in no hurry to settle down with some boring society debutante. I'd rather keep seeing you, and a weekend together would be so great, just the two of us." Bruce leaned forward and his voice thickened. "Say yes, baby, please. You know you want to."

Laura's emotions cycled from confusion and shame, to pain, then blinding anger. "You and your parents don't think I'm good enough to sit at your table, but you want to take me to a hotel in Oklahoma City? You can't even consider me for a wife, but I'd be okay as a girlfriend on the side?"

"Don't look like that," Bruce implored. "We've had fun together, and I just want to keep having fun. I never said anything about us being more than that."

Laura fought hard to keep from crying. "Going to a movie or having dinner is different from sharing a hotel room for the weekend. I can't imagine what I've done to make you think that would be okay."She trembled from head to toe, throat burning. "Take me home, right now."

"Oh, come on. Stop acting like some kind of innocent little school girl. You told me your history. What's the problem? It's not like you're a virgin ... and with your own father yet."

Laura slapped Bruce as hard as she could, almost knocking him off the bench. "He raped me," she screamed. Her hand stung like fire, but the flaming red mark on Bruce's face was worth it. Without saying a word, Laura ran away, back the way they'd come.

Bruce yelled. "Come back here, you little bitch. No girl hits me and gets away with it. Where the hell do you think you're going?"

"Leave me alone. I never want to see you again." Laura spit the words back over her shoulder.

"You know you don't mean that. Come here and I'll take you home." Bruce's words were softer, but his tone couldn't make up for what he'd said.

Laura ran even faster, staring straight ahead as she passed the ivy-covered stone walls of the church. She angled toward the road, sliding on the damp grass as she passed dark trees, lit only by the moonlight.

No more words pursued her, but Laura heard Bruce's car starting. When he drew even with her, Bruce leaned out the window and said, "It's a long way to the YWCA. Get in the car. You know I'm right."

Laura didn't turn her head or acknowledge him at all. Bruce drove alongside her and kept talking. Then he gave up and sped away. Only then did she slow down to a snail's pace, struggling to see through the tears that coursed down her face.

How could she have been so stupid? A handsome, rich guy like Bruce with his college education and a Father who owned a bank? Why, oh why had she trusted him?

Hot tears still fell as Laura reached the YWCA front door. She was late and had to listen to a lecture before being allowed to go to her room. Once there, Laura paced back and forth, from wall to wall, raging inside.

She pressed her hands into her temples, unable to keep the words inside. "What's the matter with you? Miss Emma warned you and warned you not to tell anyone about your past.

They will use whatever you tell them to hurt and manipulate you."

Over and over the same phrases reverberated inside Laura's mind, even after she stopped speaking them aloud. At long last she stopped circling the room and sat down. She had only one choice, and that was to get as far away as possible. Tulsa was a big city with plenty of room to start over. She'd be smart this time. She'd gotten along just fine without a boyfriend before.

Decision made, Laura pulled her suitcase from under the bed and started to pack her things. She left fresh clothes for the morning on the dresser, together with her comb and toothbrush, set the clock for an hour before dawn, then climbed into bed.